It's Not About the Accent

Also by Caridad Ferrer

Adiós to My Old Life

Available from MTV Books

It's Not About the Accent

caridad ferrer

POCKET BOOKS

New York   London   Toronto   Sydney

POCKET BOOKS
A Division of Simon & Schuster, Inc.
1230 Avenue of the Americas, New York, NY 10020

First MTV Books/Pocket Books trade paperback edition August 2007

Designed by Carla Jayne Little

Manufactured in the United States of America

10 9 8 7 6 5 4 3 2 1

Library of Congress Cataloging-in-Publication Data

Ferrer, Caridad.
  It's not about the accent / Caridad Ferrer. — 1st MTV Books/Pocket Books
trade paperback ed.
     p. cm.
  Summary: Caroline Darcy decides to explore—and exploit—her distant Cuban
ancestry when she goes away to college, claiming to be half-Cuban, calling herself "Car-
olina," and dying her blond hair Havana Brown, but soon faces profound consequences.
  [1. Identity—Fiction. 2. Universities and colleges—Fiction. 3. Cuban Americans—
Fiction. 4. Dating (Social customs)—Fiction. 5. Sex—Fiction. 6. Family—Fiction. 7.
Ohio—Fiction.] I. Title. II. Title: It is not about the accent.
  PZ7.F3697Its 2007
  [Fic]—dc22   2007000244

ISBN-13: 978-1-4165-2491-5
ISBN-10:   1-4165-2491-6

For information about special discounts for bulk purchases,
please contact Simon & Schuster Special Sales at 1-800-456-6798
or business@simonandschuster.com.

This one is for Mom and Abuela and the very long
line of storytellers who preceded them.
Thank you.

Acknowledgments

First off, many thanks to my great editor, Jennifer Heddle, and of course to Lauren McKenna, Erica Feldon, and the entire team at MTV Books.

Huge hugs and thanks to the world's bestest, most fabulous agent, Caren Johnson, who not only understands but also shares my deep need for Cute Shoes.

This book benefited hugely from some fantastic early readers, so to Jen, Erin, Allie, and Brandie, thank you so much. All of your suggestions were invaluable and I'm so grateful to have had your input. (And a very special shout-out to Steph for the legal advice/knowledge.)

To my treasured online communities, TeenLitAuthors, PASIC, LiveJournal, Backspace, the Treehouse, and the Playground—you all rock with your unflagging support and many, many happy hours of procrastination. And always, always, to the darling Cherries, a big, huge sloppy hug and Dating Game Kiss. You guys are amazing and really, BTCKE!

Many thanks to Thom—friend, website guru, and one of the most kickingest cartoonists around.

Alesia, you are easily one of the best partners in crime/sounding boards/friends a girl could have. Can't wait for you to move back so we can be Pretentious Coffeehouse Writers again!

Torrie, as always, couldn't have done it without you. You know just when to smack me upside the head.

Musical Geek Alert—It's almost all about the girls this time: Shakira, KT Tunstall, Natasha Bedingfield, Pink, Jonatha Brooke, and Faith Hill for being strong, unique voices who kept me company throughout the creation of this story. And in the Not Girl category, to Taylor Eigsti, whose *Lucky to Be Me* truly resonated with the themes of this book. Finally, thanks to Alejandro Sanz and his beautiful melody, "Labana," a love song to the city of my ancestors.

To my very, very patient and loving extended family—you'll never know how much it means to me to have your unflagging support. Nate and Abby, I'm so proud to be your mom, and Lewis—as always, there just aren't words.

Prologue

"**W**hat's next, Nana?"

"Now we return the chicken to the pot, add the stock and wine, and let it come to a boil."

With Nana Ellie's help, I put each piece of chicken back into the big pot, along with the other stuff, and gave it all a stir before stepping down from my stool.

"You make the best chicken and rice, Nana." I sniffed the air, practically drooling. And I had to wait nearly another *hour*.

"*We* do, sweet girl." My great-grandmother sat in her chair at the table, slicing the funny bananas—what did she call them again?—oh, yeah, plantains. They looked totally gross, with their almost-black skins and the way they were sort of slimy under the skins, but when she sliced them and fried them in oil, they turned golden and tasted as sweet as candy. She always made the plantains when we cooked any Spanish dishes, even though it usually required a trip to West Side Market to find the good ones.

Actually, 'cause Nana was way picky about her food and could cook stuff from all over the world, she had to make lots of trips to West Side, which had ingredients from everywhere and was totally the coolest place in Cleveland. Outside were stalls where the vegetable and fruit vendors haggled with the old ladies, saying they had the best green peppers or whatever. And inside the big building, it was completely awesome. There were bakeries, where grandmas from the Old Country would give you stuff like baklava or biscotti, just out of the oven, trying to convince you to buy, like, two dozen more. The butchers were also inside, with all sorts of meats and sausages and things you couldn't find anywhere else. Actually, some of it I was happy *not* to find anywhere else—because a whole pig staring at you from inside a glass case? *Ew.* But Nana's roast leg of pork? Way good.

Nana also made stuff like blinis, which she served with sour cream and caviar, which I thought was kinda *eugh*, but Nana said I needed to expand my horizons and what better way to understand a culture than through its food? But a culture where they ate fish eggs and *liked* it? Not sure how much I wanted to understand it. Better, though, was when she made little pancakes that were sort of like the blinis, but sweeter, and stuffed with strawberries and cream. She called them crepes. I just called them yummy. Almost as good as her apple pie, which had been Papa Joseph's favorite.

Following Nana's instructions, I picked up a peeled plantain and started cutting it. "Nana, how did you learn to cook so many different things?"

"You know how, Caroline."

"Yeah, I *know*," I admitted, but I loved hearing her tell the stories anyway because there was always something new. She'd had so many adventures. I'll bet my great-grandmother could live to be a hundred and forty-six and we'd never get through all her stories—she was just one of the coolest people ever. "But come on, Nana, please? We have nearly an *hour* before dinner's ready." I showed her the plantain I'd just sliced—it looked just like hers, long strips cut on the diagonal.

She smiled and one white eyebrow went up. I so wished I could do that. Spent ages standing in front of my mirror holding my left eyebrow (same as Nana's) up with my finger, trying to train the muscles to keep it up there. So far, not working.

"Well done, Caro. All right—I suppose helping me so much in the kitchen earns you a story. Which do you want?"

Awesome! I put another plantain on my cutting board. "Oh, living in the same house as the Russian expatriates in Paris. Or . . . no, no . . . how about Greece?" I nibbled the inside of my cheek, thinking. "Or the winter you spent in Venice? Or—*augh!* I can't pick. You pick."

By this point she'd put down her knife and was just laughing at me. "But you've heard these stories a hundred times."

"And I could hear them a hundred more and never get tired of them, Nana. I mean, come on, you've had adventures. Your life has been totally exciting." While mine was totally boring, living in boring old Hampshire, Ohio, and going to boring old Hampshire Elementary and just doing boring old things. Boring, boring, *boring.* With a side of dull.

Because she was Nana and always seemed to know when I was thinking stuff like this, she put her knife down again and placed her soft hand against my cheek. "Oh, sweet girl, be patient. You're young yet. After all, I was nearly twice your age before I even *thought* of having an adventure."

Twice my age? *Twice*? That would've made her . . . eighteen, nineteen, maybe. Jeez. That was for*ever* away. I'd probably wither away from the dullness of my life before then. With another sigh, I left the table, walking into the dining room, which had tons of family pictures, like the ones of Daddy when he was a baby that always made me laugh, and the ones of Papa Joseph holding me and my brother James when we were really little. I wish I could remember Papa Joseph, but I'd only been a year old when he died. He must have been so cool though—I mean, considering how much Nana loved him. And you could *see* how much she loved him, in every single picture of her, whether Papa was in the shot or was the one taking the picture. Like my favorite picture of her—wearing a flouncy skirt, a shirt that left her shoulders bare, and a big flower tucked in her hair that fell all the way down her back. She looked so wild and grown-up, like a Gypsy princess or something, glancing over her shoulder with this big smile, and you could just *tell* by the expression on her face that it was Papa Joseph who'd taken the picture. And that they were in the middle of some fantastic adventure. Far, far away from Hampshire.

Her hand stroked my long braid. "Oh, my impatient Caroline. Don't worry, sweet girl, you'll have your adventures. I promise." Leading us back to the table, she picked up her knife and kept slicing. "Now, have we discussed Grand Duke Orlovsky?"

"Isn't he the guy who gave you the recipe for borscht?"

"Yes—and he was hardly just a *guy*," she said, that eyebrow going back up. "He was Russian nobility—descended from the czars, or so he said." She shook her head and laughed.

"Yeah, what was up with all that White Russian stuff anyway?"

"Well, it's a long story."

"Nana, we have nearly an *hour* . . ."

ACT I

1

"**Y**ou got everything?"

I slammed the back hatch on my aged-but-not-so-old-it-was-actually-cool Forester and turned to face my best friend. "Yes, Mom," I drawled.

Amy wrinkled her nose in that cute way she had. "Bitch," she replied in a decidedly *not* cute voice. It's what threw people—the acid tone coming from that sweet little face and petite body. Well, the tone *and* the scary intelligence. Neither of which threw me, mostly because we'd known each other since the playpen, so I just laughed.

"Takes one to know, et cetera, et cetera."

"Yeah, yeah." She waved her hand and made a *pfft* noise. She wasn't impressed by me, either. "So seriously, Caro, do you have everything?"

I glanced again into the full-but-not-stuffed back of the wagon. "Pretty much. It's only a summer session, Ames."

"True," she agreed, "but you still have to have the essentials."

Holding up my hand, I began ticking off on my fingers, "Laptop, iPod and portable speakers the 'rents gave me for graduation, coffeemaker—"

"Books?" she broke in.

"Books," I reassured her, glancing over my shoulder at the three boxes stashed in the back of the Forester. Couldn't go anywhere without the books. "Makeup and other beauty essentials and, of course, the cute summer wardrobe."

At that, she sighed.

"Don't start with me, Amy—you helped me pick out half that stuff."

"Under duress." Yeesh, but the frown looked so wrong on that cute face.

"Bite your tongue. Spending money on our dads' credit cards is *never* an 'under duress' situation."

"Well, no . . ." For a second the frown gave way to a smile, then melted away again. "You're really, really going to do it—go through with this boneheaded scheme."

Here we went . . . again. I took a deep breath and launched into the argument I'd been perfecting over the better part of the last six months.

"Think of it as playing a part, Ames. I mean, I'm a theater major, right?" I hit a pseudo-drama queen pose, which elicited another smile. Dropping down to the grass and crossing my legs, I waited for Amy to join me, chin on her upraised knees, same way we'd sat facing each other . . . forever, practically. "I mean, really, how is it any different from when Renée Zellweger and her American accent went incognito at a London publishing house for *Bridget Jones*?"

"Aside from the fact that you're not getting paid a metric buttload of cash and aren't likely to score an Oscar nom?"

I stuck my tongue out at her. "Then think of it as exploring my roots."

"Oh, bullpuckey. What roots, Caro? You're basing all of this on the background of *one* relative—two generations removed."

"You're forgetting the part where she's the only relative I've ever felt a *real* connection with," I reminded her, my throat closing up at the thought of Nana Ellie.

Nearly five years she'd been gone and I still missed her so much. Her cooking and her soft perfumed hands and her stories of adventure and the constant assurances that I'd have my own when the time came. Well, dammit, it was time. I'd been patient and everything, marking off every year until I turned eighteen, which was when she'd set out on her first adventure—and which, as it so happened, had turned out to be a total slam dunk. So who better to emulate, right?

"Look, I'll grant the connection is important," she admitted, "but the total truth is, your roots are in the same place mine are, Caro. Right here in Hampshire where both our families have been forever. The way you talk about it, you'd think it was a leper colony or something."

"Only if lepers are boring."

"It is *not* boring." She cranked up the indignant on the tone. "It's got that whole quirky, *Pleasantville*-meets-*Northern Exposure* vibe going for it."

"The Spiritual Life Holistic Center sharing space with Temple Beth Shalom in the former Catholic church does not, in and of itself, a quirky vibe make."

"Oh, come *on*."

Eh, she had a small point, if I were honest. "All right, well, maybe a little."

Because while it was weird as hell watching people trying to hold tree pose while serenely facing off with some stained-glass saint or another, I couldn't deny it did give us a uniqueness that most of the other burgs around these parts couldn't claim. Not that that was saying much—northeast Ohio just wasn't exactly a hotbed of exotic.

"Caro, look . . . not that I'm trying to preach or tell you what to do—"

"Of course you are."

"Okay, maybe just a little." She stared down at her hands, then back up at me. "Or maybe I'm just still trying to understand why being from Hampshire is such a bad thing. I mean, it's not like it's the only thing that's ever going to define you."

"I don't know," I answered after a long moment, shaking my head. "Right now, it's the sole basis for how everyone sees me. My whole *life*, it's been the sole basis for how everyone sees me. Caroline Darcy, sixth-generation Hampshire girl, *nice* Hampshire girl, never gives her folks any trouble, a bit quiet, unless she's on the stage, then she's a pretty fair little mimic. Maybe she'll come back and help run the community theater after she's done with college."

I shook my head again. "I just feel like if I don't look for something different, Ames, if I don't fight to get out, it'll end up being the *only* thing that defines me."

Fiddling with the beads studding her flip-flops, Amy said, "I don't think you give people around here enough credit."

"Oh yeah?" The heat started prickling along my neck and shoulders. "People around here—they *think* they know me, no matter what I do. I could dress in a grass skirt and do the hula on the Village Green in the dead of winter and the most I'd get is patted on the head and told how sweet that is and does my daddy know I'm outside without my coat?" The heat faded as I sighed and looked down the shady street toward the Village Green, just visible, two blocks away. And not far past that, on the corner of Main and Third, my family's pharmacy and old-fashioned soda shop that we'd owned for—guess what?—six generations.

"I mean, no one here will ever see me as anyone other than Jimmy and Nancy's little girl or James's little sister." Staring down at my Keds, I added, "I want more than that."

"You know, I'm going to skip the whole 'you're already more

and you should know that and that's what's really important' thing because you wouldn't believe me anyway." Amy popped up and started pacing in front of me, her flip-flops snapping against her heels in a way that made me think even *they* were annoyed. "But going off to college and pretending to be Cuban? Isn't that a little extreme in the redefinition department?"

"It's not pretending." I shrugged and pulled at the summer-dry blades of grass by my feet. "Not really."

"Caro—" She dropped back down in front of me. "One relative—one—" She held up her index finger, making sure I was getting it. "Two generations back. Even if it *was* Nana Ellie and she was the coolest, it's what? One-eighth of your background?"

"It feels right," I insisted with another shrug.

"I don't get it," she said with a sigh, dropping her chin back to her knees.

"I know."

Wasn't so sure I totally got it, either, but I wasn't bullshitting her. Tapping into my Latin roots, however thin they were—reestablishing that connection to Nana Ellie—I couldn't imagine any other adventure being more exciting. Even if it didn't involve Russian dukes.

A few hours later I cruised over the final rolling hill singing along to the Shakira blaring from the stereo as I turned through the brick-and-iron gates that formed the main entrance to the University of Southern Ohio. (Go, Fighting Cougars, although God knows when anyone actually saw an actual cougar around here. I'm just sayin'.)

Anyhow, it was just me making the trek to Middlebury, a little corner of hilly real estate situated in that no-man's-land near the Pennsylvania and West Virginia borders. Mom and Dad had offered to come with, but I'd said, no, not necessary. I mean, not like this was the real deal or anything. Was just a summer session—I wouldn't even be living in the residence hall I was booked into for the regular school year, so it was more like going off to camp for six weeks.

Dad was actually kind of relieved when I said I was good driving down by myself since summer was such a busy time at our pharmacy, what with kids out of school and all the tourists who blew through Hampshire for the Colonial charm and obscure battlefields, and the National Park complete with rolling hills, flora and fauna, and tons of hiking and bike trails for the getting-close-to-Mother Earth thing. We were a prime "educational vacation" destination—the kind of place where people killed a day so they could feel all virtuous before heading up to Cleveland and the Rock and Roll Hall of Fame or down to Canton and the Pro Football Hall of Fame. And since tourists seemed to have a way of getting sick and/or injured, Dad always had plenty to occupy his time. So he calmed Mom down, since she was bummed at not getting to see one of her babies settled at college, and reassured her they'd help me do the big, official freshman year move-in come fall semester.

Which would be good, since I think we'd already dealt with the worst of the "going away to school" stuff.

Because you see, just because he was cool with my being Independent Girl didn't mean my father didn't give me a big old "drive safe, be safe" lecture, complete with an AAA card and a jumbo box of Trojans, spermicidal lubricant and everything.

"Honestly, you'd think I wouldn't have been so surprised seeing as he pulled the same stunt when James went off to Ohio State four years ago," I'd spluttered to Amy on the phone about ten seconds after Dad closed my bedroom door behind him, mission accomplished.

"Yeah, but James is a guy and the firstborn and all that good stuff," Amy pointed out. "Not a surprise you got sort of blind-sided."

"No kidding. I mean, considering it was Mom who gave me 'the talk' the first time around. And anyway, I thought dads had a thing about their little girls having sex."

Then again, when your dad happened to be the town's pharmacist . . . I guess it went with the turf—but honestly, I thought I was going to die, right there. First thought that had crossed my mind was that he'd somehow gotten inside info about last summer when I went up to Interlochen for theater camp. Not quite "this one time . . . at band camp . . ." territory, but hey, teenagers, summer heat, hormones, and Michael—who'd played Bernardo to my Anita in our production of *West Side Story*—had been cute in a gawky sort of way. And with this outrageous talent that lit him up once he was on the stage. . . . There was no resisting him then. But it was a classic summer thing and after a final romantic hurrah under the stars and a slightly teary-eyed good-bye, he'd gone back to Colorado Springs, I'd come back to Hampshire, and that had been pretty much it. But it had been really nice. Nice enough that I wasn't about to risk ruining the memory with just *any* old guy. Not like this was a big danger in Hampshire, where every eligible guy just saw me as plain old Caro Darcy, sixth-generation Hampshire girl, et cetera, et cetera . . .

But if Dad didn't somehow have the inside info, I wasn't about to give it to him. *Way* too much TMI for me—and him, too, if I had to guess, Trojans notwithstanding. I did tell him not to worry, though. And thanked him for the, um . . . gift, even if I was blushing about forty-seven shades of red as I said it.

After finding a parking spot in the lot next to Harrison Hall and getting myself checked in, I dragged my stuff upstairs to my third-floor single. Man *alive*, a shower was going to feel great, but I had one more thing to do before I could indulge. Poking through the box packed with bathroom stuff, I found the Walgreens bag I'd thrown in there last night. I reached in and pulled out step one in my "boneheaded scheme."

Two hours later, I stared at myself in the mirror. Whoa. And whoa again. This was even better than I'd hoped. Ames was so wrong. This was *not* boneheaded, or harebrained or . . . what was the other one? The one she'd gotten from her Granddad MacCallum? Oh, right. Addlepated. This wasn't going to be any of those—it was going to be absolutely *fantastico*. Digging through my backpack, I found my cell and took a quick shot. After sending it zooming to Amy's cell, I texted a quick message.

> *What do you think?*
> *Caliente, right???*

Ha. Bet I'd be able to hear the screech all the way down here when she checked *that* message. Pulling out my laptop, I fired it up and downloaded the picture from my phone. Bringing it up onscreen and enlarging it, I studied myself closely. Havana Brown: the new hair color for the new me. Man, it was *so* nice— even better than I'd envisioned. A bunch of shades darker and a world away from the blah, beige blonde I'd lived with my whole life. Thanks to spending every free minute I'd had since graduation at the community pool and easing back to SPF 15 from my normal 45, I also had a nice, bronze-y, tropical glow going that made my usually muted blue eyes stand out in a way they never had against my normally pale (and blah) complexion. Are we sort of sensing a theme here?

I studied the picture and twisted in my chair to look in the mirror again—definietly not beige anymore and not so blah. Not so easy to fade into the wallpaper.

Absolutely *fantastico*.

2

As I walked down the hallway, I put a hand to my stomach, trying to settle the quivering—not to mention the greasy burger I'd grabbed at the student union. Big mistake. But the Organic Llama, the salad and sandwich place, had been packed. Now I knew why. I'd have to figure out when the best times to go were—and would have to stock up on yogurt and munchies for my room. The closer I got to my destination, the harder my stomach started doing its thing and the more the floors vibrated. No, I hadn't indulged in anything hallucinogenic—as *if*. It was only the music throbbing from the giant second-floor rec room that joined the three dorms in the complex together. According to the registration packet I'd received at check-in yesterday, this was the Welcome Neighbor Luau. Cheesy, true, but kind of fun sounding.

"Yeah, because nothing says 'luau' like Fall Out Boy bellowing 'Dance, Dance.' " It was so loud, I could barely hear Amy's comment on my cell, as I approached the rattling double doors.

"Could be worse." I shrugged, smiling into the phone as I felt the bouncy waves of my Havana Brown hair brushing against my nearly bare shoulders and against my back in a way that for the first time in my life made me feel . . . I don't know, sexy, I guess. Sexy as me, not as a character on the stage. That was a first. "At least it beats Alan Jackson and Jimmy Buffett."

"Come again?"

"That's what James said they played at his first dorm party at OSU."

"Oh, *ugh*." I could practically feel Amy's shudders all the way back in Hampshire.

"No kidding. I mean, who gives a rat's ass if it's five o'clock somewhere? There's not enough alcohol in the world to dull the pain of having to listen to that song."

"No shit. Although I shouldn't talk. Who knows what they'll play at Michigan." All of a sudden, she switched gears, asking, "Caro, are you absolutely *sure* about this?" Poor thing, she sounded like a nervous old lady about this, but really . . . she didn't need to.

"Relax, Ames."

"You are about to breeze in there and completely bullshit your background and you're telling *me* to relax?" Her voice kept going up in pitch until I had to pull the phone away from my ear and even then, I could still hear her, loud and clear. "You're certifiable, you know that?"

"Amy, please, would you *chill*?" I ducked into a vending area that was quiet—and maybe more important, secluded. Lowering my voice, I said, "It's not so much complete bullshit as it is shifting a few facts around. Honestly, I really don't know why you're so bent about this."

"Because it's nuts isn't enough?" I could hear the pop and hiss of a soda can opening in the background. "Or how about because I have a feeling this has all sorts of bad spelled across it?" She let loose with a belch that would've made any of her four brothers proud.

"You know, it's hard to take you seriously when you rip one like that," I muttered.

"Okay, explain to me how this is going to work?" she asked, *again*, while conveniently ignoring me at the same time.

For what felt like the millionth time, I repeated, "Easy, Ames. It's a case of keeping most of the facts accurate, so that I don't trip over the embellishments." Because it so wasn't a lie—not really. "I'm still from Hampshire, my last name is still Darcy, but instead of having a great-grandmother who's Cuban, it's my mother who's Cuban, so I'm half a hot tamale." I swished the tiers of my blue ruffled skirt on the last two words.

"Why don't you just go check out the Latin American Student Alliance?" she begged. "Explore your roots that way? Then you—"

"Uh-uh," I said before she'd even finished the suggestion. "Where's the adventure in that?" I stared down at my feet in my black canvas espadrilles.

A soft thumping sound made me pull the phone away from my ear and look at it. Oh man, she was probably banging her head against the wall or her headboard again—gently, I hoped. "Your idea of adventure is so. Utterly. Bent. *Augh.*"

Okay, she wasn't going to get it—I couldn't really expect her to get it, so I wasn't going to make myself too crazy trying. Okay, lie. I had to try. If only because she was Amy and I had to have her, if not in my corner, then at least not blocking it off from the rest of the room.

"Ames, look, I can't explain it any better than I have before, so you'll just have to trust me. I have to try it this way, but I'll make you a promise—I'll totally check out the Latin American Alliance during fall semester."

"You know, that's really not the point," she said in a voice that wasn't just grumpy, but had—I don't know—an edge, I guess. It kind of scared me, truthfully, but I had to ask.

"Then what?"

I heard her take a deep breath. "You don't want to hear it, Caroline, but that's not the point, either. You don't need me telling you. You need to figure it out yourself. I guess this . . . adventure is the way you need to do it, so who am I to try to stop you?"

Okay, seriously confused, now. "You're my best friend."

"Yeah, I am." Her voice went soft, losing the edge. "As such, I've got your back and all that good best friend stuff."

Closing my eyes, I took a deep breath. I wondered if she could tell just how relieved that made me feel. Opening my eyes, I left the vending area and resumed my walk toward the rec room. "Well, time to luau, then."

"Yes, because nothing says 'luau' like Linkin Park and 'Numb.' " She made the new observation in what I called her English professor's voice.

"Don't forget Jay-Z," I said with a laugh.

"Never," she drawled. "Call or IM later, okay? Let me know how it went? After all, I have to live vicariously through you until I go off to Michigan so don't forget a single sordid detail."

"I'll take pictures," I promised, then hit the button ending the call and slipped the phone into my woven Target-special clutch before pushing the door open.

"Aloha," a voice shouted over one of the riffs from the "Numb/Encore" mash-up. I looked up into a pair of seriously blue eyes as a paper cup of festive red punch was shoved into my hand. Darned tasty red punch. Excellent for the sudden dry mouth.

"Welcome to the luau, my name's Dylan and tonight I'll be serving as your perky cruise director." Dark eyebrows rose as he joked and looked me up and down, and would you believe those gorgeous baby blues even twinkled? It was an effort not to let my jaw drop.

"Hi, I'm—"

Here we go . . . if I was going to do it, it was now or never.

"Carolina," I said with the subtle inflection and roll on the "r" that I'd practiced and repeated into my digital recorder until it became second nature. So second nature, it actually sounded natural, even though I had major-league butterflies headbanging in my stomach. Taking the hand Dylan the hottie offered, I took a deep breath and repeated, "My name is Carolina."

3

Her full name was Elisa Maribel Teresa de la Natividad Sevilla y Tabares.

You had to be wondering, right? The source of all of this? Well, that's her and she's been my hero since I found out about her when I was fourteen years old. Well, found about the *real* her. Until then, she'd only existed as Dad's Nana Ellie. *My* Nana Ellie—my best bud who'd had fabulous adventures far, far away from Hampshire and loved Papa Joseph and the rest of the family and made great meals and gave cool gifts. Like the huge Easter basket she gave me when I was seven, decorated with silk lilies of the valley and filled with tons of European chocolate. At the time I was bummed because I'd wanted Hershey's and marshmallow Peeps. Relax—my tastes have evolved. Mostly because of Nana Ellie.

Anyhow, stuck in among the chocolate was a doll with a porcelain face and dark hair, wearing a tiara and a fluffy dress that had once been white, but which, by the time I got her, was sort of a mottled ivory. When I started to complain that her dress was dirty, Mom shushed me but Nana Ellie just laughed and said that she hadn't taken such great care of her and maybe I'd do better. In the car on the way home, Mom told me the doll was very, very old and I had to be careful with her.

No problem. I mean, the doll was pretty, I guess, but it wasn't like my Barbies with their shiny dresses and the cool accessories, so I was happy enough to leave her sitting on a high shelf as decoration. Again, didn't find out until I was fourteen the significance of the doll.

So why was fourteen such a big deal? Well, because it was my freshman year of high school and the first year I had to take a language requirement. I chose Spanish and the first time I stood up in class to recite, Señora Garcia interrupted midconjugation and rattled off a question.

"Perdóname, Señorita Darcy, ¿Usted sabe hablar español?"

" 'Scuse me?" She'd blurted it out so fast that it came out sounding like one big word I couldn't decipher. I guess the blank look was enough of an answer, but she tried again—in English, at least.

"Have you ever spoken Spanish before?"

"No, Señora."

"Qué raro," she muttered, which at the time I didn't understand, both literally and figuratively.

But I owe Señora Garcia—big time. See, she was so impressed with my accent, and the fact that I took to Spanish so easily, that she actually called a conference with my parents by the end of the first grading period. Told them that she'd never had such a natural first-time student. That's when Dad said something along the lines of it maybe being a genetic thing and *I* said something along the lines of "Say *what*?"

That's when I found out about Nana Ellie's secret identity as Elisa Maribel Teresa et cetera, et cetera—the daughter of an über, *über*wealthy Cuban family. And I'm not exaggerating when I stress the über. We're talking the kind of old-money family that makes the Rockefellers look seriously nouveau and just this side of the trailer park. With not just one house in Havana, but also the country house *and* the beach house. The kind of family that had memberships to every exclusive club that catered to

Cuban high society, that traveled to Europe as casually as most people travel across town, and sent their kids to élite boarding schools and universities, in Havana, or in the States, or Europe.

Can you *imagine*?

So how did Elisa Maribel Teresa de la Natividad Sevilla y Tabares of Havana turn into Nana Ellie of Hampshire, Ohio?

Come on, you had to guess that only love could pull off that feat.

But it was love with *scandal*.

She was seventeen, just married—weird, but they got married *real* young back then—and her husband had commissioned a young American artist to paint her portrait for her eighteenth birthday. Pretty much followed that Jack and Rose scenario from *Titanic* after that, except without the iceberg and sinking ship and tragic death. They ran off to Europe—about the only things she took with her were some clothes, a few pieces of jewelry that her parents had given her, and the doll—the one she gave me. Her *quinceañera* doll—the symbolic last toy of childhood that a Latin girl receives on the occasion of her fifteenth birthday, her entrance to womanhood and society. I'm sure there's irony in there somewhere, that it's one of the few things she took with her.

They lived the Bohemian Artist's life, traveling around Europe for a few years until Nana Ellie got pregnant with Grandma—Dad's mom. Considering that the Nazis were starting to make things uncomfortable for bohemian artist types, Papa Joseph decided it was as good a time as any to give up the *Moulin Rouge* existence and take her home to Hampshire to become respectable.

He introduced her as his wife, everyone more or less said the 1930s equivalent of "cool," and they settled into a pretty uneventful life with Papa Joseph opening a photography studio and Nana becoming a typical Hampshire housewife. No one had a clue that they weren't even legally married until Papa Joseph died. That's when Nana apparently pulled the Shocking Confession routine with the family about their scandalous beginning. She could never get a divorce because to do so would have meant she'd have to give up her anonymity and if she did that, it was entirely possible her family would have come and carted her butt straight back to Cuba and, let's face it, they had the money to make it happen and make sure she never saw Papa Joseph again.

Now, Dad didn't tell me all of this—not at first. Actually, I got a lot of it from Mom, who also knew the whole story and who I think was a little more comfortable with the sharing. Made sense, I guess. She had a sort of distance from the sitch that Dad couldn't possibly have. Truthfully, I think it wigged him a little— reconciling his straight-arrow, solid Midwest-value grandparents with the young couple passionate and in love enough that they weren't gonna let a little thing like, you know, *marriage,* stand in their way.

Probably right up there with realizing your parents actually still had sex and enjoyed it.

Unfortunately Nana passed away when I was thirteen or I would've just asked her. Who knows what dirt I might've gotten— I have this feeling she might have enjoyed telling all, and . . . Well, as much as I knew her, I just really wish I could've had more of a chance to get to know the real her.

As for me, it was like everything got brighter and a whole new world of possibilities opened up. I'd finally found something special about myself, something unique. And I'm not just talking about the facility with Spanish. I mean, I had Exotic Bloodlines! With a side of Rebel, no less.

I kept it pretty much under wraps because hey, even I can

recognize the inherent weirdness in embracing it too much, especially when you live somewhere as all-American as Hampshire, but I told Amy, of course. At first she thought it was as cool as I did, the Exotic Bloodlines and all. She started thinking I'd maybe lost my mind, halfway through senior year, when it occurred to me, why *not* embrace that Cuban part of me? Play the part, as it were. Just for a little while—to see what it was like. I'd be going away to college where no one knew me, I'd been doing community theater since I was old enough to memorize lines, and clearly, acting ability was something else I'd inherited from Nana. Think about it—no one even knew that she wasn't American until her confession because she spoke English without the slightest hint of a Spanish accent. Apparently everyone had thought she'd just been an American abroad when she met Papa Joseph and she never bothered correcting that assumption.

The one thing I knew I needed to do, though, to pull it off, was to sound less like someone who'd taken four years of formal high school Spanish and more like a modern, half-Cuban teenager. That's when I started watching the Spanish-language networks that we got on satellite and lots of Gael García Bernal movies. Buying scads of music off iTunes to sing along to and reading magazines like *Latina* and *People en Español*. All the glam pictures in the mags also made me realize I'd have to change the appearance a little, hence, the Havana Brown hair and the tan and, well . . . here I was. Checking out the crowd as I sipped from another paper cup of the festive red punch and hoping that maybe Dylan the blue-eyed hottie might wander over and ask me to dance. I was definitely enjoying the newfound confidence, but didn't think I was quite up to asking a guy who looked like he did if he wanted to take a spin around the floor.

"Avoid the shish kebabs."

I looked up and promptly suffered my second attack of dry mouth as I stared into another pair of gorgeous baby blues. "Ex-excuse me?" I managed to stutter out.

"I said, avoid the shish kebabs. They're probably lethal and I'd hate to lose you before I've gotten a chance to get to know you."

4

Holy cow, did they pass out tinted contact lenses to the guys at registration or what?

Even though his hair wasn't dark, like Dylan's, but a sandy blond, it totally didn't lessen the impact. Especially considering the brows that were only a shade or two darker and had this pointed little arch that gave him a wicked, merry expression. Add in the effect of one corner of his mouth turned up in a smirk and I immediately pictured him as Shakespeare's immortal pain in the ass Puck. A very hot Puck. Who was warning me about shish kebabs.

"Lethal?"

"Yeah. My fraternity brothers brought them as their contribution and they're made with cubes of Spam, pineapple, and maraschino cherries that they soaked in bourbon."

"Oh . . . yuck." I shuddered and downed the rest of my punch.

"Exactly." He rolled his eyes and, before I knew it, had led me over to the table with the punch, far away from the shish kebabs. Smooth. Very smooth. Handing me a fresh cup of punch, he said, "I hate to give the freshies such a bad impression first night out, but clearly, my brothers have no such issues."

"Stick out that much, do I?" Now that I'd recovered—sort of—from the shock of being faced with another pair of gorgeous eyes, I was able to relax. At least as much as anyone who was completely faking a persona was able to. Oh man, was I out of my mind? No time to worry, though, because the cute Puck wannabe was talking.

"Not as much as some, but after three years of practice, I've got a good eye for the newbies."

Three years. Which meant he was probably a senior. *Whoa.* "Which was it, the scared-shitless expression or the fact that I wasn't talking to anyone?"

He leaned a shoulder against the wall next to me and openly looked me over. He wasn't a whole lot taller than me, but gave off a confidence vibe that had the butterflies headbanging in my stomach again. "You do not look scared shitless."

See? Pretty good actress. Because, oh yeah, I *was* scared—with a heavy dose of nerves on the side. Of course, it was possible he was also just feeding me a gigantic line about not looking freaked. Whatever. I was cool with that so long as he looked me over again. Because along with the butterflies, there were some nice tinglies going on, as well. I'd never really had much of a chance to hone the flirting skills outside of acting classes. Even with Michael, we'd clicked first as our characters, *then* as ourselves. Doing it the normal way . . . this was kind of fun.

"So what gave me away then?"

"The fact that you don't look a thing like anyone else around here."

I couldn't help but giggle. "Oh, you're good."

At that, he straightened and gestured to the room at large. "No, seriously. Look around. You definitely stand out."

Would you believe he looked serious? Enough to make me tear my gaze away from the blue eyes and glance around the room enough to realize he had a point. Everyone was in some variation of jeans or shorts paired with tees or polos, except for the girls who were clearly going for that trashy Paris Hilton look in microminis and backless camisoles. Clearly fashion forward wasn't exactly Middlebury's forte. And here I was in my festive blue ruffled skirt and black flowered tank with a hot pink one worn beneath, inspiration, courtesy of a recent issue of *InStyle*. My mirror had told me I looked pretty good. This guy's eyes were telling me I looked great.

"There's something different—exotic, I guess—about you."

The words shivered down my spine and made goose bumps rise on my arms. *Bingo.* I smiled with what I hoped was some mystery, then cast my eyes down and took a sip of punch. A small sip, because if I kept guzzling, I'd have to make a mad dash for the bathroom and it would be a shame to interrupt the proceedings when things were starting to get interesting.

"So, you have a name or should I just stick with 'exotic girl'?"

"Carolina Darcy." And it came out even smoother and with more of a lilt than when I introduced myself to Dylan. Looking up into his face, I could see it light up, those eyebrows rising. And again with the *bingo.*

"And where are you from, Carolina Darcy?" He tried to put the same lilt on it, but stumbled a little over the subtle roll on the "r." Never mind. It was cute that he tried.

"Hampshire."

"No."

"Seriously."

"No way." He shook his head. "I've met people from Hampshire. There is just no way."

Hey, wait a minute . . . "Maybe it's high on the vanilla scale, but it's not exactly some sort of Stepford, spitting out homogeneous assembly-line robots."

Wow, he actually jerked back physically. I almost did, too—who knew I could sound that fierce? And about Hampshire, no less? But he recovered pretty quick, just lifting the corner of his mouth in that smirk and saying, "Obviously not, if you come from there. Last thing you are is assembly-line material."

Man, he was *good*. I couldn't help but wonder if all college guys were this smooth or if he was just exceptionally gifted.

"Well, thanks." I relaxed back against the wall and ran my thumb along the rim of my cup. If I kept moving my hands, he couldn't see them shaking. "So, do you have a name or should I just stick with 'my hero,' since you saved me from the shish kebabs of doom?"

He threw his head back and let loose with a laugh that was loud enough to carry over the music, his full-out smile revealing an unbelievable set of dimples. Oh man, this was starting to be completely not fair. Not that anyone would ever mistake him for an out-and-out pretty boy—the individual features weren't put together that well—but honestly, *no* guy should be allowed a set of dimples to go along with those eyes. Or if it was going to be allowed, he should come with a warning label so a girl at least stood a fighting chance.

"While I wouldn't object to 'my hero,' I think I'll settle for Erik." He reached out and took one of my hands in his, shaking it. "Erik Larsen."

Considering how my stomach jumped up into my throat at that first contact, it was amazing I was able to get "Good to meet you, Erik Larsen" out in a reasonably normal tone of voice.

"So, what is it that keeps you from being assembly-line material, Miss Carolina?"

Huh? Assembly line? Then the second he released my hand, it made sense again, even though I could still feel the cool, dry clasp of his fingers around mine. Warning labels, I'm telling you.

But now that I remembered what he was referring to, my stomach jumped up into my throat again. If I was going to do this—*really* try to pull this off—this would be the first test.

"Oh, there's nothing really that different about me."

"Oh yeah there is, and it's not just the hot outfit. Come on," he urged, leaning a little closer. "You can tell me. If only because I saved you from the shish kebabs."

I tried to shrug in a nonchalant manner. "Honestly, there really isn't . . . not unless you consider being Cuban as different."

And chalk up the third *bingo* moment to complete the trifecta.

"A Cuban girl from Hampshire and you don't think that qualifies as different?"

I shrugged again. "In the immortal words of Popeye: I yam what I yam."

"A Cuban girl from Hampshire who quotes Popeye?" He put his hand to his chest in this really cheesy, showy move. "I think I've died and gone to heaven."

"Oh, stop," I giggled. "Only half Cuban, so it's not *quite* so exotic."

He dropped the hand. "More than what you usually get around these parts."

See? I wasn't the only one who thought parts of Ohio were seriously lacking in exotic.

"So what's the other half?" he asked.

"Just plain old American."

He leaned his shoulder against the wall again, but unless someone had slipped a little something into the punch and I was imagining things, he was a little bit closer than he'd started out. We were starting to seriously edge into each other's personal bubbles. Cool with me.

"Guess that Cuban half is pretty powerful then."

"Yeah?"

"Yeah. Definitely trumps the plain old American, big time." His mouth quirked up again. "Would you like to dance, Carolina Darcy?"

As he asked the question, I realized that the frantic tunes that had dominated since I'd gotten here had finally eased back into something slow and sway-worthy. "Yeah."

And good thing one-word answers seemed to be doing the trick. But wouldn't you know it, no sooner had he taken my cup—setting it on a nearby table and taken my hand in his—than a cheerful "Yo, Erik—hold up, man" rang out over John Legend's sexy vocals.

"Nichols, can't you see I'm about to take this lovely lady out for a spin on the dance floor? Your timing blows bears, dude."

"Oh shit, sorry, bro." The skinny guy who'd approached at least looked apologetic, even as he half smiled, half leered. It was a toss-up as to whether I felt flattered or creeped out. I settled for taking a step back—grabbing some breathing room.

"So, what's up—and make it quick, wouldja, so I can grab at least half this song."

"Chill, dude. I'll get the DJ to play another groiny chart."

Okay, definitely leering—and crude to boot. Charming. Erik apparently thought as much, since he smacked the guy upside the head and snapped, "Jesus, Nichols. Show a little respect. No wonder you can't get a chick to date you more than once."

"Once with me is all they can handle." Then he winked in a way that suggested he wasn't taking himself too seriously. I relaxed some. You know, he was just a college guy. Like my brother and Amy's brothers had all been at one point or another. High on the weenie scale, but fairly harmless.

"Nichols . . ."

"All right, all right. Sorry. I just wanted you to meet someone who's thinking of pledging this fall."

"Oh, hey, that's great." He turned to me. "I'm sorry. I'm pledge master this year and I kind of have to . . ."

"It's okay. Another song." I started to move away so he could do whatever fraternity pledge master/secret handshake/hoodoo-voodoo thing he needed to do, but before I could get too far he reached out and grabbed my hand again.

"It's cool. Since it's summer this isn't actually official. Stay close?"

How could I say no when he turned that full smile with the dimples on me? More importantly, why would I want to?

"Pete, this is Erik, this year's pledge master; Erik, this is Pete. He's a ju-co transfer."

"Hey, Pete, good to meet you." Releasing my hand, Erik reached out and shook the hand of the tall, dark-haired guy standing next to Nichols the Classless. The guy who'd been so quiet I hadn't realized he was even there until right now. Of course, I'd been so focused on Erik and his seriously expert flirt-ing, a squad of jets could've landed in the room and I might've missed it.

"Nice to meet you, too. And I prefer Peter, actually," the guy corrected as he returned Erik's handshake.

"Sorry," Erik said with a smile as he released Peter's hand and casually slung his arm over my shoulder, making me nearly jump out of my skin. Oh, *mama*. "You'll have to excuse Nichols—he has trouble with most words over one syllable."

"No big. Hi, I'm Peter."

I was so busy concentrating on the weight of Erik's arm on my shoulder that it took me a second to realize that Peter was talking to me. Luckily, Erik jumped in and rescued me.

"Excuse me, Peter. My manners are going almost as much to shit as Nichols's. This is Carolina Darcy."

Poor guy—still stumbling over that rolling "r," but he sounded so darned charming doing it. However, it sounded all the more obvious when Peter shook my hand and said "Pleased to meet you, Carolina" without stumbling and *with* the subtle roll. The high school Spanish must've stuck.

While Erik launched into his shtick about why their frat was the one frat to rule them all and why all the others were losers—without actually saying that, understand—I let my gaze wander again. I bit back a laugh as I saw some people sampling the shish kebabs over at the buffet and swallowed a sigh as I watched all the other people out on the floor dancing . . . swaying, actually, hips plastered nice and close together, to the slow, sultry tune. I wanted to be out there, dammit. Preferably with Erik, although if Dylan happened by, not sure I would've turned him down, either.

As I continued to people watch, I started to get the weird feeling that *I* was being stared at. Trying to be subtle as I checked out my immediate surroundings, I saw that the Spidey sense hadn't been off. Nichols was staring at me—or more accurately, my boobs—with an expression that was definitely back toward leer territory. But hey, *that* I'd been dealing with since they'd made their appearance with a vengeance in eighth grade, so not like it was something new. Maybe the guys back in Hampshire only saw me as plain, old Caro Darcy, but that never stopped them from eyeing the 36Ds, even if they didn't realize they were doing it. They were guys, after all. The staring never got any easier, though. I freakin' *hated* feeling like an object—or two. Heat raging up from the scoop neck of my tank and over my face, I glared at Nichols hard enough that his eyes widened and his glance dropped away. Which made me think that maybe he hadn't been aware that he'd been staring, so I was able to relax again. At least until I realized someone was *still* looking at me.

Peter. Although he was a lot more subtle about it, only sliding the occasional glance my direction and it wasn't at my chest, but at me in general.

Man, I was really starting to wonder if I shouldn't have ex-plored my roots—or at least dyed them Havana Brown—a *long* time ago.

Ames825: So, how was your evening or do I even need to ask?

Caro_D: Be nice or I won't say a WORD about the cute fraternity guys.

Ames825: Cute fraternity guys?

Caro_D: Or the megahot R.A. . . .

Ames825: <behaving now>

Caro_D: Thought so. ☺

Ames825: Well? Fraternity guys? And what were frater-nity guys doing at a dorm party anyway?

Caro_D: Apparently, the Greeks are required to shut down their houses for the summer. Something about wanting to discourage the exclusivity vibe and have them do the blending thing with the rest of the student body. At least in theory. The ones who come for summer session all congregate at the same dorms anyhow, so not like it's that big a difference.

Ames825: So was there general ogling going on or one guy in particular?

Caro_D: <shocked> What are you, a mind-reader or something?

Ames825: So there WAS one guy—I knew it! You were giving off some serious vibage.

Caro_D: I was?

Ames825: Oh yeah. Very vibey vibrations coming through the transmission.

Caro_D: Uh-huh. Whatever. Anyhow, yes, there was one guy and he was a total Puck.

Ames825: His name was Puck?? He MUST be a frat boy. :-P

Caro_D: <grins> No . . . his name is Erik, but he reminded me of the perfect Puck.

Ames825: Could be good . . . could be bad.

Caro_D: Good thing, I think. He dances decently, got me punch, warned me away from the Shish Kebabs o' Doom.

Ames825: The WHAT?

Caro_D: Story for the phone, Ames.

Ames825: k

Ames825: Did you do it?

Caro_D: Worked like a total charm—he looked intrigued and interested and totally and completely bought it.

Ames825: I was afraid you'd say that. <sigh>

Caro_D: It's going to be okay.

Ames825: I was afraid you'd say that, too.

5

"**M**ay I?"

I glanced up from my history text to find the quiet, dark-haired guy from the luau the other night—Peter, I think?—standing by my table, a brown, recycled paper bag from the Organic Llama and a drink in one hand, his backpack in the other.

Looking around, I saw that the rest of the Llama's outdoor tables were full. Not surprising since it was a fantastic day—sunny, not too hot, even the occasional light breeze. Couldn't blame him for wanting to sit out here, especially if he'd just been cooped up in a classroom for nearly three hours like I had. Upside of summer classes: get a heinous course done with in six weeks instead of fourteen. Downside: the actual classes were a lot longer.

"Sure." I waved at the empty seat opposite mine.

"Thanks." As he settled himself, dropping his backpack to the concrete patio and pulling his sandwich and Terra Chips from the bag, he reintroduced himself. "Don't know if you remember from the other night, I'm Peter."

Cool, I did remember right. "Right. And I'm—"

"Carolina," he interrupted, once again putting the subtle lilt and roll and making me smile. And shiver a little, truth be known. You know, as cute as it sounded when Erik tried saying it (and yeah, he'd tried more than a few times since the other night), there was something about hearing it said right that sent this warm little tingle through me. I'd take it as a sign that I *was* doing the right thing, no matter what Ames said. And said . . . and said . . .

"You remembered."

"Yeah. Nice name."

Wait a minute. Something in how he said that—just as casual as the folks back home might say, "hot out there, today, isn't it?"—left me feeling kind of prickly and uncomfortable. And prompted me, for some bizarre, unknown reason, to say, "You can call me Caro, if you want. Most people do."

He glanced up from unwrapping his sandwich. "Do you prefer one over the other?"

Now, don't ask me why, but the question—every bit as casual-sounding as his observation about my name—had this feeling of an unexpected moment of truth, for yet some *other* bizarre, unknown reason.

"Not really." I figured I'd leave it up to him. Which did he see me as?

He shrugged. "Okay."

Okay? *Okay?* That was it? I sat there feeling like I'd somehow dodged a bullet, yet cranky about it at the same time. Well, crap.

"Hey, you know, don't let me interrupt your studying."

Well, then, a change of subject from my name. Probably a good thing. Since I hadn't imagined something so minor requiring so much internal drama. I stuck my lunch receipt in place as a bookmark and set the text on top of my backpack. "It's okay. Not really studying—more reading ahead for pleasure."

As he reached into his open bag of chips, his gaze shifted over to the book I'd been reading. "History's pleasure reading for you?"

"Yeah," I said, trying to mask the utter lameness of my confession behind a bite of grilled chicken-and-veggie wrap. But then again, I was a theater wonk. Not like I hadn't been embracing my inner dweeb for a long time, so what was one more instance? After a sip from my bottled Tazo, I added, "I figured since it was summer, I'd take one requirement I knew I'd love and one that would be an ass-kicker. Only six weeks of pain that way."

"Makes sense." We went quiet then, me finishing my wrap while he started in on what looked like tuna on wheat, the occasional crunch of a chip breaking the silence. "So what's the ass-kicker?"

I look up from the giant chocolate cookie I hadn't been able to resist. Which I probably needed to resist if I wanted the hot tamale wardrobe to retain its current hot status and not look like it was wrapped around an actual squishy tamale.

"Math analysis and trig." I shuddered, then closed my eyes at the combo of chocolate and macadamia nuts hitting the taste buds. Oh crud, I should've resisted. Because now that I knew how good the Llama's cookies were, it was going to be hard to resist. Wonder where the university's fitness center was? My eyes flew open at his quiet laugh, my skin feeling like I had instant major sunburn happening.

"Do I look that stupid?" And did I have crumbs on my face?

"Huh?"

"I was practically having a meltdown over the cookie— figured I looked kind of stupid in my bliss."

He looked at me, obviously confused, and shook his head. "No, wasn't laughing at that." Confused gave way to a grin. "Are you kidding? I don't *ever* laugh at women and chocolate. I have two older sisters. They taught me well—not to mention kicked my ass more than a few times."

Oh. Part of me admired that and wished that I'd been the

older one so I could've kicked James's ass when he was being a jerk; the more prominent, closer-to-the-surface part of me was hoping for a convenient hole to open up right under my chair because now I was really feeling like a total idiot. Didn't stop me, of course—

"So what were you laughing at?"

He lifted the bag of chips and tipped his head back for the last of the crumbs, the sunlight glinting off the small silver hoop he wore in one ear. "Irony," he finally answered, crumpling up the empty bag. "History was always one of my ass-kickers, math was fun."

"Fun?" Clearly, I was sharing my table with a twisted soul.

"Yeah." Shoving his garbage into the Organic Llama bag and pushing it aside, he leaned back in his chair with his soda. "But I'm kind of surprised that you say math is your ass-kicker. Math analysis and trig isn't exactly a lightweight class, so you can't be all that bad at it."

I snorted, choking down the swig of tea I'd just taken. "I got beyond lucky during the placement exams." If you could call it luck. "Not so lucky that I qualified for any credits, though, so not only do I still have to take the whole six credits' worth of math to fulfill the general studies requirement, it has to be with harder classes." Which meant calculus after this one—provided I survived. Feel my joy.

"I can help you out." Another shrug as he made the offer along with that same casual tone from before. Casual enough that it sounded more like some obligatory, "you let me share your table with you, I suppose I gotta be nice in return" offer, rather than the genuine article.

My turn to shrug, even as I felt all prickly again. "Obligatory" didn't exactly do wonders for me. "Thanks, but it's all right. I'll probably muddle through." I stood and tossed my garbage into a nearby can. Returning the history text to my backpack, I grabbed what was left of the chocolate cookie and made to leave. He followed my lead, tossing his garbage and slinging his backpack over his shoulder.

We made our way from the Llama's patio to one of the many paths leading away from the huge student union complex. Somehow, through God knows how many renovations and expansions and additions over the past century, the union had still managed to stay smack-dab in the middle of campus. On the map I'd received with my registration packet, it looked like a deformed fly caught in the middle of a really psychotic-looking spiderweb. In reality, it was a lot more attractive, all tree-lined flagstone pathways leading away from the sprawling brick building. And of all the pathways Peter could've veered off on, wouldn't you know, he went ahead and stayed on the one I was on, falling into step beside me.

A light touch brushed across my shoulder, making me look up. "Seriously, I don't mind. Maybe it won't be so ass-kicking with a little help."

His tone didn't sound quite so obligatory this time around— the gaze seemed pretty sincere, too.

"Are you serious?" Because if he was . . . maybe I wasn't big on obligatory, but I also wasn't one to look a gift horse in the mouth. And after my first three-hour class this morning, I already knew this was a course I did *not* want to take over if I didn't have to.

"Yeah, sure. Wouldn't offer if I wasn't."

I didn't point out how noncommittal he'd sounded when he made the offer the first time. Didn't really know him, after all, and why embarrass either of us? So I settled for breaking what was left of the enormous cookie in half and holding it out—a peace offering, even if he didn't realize it.

One eyebrow went up—seriously, was I the only person in the universe who couldn't do that? "You're parting with chocolate?"

"You're offering to babysit me through math analysis. Seems only fair." I grinned and bit into the cookie portion I still held.

"My sisters would say it's a completely unfair exchange—not that I'm objecting," he added, lunging for the cookie as I feigned snatching it back while laughing at the desperate look on his face.

More quiet between us as we walked, eating the cookie. Comfortable, like we didn't need to force conversation. Without the extraneous chatter, I fell into my habit of keying into the sights and sounds surrounding me, filing them away for future reference. People yelling across quads to each other, throwing Frisbees or tossing footballs; some sprawled out on blankets, sunbathing as they studied or—for those who were paired up—didn't. Music drifting from open windows, snatches of Kanye and Nickelback and the Raconteurs and Sugarland. Just the warp and woof of campus life on a warm July afternoon.

Approaching the dorm complex, I asked Peter, "So, what dorm are you in?"

He turned his head toward me, a funny expression on his face. "Harrison."

"Hey, that's mine, too—at least for the summer."

"I know." That funny expression was still on his face as we reached the front door and he swiped his key card through the electronic lock. "We're on the same floor."

"No way!" Not sure why I was so shocked since Harrison wasn't exactly a huge dorm—five floors and only about twelve rooms per floor. It almost served more as a bridge between Taft and Garfield, wedged the way it was between the two much bigger dorms in the complex. "Really?"

He held the door open and waited for me pass through. "Really." He followed as I opened another door and started up the stairs. The elevator wasn't the most reliable thing on the planet and besides, had half a cake plate-size cookie to work off. "I've seen you a couple of times, but you've seemed kind of . . . preoccupied."

"I did? With what?" But even before the words finished echoing around the stairwell, I felt a scorching wave of heat rushing down from my face under the neck of my T-shirt and all the way to my toes. Oh my God. He must have seen me with Erik. Because—let's be honest—he'd been a major source of preoccupation since the second he turned that Puck's grin on me and warned me away from the shish kebabs. I'd seen him every night since then, spending time laughing and doing the "get to know each other" dance at the various floor parties that seemed to be a big summer thing around campus. And each night, he'd walk me back to my room and we'd stand outside my door and talk and, well . . . more than talk. Thank God the entrance to my room was in a bit of an alcove that had lots of shadows. Shadows that had hopefully masked some of where Erik's hands wandered as he kissed me good night. But I still wondered how much Peter might have seen.

Yeah, I *know* we could've had more privacy in my room and it wasn't like I had a nosy roommate to work around, but things with Erik were still new. I was only just getting to know him. Wasn't ready yet to go inviting him into my room with its temptation of the jumbo box of Trojans.

I pushed open the door onto the third floor and a welcome gust of fresh, artificially chilled air washed over my skin, cooling me down. Sort of.

"This is me," he said. I finally lifted my gaze from where it had been firmly fixed on my black pseudo-designer flip-flops for nearly three flights of stairs to find that we were standing out-side a room door. Not quite the room at the end of the hall, but just far enough away from mine that I breathed a sigh of relief. Imagine if he'd been my next-door or across-the-hall neighbor? How big a bonehead would I have felt like *then*?

"Listen, I meant it about helping with the math—if you want me to."

"Th-thanks." My gaze darted down the hall, eyeing my room, my mind still reviewing last night's door escapades and trying to remember how far Erik had unbuttoned my shirt. Oh, hell—what did it matter? Not like Peter was pulling judgment. He was just making an observation—an accurate one, as it happened. I *had* been preoccupied.

Relaxing some, I was finally able to smile as I shifted my backpack on my shoulder, feeling the weight of the cursed math text. "I'll probably take you up on that, then. As long as you're sure you won't mind a frantic three a.m. pounding on your door right before a test."

"I think I can handle it." Swiping his card again and punching in his key code on the numbered pad, he tossed his backpack through the open door and leaned against the jamb. "Thanks again for the cookie."

"My pleasure." I lifted a hand and turned to go. "See you around."

"See you, Caro."

With my mind already thinking ahead to the studying I'd need to do this afternoon if I wanted to go to a party with Erik tonight, and the burning question of what I was going to wear, it wasn't until much later that I realized what name Peter had called me.

6

"**Y**ou good?"

"Mm . . . great, thanks." I took the plastic cup Erik handed me and scooted over on the sofa to make room for him without crowding into the couple on my other side, who were busy cramming their tongues down each other's throats. "Still tingly."

I took a sip of icy beer, already prepped to stifle a shudder, because . . . beer? Ugh. However, given that my other option was something called "Hairy Buffalo" punch, heavy on the many different alcohols that gave it the hairy, and that I was going to need something of a clear head for my math quiz tomorrow, I was ready to put up with the beer. Beggars can't be choosers, and like I'd just said to Erik, I was still tingly—at least my mouth was.

"Dinner was great, wasn't it?"

"Yeah, it was. Thanks again."

"Totally my pleasure. Figured you'd enjoy something closer to your Mom's home cooking than campus food."

I didn't say a word, just smiled and took another sip of beer. Because it *had* been a sweet gesture and Señor Sparky's chimichanga had been high on the awesome and mouth-tingly scale. No point in busting Erik's bubble by informing him there was a world of difference between Mexican and Cuban cuisine and if anyone ever cooked Cuban in my house, it was me, since Mom was more about the meatloaf and mashed potatoes—

when she cooked at all. Not exactly her forte the way it was mine. Anyway, I loved Mexican food; Nana Ellie had made killer fajitas.

"Come on, babe." Erik's arm around my shoulders pulled me closer against him. "No point disturbing them." And there went those wicked eyebrows as he stared past me at the tonsil swabbers.

"No worse than we were last night."

"Yeah, but we didn't do it with an audience."

"True," I agreed. And *tried* not to hear Peter's voice, mentioning how preoccupied I'd seemed. But I did. *Not* what I wanted to be hearing. Another sip of beer would help with shoving that out of my head, right? Right. And I couldn't deny the brew was going down smoother than it had been the past couple of nights. Somehow didn't seem so vile.

"Ready for another?"

I glanced down into my nearly empty glass. "Wow. Yeah, I guess I am."

"The Zetas have the bucks to get the good import beer," he said as he waved at one of his fraternity brothers who was hovering near the keg and gestured to our empty glasses. "They're assholes, otherwise, but for good beer and an off-campus party? We can deal with their assholery for a few hours." A second later, fresh beers were presented to us, Erik exchanging some complicated handshake thing with the guy who'd brought them over.

"Must be nice, being pledge master, making the underlings step and fetch."

"Oh no, we'd never make the underlings step and fetch." He took a long swig of his beer, emptying nearly half the glass. Straightening and drawing his eyebrows together, he adopted a stern tone. "According to the campus Greek honor code and the decree from our national office, we're not permitted to make pledges or first-year members perform demeaning or menial tasks. Anything they do, they do of their own free volition and out of a sincere desire to serve their fellow brothers."

"How very utopian."

His face relaxed and he grinned. "On paper, maybe."

I giggled and stifled a small burp. "You're such a bad boy."

Another long swig that emptied his glass, which he set on the floor before pulling me even closer against him and whispering in my ear, "Babe, I'd love to show you just how bad I can be."

You know, in all honesty, I wasn't crazy about this new thing where he called me "babe" all the time, but I had to figure it was because he had such trouble with Carolina. Yet . . . I wasn't making any move to tell him to call me Caro. Weird. So I settled for another drink of beer, followed by a nuzzle against his neck along with a small bite.

"You're not the only one who can be bad, you know," I whispered in his ear.

"How bad are you willing to be?"

I drew back, far enough to see him pulling something from his pocket.

"Oh. *That* kind of bad? Is that such a good idea?"

"We're off-campus, babe. We're golden." A lighter followed from his pocket, the flame turning the end of the joint a soft, glowing red in the semidark basement. After taking a deep drag and holding it for the required however many seconds, he blew out a steady stream of smoke, then leaned in and whispered, "And who knows what kinds of bad this might lead us to?"

Had news for him—probably not anything terribly bad, and more's the pity. Pot didn't do a thing for me, other than give me wicked munchies and a headache. I'd just sit around while the rest of my friends giggled like loons and wait for something—

anything—to happen. You know what usually happened? *I* had to make the munchies run because I was the only one straight enough to drive.

Bogus, man.

"Come on, Carolina."

Well, listen to that. That was as close to correct as I'd ever heard him say my name—on the first try, even. Maybe this was better stuff than what we'd smoked back in Hampshire. Lifting the joint to my lips, I took in a medium-size drag, remembering to suck it all the way down with a slight breath afterward, just like James had shown me. Go figure, my big brother had shown me proper pot-smoking techniques. The one time he wasn't a total jerk.

"You've done this before," Erik observed, taking the joint back.

I nodded, my lungs burning, the smoke tickling its way back up my throat. "Yeah," I breathed out, before taking in a clean breath.

We sat there, trading the joint back and forth, while the party ebbed and flowed around us. At least, that's how it was starting to feel. At some point, the Tunnel of Love couple beside us took off, probably in search of a bed, and can I say how relieved that made me feel? More room on the sofa. I stretched out, my head in Erik's lap, turning my face toward his stomach and kissing the small bit of skin visible where he'd left his bottom two shirt buttons undone.

"Hey."

I turned my face up in time to see Erik's face lowering, as if it were in super slo-mo . . . getting larger as it got closer, close enough for me to see how tight he was holding his lips together. When they finally met mine, they parted and I could feel his breath, hot and smoky, sharing the last toke off the joint. Breathing it in, I lay back, marveling at how cool his face looked as it receded, watching him lift yet another beer that seemed to have appeared out of nowhere and take a drink; feeling his hand, cool and damp from the glass, running up my leg, ankle to thigh, little tingly vibrations rumbling through every muscle. Vibrations that grew into a more intense throbbing as I slowly released the breath I'd been holding for what felt like forever.

"Dance for me," I heard in my ear.

I wanted to say something, but my tongue felt thick, my lips dry. Wetting them with a sip of beer from the glass he held for me, I finally managed, "You want me to dance?"

His lips moved slowly, the words a beat behind as he said, "Yeah. For me."

I realized, lying there, that all those tingly vibrations and the intense throbbing weren't coming just from me, but from the music that suddenly felt like a blanket wrapped around us. Had there been music all along?

I shook my head ever so slowly, the skin of his thigh hot against the back of my neck. "I don't think I can move."

"For me, babe. Please?"

I took another sip of beer, closing my eyes against the feel of his fingers twisted in my hair, cradling my head. Suddenly, it's all I wanted to do. Respond to the rhythms, move to the beats. Do it all for him. Opening my eyes, I whispered, "Okay."

He blinked, like he was processing, then smiled. "Dance for me, Carolina."

Oh man . . . his voice saying my name sounded so beautiful. Made me feel beautiful. Made me think maybe dancing wasn't what I needed to be doing. But he wanted me to dance for him—I wanted to dance for him.

I rolled off the sofa and onto my knees, my hands resting on his thighs as I took a second to let the music flow into me, become part of me. Sean Paul, Joss Stone . . . sultry, sexy, completely in tune with how I was feeling. Lowering my head, I let my hair drag along Erik's legs, my hands following, backing away until I had enough room to stand, my bare toes curling into carpet that felt plush and thick, my hips swaying. I ran my hands up my sides, my neck, through my hair, blowing a kiss at the dazed smile on Erik's face.

The more I danced, the hotter I felt. I unbuttoned my short-sleeved shirt, enough so that cool air washed over the thin, stretchy camisole I wore beneath. Still wasn't enough, so I started swishing my skirt around, generating a breeze that felt so good, I just kept lifting the hem higher and higher, turning faster and faster, sweat trickling down my neck and between my breasts as the song built to a climax. After one final spin, I collapsed in a breathless, laughing heap next to Erik, taking the beer from him and downing what was left in one huge gulp, the room swirling and spinning in a kaleidoscope of colors and patterns.

"Wanna go?" Erik's breath was hot in my ear.

"I thought you'd never ask."

7

*O*h my God, why did I ever think it was a good idea to use Pink as my alarm?

Why is there a wad of cotton stuffed in my mouth?

And why does my bed feel so crowded?

Crowded?

Shoving my hair out of my face, I carefully turned over, trying to ignore that ominous pitch-and-roll number my stomach was doing. I had to see what this crowded thing was about— Oh man . . . Erik. Asleep on his side, my cheerful plaid sheet pulled to his waist, the length of his back—his very bare back—visible above purple and lime green checks that were suddenly making gremlins tap dance behind my eyes. And you know, I didn't dare lower the sheet the fraction of an inch it would take to see . . . I mean, I was still wearing my camisole, even though it was shoved up to just under my boobs, and running my palm along my hip confirmed that yep, bikini underwear was up and in place.

But that didn't mean a thing, did it? Other than I might have pulled the dainties back on after . . . after we . . . oh God, *did* we? I just couldn't remember.

I could remember dinner at Señor Sparky's and the party at that off-campus house. I remembered the beer not tasting as vile as usual and sharing a joint with Erik and being surprised when I actually copped a buzz. Then . . . dancing? Did I dance?

I had some vague recollection of spinning and twirling, but that could just as easily have been the room moving around me. Kind of like it was doing right now.

Groaning, I dropped my head into my hands and shook it back and forth, doing my best to ignore the gremlins as the little bastards began performing the Lord of the Dance along the interior of my skull. Trying to ignore Pink bitching about stupid girls. Oh shit, oh shit, oh *shit*.

"Babe?"

I nearly jumped out of my skin as I felt a warm hand stroke the bare skin of my stomach, then had to swallow hard as the jumping made my stomach do that pitch-and-roll thing again. Swallowing again, I finally managed, "Yeah?" although I didn't *dare* take my hands away from my face.

"You all right?"

No, I wanted to shriek, *I'm not all right!* I barely know you and I have no clue if you and I fucked liked bunnies or not, and if we did, I can't even remember it, and I feel like I'm going to hurl all over these stupid, cheerful sheets. So no, I'm definitely. Not. All. Right.

What I *said* was, "I'm okay."

"You don't look so okay." His hand mercifully left my stomach; a second later, I felt it stroking my hair. "At least not what I can see of you."

I could feel him shifting next to me, felt the smooth pull of the cotton sheet against my legs, and even though I was scared to, I peeked through my fingers, taking a deep breath at the barest glimpse of a black waistband. Not that that meant any more than my still wearing underwear did, but somehow . . . it made me feel better. Enough so that when his fingers brushed against the backs of my hands and curled around my wrists, I let him pull them away from my face. Still couldn't look him in the eye, though. One, because it was seriously bright in my room—even with the shades drawn—and I knew the brain gremlins would have a field day if I looked up into all that brightness; and two, well, because I just couldn't look him in the eye.

"Are you going to be sick?"

"I don't think so."

"Are you going to look at me?"

"I—I don't know."

"Carolina, did I do something wrong?"

"I . . ." Oh God, how could I say it? Admit that—? But I had to know.

"I . . ." My skin prickled and tightened as heat started spreading from my scalp and over my face. Yanking my hands free from his, I covered my face again. "I don't know if you did anything wrong. I-I don't know if I—if we . . ."

His hands were back on my hair, stroking the tangled mess of it back from my face. "We didn't."

Slowly, I lowered my hands and finally lifted my head just far enough to meet his gaze—stone dead serious for the first time since I'd met him.

"We didn't have sex, babe." Then the serious look was gone, replaced by the wicked Puck's grin. "Not for lack of wanting to on my part—or yours," he added with a wink that made me blush all over again.

"Then why didn't we?"

"Because I was worried about this kind of scenario." He eased back onto my pillows, propping his head on one hand and stroking my thigh with the other. "You were pretty out of it. Didn't seem right, much as we both might've wanted to."

Goo. If I could have, I would've melted right into a puddle of goo, right then and there. A guy not taking advantage of a sure thing? It had to be completely unheard of.

He flopped over onto his back, folding his hands behind his head. "I thought you smoked before?"

Wow. If I hadn't noticed last night, I was noticing now. He had a really nice chest. Equally nice arms. Stomach. And, erm . . . clearly, he thought *I* was okay, even hungover, given the way the sheet was moving below his waist. I had to fish deep into the mental recesses to recall what he'd just asked.

"Uh—I have. But either what we smoked last night was a lot stronger than anything I've had before or maybe it was because I was drinking, too, but I've never reacted like that."

"It was pretty high-quality shit."

Right. Well, then, I think in the future I'd pass, if high-quality shit brought on this level of brain gremlin. While I'd quit feeling like I was going to throw up, my head still felt like it was going to explode.

"Carolina?"

We were back to stumbling slightly over my name, but that was okay. "Yeah?"

"Now that we're both more or less sober, can I ask you something?"

"Sure."

"It *is* something you want to do, right? With me?"

Oh man, back to that goo status, because staring at me, he didn't look wicked or merry or serious but . . . kind of vulnerable and all sorts of adorable. God, that was sexy.

"Oh yeah. But maybe not so fast, though," I rushed in to add in case he got the wrong idea from the quick-and-breathless answer. "I—I know this probably sounds stupid, considering how far we've already gone and how close it sounds like we got last night, but I'd kind of like to, you know, take our time. Get to know each other a little better."

"That's cool." His fingers brushed against my cheek as he

grinned. "We'll never do any more than you want to, babe. That's a promise."

Smiling back wasn't difficult at all. "You know, if I wasn't totally sure that I had dragon breath, I'd kiss you right now, Erik."

"Your breath can't be any more dragon than mine." He pulled me—gently, thank goodness—on top of him, kissing me, his arms stroking my back and shoulders.

Oh, this was just way too romantic for eight forty-seven in the morning. I blinked, making sure I was seeing the numbers on my clock right—eight freakin' forty-seven! As I stared, the seven blinked, then became a bright glaring eight.

I scrambled off the bed, grabbing my robe from the back of the door and my bathroom basket off the dresser. My stomach lurched and my head started spinning again, screaming at the sudden movement, but they would have to deal. I had to get a move on.

"Shit, shit . . . oh God."

"What is it?"

"I have got to be across campus and taking a math quiz in—" I stopped rummaging through a drawer for clean underwear long enough to check the clock again: eight forty-nine. "In twenty-one minutes."

He swung his legs over the edge of the bed and grabbed his shorts from the floor, slipping them on. "Relax, babe. You can be a couple minutes late, can't you?"

Relax? *Relax*? He was kidding, right? "I can't, Erik. The prof said if we were late, the door would be locked and wouldn't be reopened until the quiz was over. And if you miss a quiz without a good reason, it's a double zero."

"Are you serious?"

"As a heart attack." Brushing teeth, deodorant, and fresh underwear were going to have to do it. No time for a shower, even of the just-get-wet variety. Or coffee, blast it.

"That's brutal."

"No kidding." I brushed a quick kiss against his mouth. "I'm sorry, Erik, I have *got* to go. Let yourself out, okay?" I shoved my key card in my robe's pocket, but before I could open the door, felt myself pulled back.

"See you later?" he whispered in my ear.

"Yes, yes, yes, later." Another kiss and I was out the door and running toward the bathroom, cursing those stupid dancing head gremlins the whole way.

8

Shit.

I stared down at the paper in my hands.

Double shit.

Beside me, metal scraped against concrete loud and shrill, startling me into dropping the paper.

"Shit." Felt so good to say it out loud, I considered saying it again, but nixed the idea since my head still felt like it was going to split open.

Instead, I started to lean down to pick it up, carefully, because I didn't want my brains to leak out of my ears or anything, but before I could even prop a supporting hand on the arm of my chair, it was back on the table in front of me. Squinting through the super antiglare lenses of the Maui Jim shades that had been my graduation gift from James, I found Peter settling in across from me, not looking my way, as he dropped his backpack and a box into an empty chair.

"You okay?"

I was getting a lot of that today. Guy who sat next to me in trig had asked the same thing.

"Do I look okay?" I snapped, then sighed. "Sorry. Rough morning."

He shrugged, nodding at the paper lying in front of me. "Kind of guessed."

I glared again at the big 71% that the professor's teaching

assistant had written in sparkly pink gel pen. And circled. Perky bitch. Who was almost done with a master's in some obscenely difficult and obscure math major, so I guess she was entitled to write my sucky score in whatever sparkly color she chose.

"Yeah," I said on another sigh. "Sucks when a seventy-one goes from being a C to an almost F."

"One of those little college perks no one ever tells you about." He laughed and shifted in his chair, making the legs scrape against the concrete again and me cringe and rub at my forehead.

"Hey, ease up on the freakin' chair, would you?"

He stared at me across the table for a long minute. "Right. Sorry." Without another word, he stood and disappeared into the union. Well, that was just a stellar move on my part, wasn't it? Watch Caro be a bitch—drive perfectly nice guys off. Then again, he'd left his backpack and that box on the chair. So not gone for good. Probably just long enough to find a pitcher of water to dump on my stupid, cranky head. I dropped said head onto my folded arms and started wishing really hard for someone to take me out back and shoot me. Put me out of my misery.

"Here. This should help."

Lifting my head, I accepted the bottle of Tazo green tea, wincing at the *pop* of the cap as I loosened it. "Thanks." I took a careful sip before gently rolling the icy bottle against my forehead. Lord, but that felt good. Even the frigid condensation dripping down along the side of my face was refreshing.

"You know, it's not the smoothest move to go into a quiz with a hangover. Especially for a class you already know is hard." A single expressive eyebrow rose over the rims of his dark aviators.

"Tell me something I don't know." I took another careful sip of tea and rested my cheek on the bottle. "I didn't exactly plan to, you know."

"No one ever does." He looked up from his sandwich and the smile on his face was a dead giveaway.

I should've said thanks. Or maybe smiled back in the shared knowledge that most people were idiots at some point or another during college. But instead, I whined. A nice, pathetic "please tell me that's not tuna" whine served with a side of pitiful as I watched him fold back the wax paper. Because it had turned wicked hot and humid and it probably wouldn't take long for that bad boy to go fragrant in a way only the Chicken of the Sea could. Wasn't sure I could deal.

"Smoked turkey and Havarti on rye." He smiled again, but with a definite shade of evil. "Want some?"

Okay, not completely undeserved. But still, I shot him a dirty look before closing my eyes and taking a deep breath. The harsh rip of tearing paper only made me close them tighter. Was he *trying* to kill me?

"Here, Caro."

"Peter, I really don't want any of your sandwich." Really, *really* didn't, even though I usually was all over anything with Harvarti. Not to mention, hadn't eaten anything since the chimichanga last night.

"Not the sandwich. Just open your eyes."

I did. Cautiously, mind you. But I did.

Oh my God.

"Those ought to help settle your stomach."

"Yeah," I agreed weakly, picking up one of the flat, round cookies with all the decorative stamping around the edges. "They should." Galletas María. Nana Ellie had always given me the weird cross between a cracker and a cookie when I had an upset tummy. Or even when I didn't. That's when she would spread them with cream cheese and guava jelly and call them dessert.

"Where did you get these?" I couldn't stop staring at the one in my hand, feeling all the memories; feeling Nana, rubbing my back or brushing my hair. Feeling the beginnings of tears behind my eyes, so sudden that I had to blink really hard to keep them from falling. *Nooo* . . . I'm not a total head case, going all weepy over a damn cookie.

"My mom sent me a big care package. She's convinced I'm going to starve, being so far away from her influence."

"Your mom?" My gaze shifted from the *galleta* to the now-open box sitting on the chair between us, the tape that must have been the source of the ripping noise hanging off one end.

"Yeah. She Googled, if you can believe that. Figured there wasn't any place closer than Pittsburgh to potentially pick up any Cuban food and you know how they are—'*¿mi'jo, cómo piensas a comer?*' " he singsonged in this high-pitched voice. "Never mind I told her about the union and about all the restaurants that are within spitting distance practically and that there's a kitchen in the dorm. I'm *still* gonna starve if she doesn't make sure I've got the right food."

Staring from him to the box, to him and back to the box again, I could barely believe what I was hearing or seeing. Him, in one phrase, speaking Spanish that didn't have the sound of the formal high school variety. In the box, a veritable cornucopia of snacks and tidbits, most of them with Spanish names. Most of which I'd seen or eaten at some time or another during my childhood. At West Side Market, in Nana's kitchen, never realizing their significance—why she always tended to have them around—at least, not until much later.

I glanced at the cardboard flap facing me, with the name written on it in a nice, Mom-like print:

Peter Agosto. I suddenly realized I'd never gotten his last name. Not obvious, but it might've given me a clue. Plus, just in case the name, the fluent Spanish, and the reference to the *Cuban mom* wasn't quite enough . . . well, on the upper left of the flap, in that same nice print, was the return address. The Miami return address.

You know, and here I'd thought I was going to be so unique.

"You're Cuban." I finally bit into the cookie, mostly so I wouldn't dissolve into hysterical laughter.

"Well, my parents are. I was born in Miami, though."

"I can't believe it." I was having a serious *Casablanca*, "of all the gin joints in the world" sort of moment. I mean, what were the odds, right? "How'd you wind up here?"

"USO's got one of the best computer graphics programs in the country." His head was down, poking around in the box, until he finally came up with a bag of what looked like chips, but on second glance were—oh God, no—*chicharrones*. My stomach lurched at the sight of the deep-fried pork rinds. Nana had tried once to get me to eat those. Emphasis on the word *tried*. There were some lines I just wouldn't cross.

"Peter, please don't."

He paused with his hand inside the bag, looking down, then at me. "Oh—sorry." Tossing the bag back in the box, he grabbed a few of the *galletas* instead.

"Why can't you believe it?" He polished off one cookie in two bites, washing it down with Coke. "Cuban from Miami; going away to college. This is not uncommon stuff. On paper, you're the anomaly—Cuban girl from Ohio."

"Half," I muttered, lifting my tea and hoping I didn't have a big neon LIAR! flashing over my head. "And how'd you know that anyway?"

"Erik and that other guy, Nichols, they were talking about it when you excused yourself to go to the bathroom the other night. They think it's hot." And Peter shrugged in a way that made it clear he didn't think it was any big deal.

Honestly, I wasn't sure whether to be insulted or relieved.

"You do speak Spanish, right?" he suddenly asked. "I didn't just make a jerk of myself, assuming—"

"No, you didn't," I reassured him. Reassured myself. "I do speak it. With, uh—" I fumbled for something . . . anything . . . I could *so* get busted here, Havana Brown hair or not. "A slight accent." Yeah, that would work. "Since my dad doesn't speak Spanish, we speak English more often than not around our house." Finally, something that was true.

"Cool."

Yes, very much with the cool. He seemed to be buying it.

"My parents are like that, too. Made sure we all knew our Spanish, inside and out, but that English came first. We know too many people who've never bothered to learn English—it's too easy in Miami, you know? And makes it difficult everywhere else. My parents, they get it—how it's not easy when you have to leave everything you know and you compensate by hanging on to anything you possibly can, but at the same time, my mom, especially, really hates the immigrant stereotype."

He laughed and polished off another cookie, nodding his head at the box of food. "The Cuban mom stereotype on the other hand? That, she's good with."

The more he spoke, the more every muscle unclenched, each breath coming easier than the last. I'd given him my explanation and he was good with it. In fact, none of it seemed to be any big deal to him. It's just how things were.

"Are they helping?"

I stared down at the napkin on which he'd given me the *galletas*, surprised to find them gone, along with most of my tea.

"Yeah, they are." But below the napkin, I could still see that stupid, horrible, pink 71% on the stupid, horrible quiz. "With the hangover, at least."

He pulled the quiz toward him, turning it around so he could see all my boneheaded mistakes in their full glory. "What's this mean for your overall grade?"

"It's only the first quiz, but overall, it means I'd better get my butt in gear."

He slid the test back across the table. "Offer still stands. You busy this afternoon?"

"Actually, yeah." I checked my watch and swallowed the last of my tea. "History in twenty minutes." Which would at least be a lot easier to sit through, now that I didn't feel like my head was about to dissolve.

"Well, whenever, then." His head was down so I couldn't see his face, and even though his voice held that same noncommittal tone as the first time he made the offer, I was starting to get that that's not what it meant at all.

"I'm probably going to take it easy tonight." Even if I got together with Erik, maybe we could do something more low-key, like a movie. No drinking. And *definitely* no pot. "But I don't have anything specific planned for the weekend." Other than lots of studying so I didn't screw up like this again.

A piece of paper with a number written on it landed on top of the test, obscuring the 71%.

"My cell," he said. "Call whenever. Or you can just knock on the door. I've got no special plans, either."

Nope. Not noncommittal. Carefully folding the paper, I tucked it into a small zippered pocket in my backpack.

"Thanks, Peter."

"Anytime, *amiga*."

9

To: CaroDarcy@uso.harrison.edu
From: AMac@hampshire.net
Subject: What's up?

To: CaroDarcy@uso.harrison.edu
From: AMac@hampshire.net
Subject: Where are you?

To: CaroDarcy@uso.harrison.edu
From: AMac@hampshire.net
Subject: I'm starting to get worried . . .

To: CaroDarcy@uso.harrison.edu
From: AMac@hampshire.net
Subject: You'd better be trapped under
furniture!

And those were just the first four e-mails. There were—isolating
Ames's e-mail from the ones from Mom, the official ones from
school, the one that looked like it was probably some gross joke
from James, and the spam for Hoodia and Cialis—nine total
from her. From the past two days alone. She was going to absolutely kill me.

To: AMac@hampshire.net
From: CaroDarcy@uso.harrison.edu
Subject: I am SOOOOO sorry.

Dear Ames,
Yes, I know I suck like a sucking thing. I'm sorry. It's been
a weird couple of days—

Like she *knew*, my cell phone blared her customized ringtone,
her number flashing on the screen.

"What've you got, sensors or something?"

"I swear to God, Caro Darcy, you'd better have been trapped
under furniture or something."

"I've been busy." And I sort of wished she'd waited at least
five more minutes to call. Then my coffee could've finished
brewing and I could be mainlining caffeine while dealing with
her cross-examining ass.

"Business, pleasure, or some combination of the two?"

"And the difference would be?"

"How much I'm going to have to kill you when you get home.
Busy with school is acceptable. Especially knowing how much
you *love* that trig class. But if it's been all party, party, party and
you've been holding out—"

"Come on, Ames, it's only been a couple of days since I last
talked to you." A couple of very eventful days. "I haven't even
spoken to my parents since I got here except to let them know I
arrived safely and that my first couple of classes went well." We
wouldn't talk about the first trig quiz. I stood and crossed to my
dresser where I had my coffeemaker set up. Thank God for the
auto-stop feature. It would at least pause long enough to let me
pour my first cup.

"Yeah, but that's your parents. You're not expected to actually speak to them other than to let them know that you arrived safely and your first couple of classes went well. This is me we're talking about," she whined. "Your lifelong best friend. To whom you have a certain obligation, especially when I'm stuck back at home and working at the restaurant."

"It's a very nice restaurant." Her aunt and uncle had bought a historic mill years ago and converted it to a restaurant. Not a bad gig, actually, especially after they got the three-star rating and a glowing review in *Bon Appetit* magazine. "And at least this summer you're a host, not a waitress, and get to wear cute outfits of your own choosing."

"Yeah, yeah, what*ever*. Not me we're talking about here. What's been going on?"

Reaching into my minifridge, I grabbed the cream and stirred some into my coffee along with some sugar. "Where do you want me to start?"

Her voice was properly astonished. "Like you said, it's only been a couple of days."

"A lot's happened." I smiled as I felt arms come around me from behind, one extending to the coffeemaker and pouring coffee into the second mug I already had set out.

"Morning, babe," I heard in the ear that didn't have the cell phone pressed against it.

"Oh my God, you've got *company*?"

"Yeah." I took a sip of coffee and bit back a giggle as Erik brushed aside my hair and nuzzled the back of my neck.

"Puck?"

"Yeah." I slapped his hands away as they started drifting up from my waist to cup my breasts over my T-shirt. He sure did like them. And was very nice to them, but it was just way too distracting. He knew it, too. Taking his coffee, he flopped back onto my bed and gave me this totally unrepentant grin when I shook my finger at him.

"Do I need to let you go?"

"Not really."

"Oh, already had our morning slap and tickle, have we?"

"Ex-ex*cuse* me?" Hot coffee up the nose *hurt*, dammit. Slap and tickle? Where did she get this stuff? "You've been reading Victorian romance novels again, haven't you?"

"Hey, some of us don't have the kind of leisure-time activities that others do."

Glancing over at Erik, who'd picked up my well-worn copy of *The Mambo Kings Play Songs of Love* from the stack of books on the night table and was reading the back, I dropped my voice. "It's not like that, Ames."

She was quiet as she registered what I'd said, along with what I hadn't said. The gift of the lifelong best friend, you know? "But he did spend the night?" she finally asked.

"Yeah."

"So you're kind of serious about him already."

Was I? I looked over my shoulder at him again. His spending the night the first time had been a fluke. An accident of timing, too much beer, and a really strong doobie. Last night, though, had been the low-key night I'd wanted; ordering pizza, watching DVDs—okay, having the DVDs on as background noise. And when he'd asked if he could spend the night again—just spend the night, no pressure—it was something I'd really, really wanted. I mean, I'd have to be nuts not to. He was, if not the most conventionally gorgeous guy on the planet, certainly sexy as all get out. Had a wicked funny sense of humor and was smart enough to do well in his classes with minimal studying. Okay, that last part was probably a flaw.

So, no, hadn't even had to think twice when he asked, truthfully.

"Yeah, I guess I am."

Her long sigh was kind of unexpected.

"What?"

"Nothing."

"Yeah, right," I scoffed. "Come on. Out with it before you explode."

"Aside from the fact that you've been at college all of, what, a week?"

Yeah, okay. She maybe had a point there.

"And you haven't had so much as a date since what'shisface at Interlochen?"

Well, *yeah*. There was also that. But before I could remind her that his name had been Michael and, you know, I would've dated some of the guys back in Hampshire if they'd ever actually noticed me enough to *ask*, she was on to her next point.

"*And* he still thinks you're Carolina, right?

Oh. "Well, yeah."

"You're so gonna have to come clean at some point. At least by the time the rehearsal dinner rolls around."

I snorted. "Oh, puh-*leeze*." I mean, really—I only *had* been at college a week.

"Oh puh-leeze, my ass. What if he wants to meet your parents? If you guys do get even marginally serious, that wouldn't be beyond the pale, would it? Then you'd really have some 'splainin' to do, Lucy."

"Uh—"

"Exactly." How could someone *look* smug over the phone? Because I knew she was sitting there, probably nursing her own cup of coffee, and looking, well, smug.

"Bitch."

"I live to serve." Now she sounded like her usual acerbic self. But with an undertone of worry. "Look, I'm guessing you can't really talk now, so either call me later with all the deets or at least e-mail. I'm on shift from four till close."

"Okay."

"Later, hussy."

"Shut up." But she'd already hung up, even though I could hear her evil cackle echoing in my ear. Flipping my phone closed, I turned to Erik.

"Now, what if that'd been my parents?"

"Your body language, the tone of your voice would've been completely different, babe." He just sat back, sipping his coffee, like no big deal. "And I would've been as quiet as an itty-bitty church mouse."

I shook my head and laughed. "What on earth are you going to do with that psych major? Other than be overly qualified to say, 'You want fries with that?' "

He threw a hand up and shrugged. "Go to law school, what else?"

Even while I laughed along with him, I had to brush aside a flash of panic. Because really, what if Erik hadn't guessed right and it *had* been my parents? Trojans or not, I couldn't see either of them being all that pleased I was entertaining overnight guests. Especially after less than a week away from home. Damn Amy for pointing out that little fact.

But nothing *had* happened—much. Certainly not the main event and that's what really mattered in the long run, wasn't it?

"Careful!" I held my mug up so it wouldn't spill as Erik pulled me down beside him on the bed. Taking it from me, he set it on the night table next to his before rolling over on top of me.

"So that was your best friend?"

"Yeah."

"Giving you the third degree about *moi*?"

I grinned up at him, stroking my fingers through his short, spiky hair, making it go in even more directions. "Since you made it obvious you were here, yeah. And predictably, she reacted like a nervous *tía*." At his blank look, I clarified: "Auntie."

"Oh." His face cleared. "She's not Cuban, too, is she?"

Picturing hazel-eyed, red-headed Amy, I giggled. "Nope. Good Scottish and German stock for her." Like a lot of my background. With that one little exception, of course.

"See, that's more what I'd expect out of Hampshire." His arms tightened around me. "You really are unique, aren't you, Carolina?"

Tried like hell to ignore the mocking "You'll have to come clean," delivered in Amy's dry tones, ringing in my ears, as Erik did a fantastic job of showing me just how unique he thought I was for the next few minutes. Alas, we both felt the need to come up for air or it was something I could have happily kept doing, like . . . for the rest of the day.

"Okay, it's Saturday, it's gorgeous outside, what do you say we go out to Lake George for the day?"

My stomach sank straight down to my toes. "I can't."

"Why not?"

"I've really got to study, Erik." Despite my intense desire to stay attached at the lips for the rest of the day, studying was actually what I'd planned to do. Exhibit some backbone and get back on track with the classwork. After all, that was why I was here. School. Not the extracurriculars. No matter how fun they were. "Especially after the way I blew chunks on that quiz. Plus, I've got a ton of homework for both of my classes."

"Is that all?" Those potent baby blues crinkled at the corners, making my stomach clench, just before he lowered his head and began dropping a line of light, teasing kisses along my neck, just above the edge of my T-shirt.

"Just bring your books and study out by the lake. There are a ton of shady trees, we'll find you a quiet spot. I'll even bring one of those portable tailgating chairs with the built-in cup holders so you can study in comfort. I'll keep you supplied with food and drink and make sure the rest of the crew leaves you alone."

"R-rest of the crew?" Man, those little kisses along my neck were definitely distracting, making my insides do the samba.

"Yeah. It's kind of a summer thing—like the floor parties. People always go out to the lake on Saturdays, grill, drink beer, play volleyball, swim. Just a good time."

And I was supposed to study under those conditions? The thought of Erik in a bathing suit alone . . .

"I can't, Erik." But I wanted to. I wanted to stomp my feet and whine and wish that I hadn't done quite so well on my stupid placement exam and didn't have to take trig. "I really wish I could, but I just can't."

Air washed over my body as he rolled off and sat up. "You sure?"

"Yeah." And I felt like a total loser saying it. The lake, a grilled hot dog or two, splashing around in the water with Erik all sounded infinitely preferable, dammit. But I just couldn't justify it. Even under the guise of irresponsible college freshman.

"I could stay and keep you company while you study."

I didn't need the telltale prickling of my skin to let me know that was definitely obligatory. I could read it all over his face. And while it was nice that he was willing . . . no. I didn't like obligatory from him any more than I'd liked it when I thought it was coming from Peter.

"Erik, that's really sweet of you, but how much studying do you honestly think we'd get done?" Tried to smile. Tried to make a joke. Then I swallowed and said what I knew he wanted me to say. "You go ahead and go, though."

And tried really hard not to envision nubile sorority girls in teeny thong bikinis bouncing around as they lunged for a volleyball and not-so-accidentally fell chest- or ass-first into the nearest hard body. Your standard-issue nightmare.

Crap. Okay, yeah, I was definitely a little more serious—and jealous—than I should be. Great way to send a guy running for the hills.

"You sure?"

"Yeah," I sighed.

"Hey."

I kept my stare fixed on my bedspread. "What?"

"We'll go out tonight."

"Sure." If he wasn't too worn-out from chasing volleybimbos.

He cupped my face in his hands and made me look up. "I want to go to the lake with you. I'd love to convince you it would be in your best interests, but I think I've corrupted you enough this week, so I'll cry into my beer until I can see you tonight."

Damn him, I couldn't help but smile at that mock-pitiful face he was putting on. "Liar."

He pulled back and gasped. "You don't believe I'm going to cry into my beer?"

"No. I don't believe it's only going to be beer, singular."

The look on his face was absolutely priceless, just total shock, before falling back against the pillows, laughing his ass off.

"God, I really like you, Carolina."

Which sounded really genuine and made me feel really good and gave me the guts to say, "I really like you, too, Erik" without feeling like I was going to send him screaming.

Unfortunately, that was about the last of the good for the next couple hours. After kissing Erik good-bye and writing Amy a really long and fairly detailed e-mail (left out *some* stuff), I tried to settle down with the dreaded trig while I was still reasonably fresh. I could at least give this a go on my own before I went begging for help, right?

Wrong.

Some backbone I had. Wasn't even an hour before I finally caved. Told myself that it was early, I didn't want to bug him; I was sober now, I could do this. But let's face it—it was pride, pure and simple. Outside of Erik, Peter was the only other person who knew how stupid I'd been in going into that quiz with a hangover. The fact that he'd offered to help me rubbed salt in the wound, even if it wasn't meant that way.

However, this was my grade we were talking about. And possibly having to take the class over again. My pride would just have to deal if it meant not going through this hell again, which was why I found myself trudging down the hall and knocking at his door.

"Hey."

"I hope it's not too early."

"It's nearly eleven in the morning, Caro."

I shrugged. "It's Saturday morning. Or you could be a night owl, for all I know." Or could have been out late partying or had an overnight guest, like I had. Gads, but I was a moron. An arrogant moron. Skipping on down here, *tra la la*, like he had no life other than helping out my sorry ass.

"I *am* sort of a night owl." He shrugged right back at me. "But for the record, I'm almost always up by ten, even on the weekends." Opening the door wider, he stepped aside to let me pass through. "You want some coffee before we get started?"

10

"**H**ere."

"Thanks," I muttered, barely looking up from the problem I was working on as he set a mug down in front of me. I sank back into the intricacies of solving what seemed like the World's Most Impossible Problem—at least, until a sudden jerk of my arm sent a black streak across the paper.

"Shit."

"Sorry, Caro."

Again, didn't look up, this time concentrating on erasing the mark without erasing the work I thought—hoped—was right. "Not your fault you're as relentlessly left-handed as I am right-handed," I said as I blew away eraser crumbs and surveyed the remains.

"Yeah, but it wouldn't be such a problem if I rearranged the desks."

"Which would be stupid," I answered for what seemed like the eighty-fourth time since we'd started studying together. "Since this is your room, with your desks, and should be arranged any damn way you like. However—" I picked up my mug and stood up from the desk chair, crossing the room to his bed, where I sat down. "—since I'm done for the moment with the 'problem that will not die,' I think I'll give my brain a break and read through my next history assignment."

He glanced to his left at the paper I'd left on the dorm-issue desk. "Okay, I'll look at that as soon as I'm done with the layer on this graphic."

Thumbing through the book he'd been reaching for when he jostled my arm, he turned his attention back to the image he had blown up to enormous proportions on the thirty-inch monitor resting on his computer desk. Until two weeks ago, I'd never even imagined there could be such a huge computer monitor. Now I barely noticed it, even though it still twigged me on occasion to glance up and be faced with something blown up so huge I couldn't even tell what it was, then when he brought it back down to normal size, it turned out to be nothing more than a curled-up flower petal or something equally innocuous. Talk about your new perspectives. Otherwise, though, just part of the landscape of Peter's room, along with the art prints, family pics, and books. Lots and lots of books, just like me and Amy. Well, not quite. His weren't so much classic modern lit, screenplays, and chick novels with peppy covers as they were graphic design, color theory, HTML, and *manga*.

"How'd your quiz go, by the way?"

"Eighty-seven. It's there in my notebook." I waved at the desk, even though he had his back to me and couldn't see.

"That average is movin' on up."

"To the East Side." I smiled at his back. "Couldn't have done it without your help."

"Come on—you've done your part. Not going into quizzes totally baked has to have helped."

My smiling at his back turned into sticking my tongue out. When he started laughing, I realized he could see everything I was doing in the monitor's reflection. "You suck, you know that?" Which only made him laugh harder.

"And isn't it time to let that die? Maybe move on to new material?"

Now he spun his chair around to face me. "But why, when I can continue to get such great mileage out of what I've currently got?" A huge grin split his face, making me lob one of his pillows at his smug ass.

"You know, if you weren't such a help with this math crap . . ."

He deflected the pillow, which was pretty impressive, considering how hard he was laughing. "Yeah, yeah, I know. Horrible, painful torture, like making me watch all four million hours of Ken Burns's *The Civil War* in one sitting." He rolled his eyes so hard, I think it was only the lenses of the silver wire-rims he wore for reading and working at the computer that kept them from popping out of his head. Jerk.

"Go back to the Battle of Antietam while I check this out."

After sticking my tongue out at him once more for good measure, silence dropped over the room, broken only by Faith Hill's soft vocals. Tell you what, if finding out Peter was Cuban had been a surprise, looking through his music collection had nearly sent me spiraling into shock. Guy had some of *everything*, I swear. From Pearl Jam to Kanye to the Dixie Chicks to Dashboard Confessional to Mary J. Blige—it was like musical whiplash.

"My sisters fall in love with a trend, buy all the CDs, then they get bored and I get the leftovers," he'd explained when he noticed how far out my eyes bugged the first time I browsed his CD portfolio. And while he had his share of the Music to Headbang By—like every other guy on the planet—it hadn't taken long to figure out that for studying, it was the female singers that did it for him. The pop-country chicks, like Faith and Shania.

Which was cool by me. Made for a kind of soothing break from the Juanes and Daddy Yankee I made a point to listen to when Erik was around.

No, I hadn't come clean yet, even though Amy made a

point to mention it, oh, every time she called or e-mailed. Usually as an aside, or a postscript, but she always mentioned it. Subtle she wasn't. But Erick *so* totally dug it . . . and it felt so natural around him. I was to a point where I hardly even had to think about it; just drop a Spanish word in now and then, especially if they were sweet nothings I could whisper in his ear. Answer all his questions about the Cuban side of my family, just making sure to say "*mami*" and not "mom" or, even worse, "Nana Ellie."

Okay, so it wasn't *all* natural. But it wasn't all that hard, either. Especially when he was constantly telling me how gorgeous I was, how sexy, how *exotic*. When he showed me how gorgeous he thought I was, how sexy, how *exotic*. And I was supposed to give that up and confess to being blah-beige Caro? Amy had to be out of her tiny little mind.

As if on cue, my cell rang, startling me and making me realize I'd drifted off into Happy Daydream Land and hadn't read more than a sentence of the chapter I'd sworn I would finish before tonight.

"Hey, sexy señorita."

"Hey you. Done with class already?" Was it seriously going on four-thirty?

" 'Already,' she says. Yeah, I'm done. How about you? What're you up to?"

"Being a good, virtuous girl and studying."

"Veritable saint. How'd your quiz go today?"

"Eighty-seven."

"See, told you not to stress."

I smiled in Peter's direction, even though he couldn't see it, since he had his head down, checking my homework problem. "Yeah, took some doing, but getting there."

"Am I still picking you up at eight?"

Twisting the end of my ponytail around my finger, I did some quick mental calculations. "Could we push that forward a half hour or so?"

"Yeah, sure. What's up?"

"Well, for one thing, I want to finish up the studying, so I can party with a clear conscience. Peter's just checking over my math right now, and I have some history I want to read." And then I had to do a touch-up on the hair, since I'd noticed a few blonde roots making an appearance among the Havana Brown. And that just wouldn't do.

"Why are you studying with him again? I thought you said you got an eighty-seven." It was just my imagination that he sounded a little testy, right?

"Well, yeah, how do you think I did that?"

"Because you're brilliant, babe." Yeah, definitely just my imagination.

"Flatterer." I laughed into the phone. "How far do you think that'll get you?"

"Hopefully past third base one of these days." Sounding like he was only half joking there. Poor guy. He'd been so patient and totally true to his word, not pushing and only going as far as I felt comfortable.

"Soon, *mi vida.*" One of his favorite sweet nothings, one that never failed to make him breathe just that little bit faster. Out of the corner of my eye, I could see Peter's head lift, tilt my direction slightly, then turn away as he shifted to face the desk. I lowered my voice further. "I'll see you later, okay?"

"Wear something that'll look gorgeous on the dance floor, babe. I want to see you dance again."

I crossed my legs tight. "Okay. Later."

Returning the phone to my backpack, I picked up my history text and tried to remember what was so fascinating about freakin' Antietam. Civil War. Big battle. Lots of casualties. Right. The same could be said for most of them.

"You did good."

"Huh?" Still hadn't read more than a sentence about the damn battle.

"On this problem. " Peter rolled his chair over toward the bed until it was right alongside. "You made a goof that sent it off on a wrong tangent, but it was near the end, so it's an easy fix. If it would've been on a test, you still would have gotten most of the credit for it."

For the next few minutes, he showed me where I'd made my mistake, told me I wasn't a dunderhead when I insisted I was, and watched as I fixed it.

"You see how easy that was?"

"Yeah, actually, it was." Called for a major sigh of relief as I closed the notebook and set it aside in favor of my history text.

"I thought you had a date."

I lowered the book and stared over the top of it. Peter had rolled the chair over to his minifridge, grabbing a Coke and a bottled Tazo tea. Leaning forward to accept the tea, I asked, "Do you need me to leave?"

"Me? No. I just, um . . . it sounded like . . ." As he fiddled with the cap on the bottle, his skin flushed red. Another reason I might never have guessed his background—that skin that was just as fair as mine. That is, as fair as mine was when I wasn't slathering it with gobs of Neutrogena tinted moisturizer to help maintain the original pool glow.

"Peter, seriously, if you need me to leave, I can. I mean, I've already been here all afternoon . . ."

Just score another one for the clueless dolt and her assumptions that the guy has no life. Jeez. Grabbing my notebook, I started to shove it in my backpack.

"Caro, wait. You don't have to leave, I just thought you and Erik—"

Where was my history notebook? "Not until tonight."

"You don't have to leave," he repeated. Glancing up, I saw him shrug as he finally unscrewed the cap. "I like having the company while I work."

Slowly, I sat up, having finally located my history notebook on the floor. "Yeah . . . me, too." I'd been studying with Ames forever. It felt sort of bizarre not having anyone around while I studied. I guess I'd have to get used to it at some point, but I was just as happy not to have to—not just yet.

"Okay then." He didn't say anything more, just turned back to his computer while I went back to the Civil War. Finally, after long shadows started drifting across the textbook's pages and Sherman had finished with his March to the Sea, I declared myself as crispy as Atlanta and decided to call it a day.

"God."

Peter spun his chair around at my sigh. He wasn't working on his graphics project anymore, I noticed, but had a huge Sudoku grid going that made my brain hurt just to look at it. Following my gaze, he grinned, then moved the mouse; a second later, the screensaver activated, soothing swirls of color that flowed across the giant screen. "What?"

"It never fails to get me—no matter how many times we study these wars, these battles—just how brutal people can be." I waved at the textbook, sitting closed now, on the pillow. "It's horrifying, but fascinating, too, you know?"

"Yeah," he agreed, nodding. "Especially considering how we keep doing it over and over, never really learning from the lessons of the past."

My jaw dropped. "Wait a minute, I thought you said history was your ass-kicker."

"Trying to keep the dates and facts straight, yeah." Another one of those noncommittal shrugs. "But trying to figure out what drives people to do the things they do is pretty interesting."

"Yeah." I nodded, feeling a flash of recognition. "I think so, too."

"It's probably what'll make you a great theater major, that knack for observation."

This time, my jaw dropped so darned far, I could've sworn I felt the industrial dorm carpet grazing the underside of my chin.

"What?" he asked.

"You are totally the first person who's ever gotten that." That love I had for looking around, for making notes of things both ordinary and unique, that I then tried to bring to every role I took on, where I tried to give it something new. In a way, it's what I was doing with this Carolina persona—taking all the nuances remembered from Nana, the little things I'd picked up from television or magazines, and turning them into this new, believable person.

"Shouldn't be such a surprise, should it?" He leaned forward, propping his elbows on his knees. "I do the same thing, finding the extraordinary in the ordinary. It's just expressed in a visual medium, while yours is more behavioral."

I mulled that over, turning the idea over in my mind. "Yeah . . . yeah," I said, hearing his words again. "You're absolutely right." And this had to be the coolest, most intellectual conversation I'd ever had in my entire life. One I totally didn't want to bail on, but . . . I looked at my watch. *Gah*. I was going to have to get going if I wanted to do the Havana Brown touch-up and look suitably exotic and fabulous.

"Are you coming tonight?" I asked as I began shoving my notebooks and texts and all my other assorted crap into my backpack.

"On your date?" he laughed.

"It's not a date. Well, it is," I amended when his eyebrows went up, "but it's another one of the dorm party-dance thingies." A halfway-through-the-summer-session blowout bash. And everyone thought Ohio State was the state party school. Ha.

"Maybe I'll come by for a bit."

A thought suddenly occurred to me— "You haven't really been to anything since the first night, have you?"

He stood and walked over to the fridge, grabbing yet another Coke. No wonder he was a night owl with all the caffeine he ingested.

"Nope," he finally said. "I did the party scene my freshman year, Caro. I'm kind of over it."

Okay, I got that, even as I blushed, realizing that's exactly what I was doing—freshman, party scene, et cetera, et cetera. "I thought you were going to pledge, though." And pledging tended to mean parties. Lots of them.

"God *no*," he choked out around a swig of pop.

"But—" That first night, Nichols had brought Peter over, introduced him as a transfer, said he was thinking of pledging . . .

"That Nichols jackass cornered me and would *not* stop talking about the stupid frat. Kept saying that the pledge master was right over there, 'come on, dude, just come meet him, just for a second,' and I finally said yes, just to shut him up. Then we barged on over and interrupted you guys."

Oh. That's right. Erik and I had been about to dance. John Legend. Groiny chart. "Nichols is such a dolt."

"Seriously," Peter agreed. "That alone would be enough to keep me from pledging—the idea that I'd have to kowtow to the likes of his power-tripping ass. And anyway, I'm moving to an apartment in the fall. I'm not about to give that up so I can move into a fraternity house where it's a kegger every night and if you don't join in, you're some sorry loser. It's bullshit."

It hit me then that he wouldn't be right down the hall anymore in just a couple of weeks. Not that he would've been anyway, since *I* was going to be in a different dorm come fall, but I hadn't really thought about it beyond that. "Apartment—wow. That'll be cool."

He nodded. "Only reason I'm not there already is that they're not going to be done until September. It's the new complex on the other side of the football stadium."

Whoa. Seriously nice. I had entertained thoughts of begging Mom and Dad that maybe by junior year, if I kept really good grades and maybe sold myself into white slavery to earn at least part of the rent, maybe I could get an apartment.

"Man, Peter, I'm so pea green with envy, you wouldn't believe. Especially since I'm probably going to end up in a cramped dorm room with some psychotic cheerleader named Bambi as a roommate."

"You have no idea how long I've been waiting for this," he said, his eyes lighting up. He had really interesting eyes—brown, but not dark. More amber, although I'd noticed them changing some with his moods, going lighter or darker. Right now, they were bright as he said, "First time I've ever lived on my own, since I stayed at home while I went to Miami-Dade so I could save money. Took three years to finish my associate degree so I could really concentrate on each class—get the best grades possible so I could score some scholarship cash."

And all that with a web design business on the side, which he'd told me about the first time we'd studied together. A small operation that he intended to keep building once he finished with his master's, which was his ultimate goal.

"I did everything I could to guarantee that I'd be able to live completely on my own for the next few years and just do nothing but concentrate on my classes and my business. Boy," he said with a short laugh, "was my ex pissed."

"Ex?" I chanced another glance down at my watch. I was on the verge of running late, but this was getting too interesting.

"Well, she wasn't my ex at the time. She wanted to get married."

"Married?"

His smile faded as he sighed and nodded. "She'd been making these 'it'd be great to settle down' noises and, like an ass, I didn't say anything. Hell, I thought she meant *after* I was done with school. Assuming we even lasted that long."

For such a smart guy—kind of a dope. "Which, she didn't, of course."

"Nope." He sighed and dropped back into his chair, rubbing the back of his neck. "Josie had it all worked out—we'd get married in a little ceremony in June, then come up here while I did my work and she did hers."

I was almost afraid to ask and, you know, it probably wasn't any of my business, but hey, he's the one who brought it up. "Which was—"

"Taking care of me and having kids, not necessarily in that order."

"Oh God."

"Him and every saint I had to call on to deal with the sitch. Especially since her parents were all for it—were completely prepared to help support us financially so we wouldn't have to struggle once we had kids, maybe buy us a house. Her mom even talked about them maybe moving up here to help look after the kids." He shoved his hands through his hair. "Jesus, Caro, they had me with kids, plural, when marriage wasn't even a faint blip on my radar."

Wow. I could only begin to imagine the horror of that scenario. What was he—twenty-one? Chick *had* to be insane. "But still, you got out of it and you're here."

He nodded again. "And Josie's back in Miami, probably still calling me every kind of a *pendejo* she can think of and lighting candles that I should fall victim to some unfortunate, horrible, and probably disfiguring accident."

"Hell hath no fury, dude," I reminded him. And to be scorned in favor of graphic design classes and living alone when she'd been thinking Happily Ever After and Hush Little Baby . . . yikes.

"I know, I *know.*" The hands came up, as if in surrender. "But it was for the best, not that she'll ever get that. There's no way I'm ready to be anybody's husband, let alone a father, for God's sake. I just . . . need to do this my way." His gaze met mine, dark and serious, behind his glasses. *"Me entiendes?"*

Little icy prickles ran down my spine as my breath jammed in my throat at his words. Oh my God, did I *ever* understand him.

"Sí," I said slowly, my hand tightening around the straps of my backpack. *"Te entiendo."*

11

All he did was stare. Just stood in the doorway after I opened it and stared while I sent up a little silent thanks to the fashion gods. Well, and the Internet. Because I'd been doing a little studying a few days back . . . had taken a little break . . . done a little online window shopping, and come across this little red dress on Anthropologie's website that screamed "buy me!" I couldn't whip out my credit card fast enough.

And while I'd probably be paying this puppy off for the next four months, considering the way Erik was staring at me? Really, I could almost hear that ancient knight from *Indiana Jones and the Last Crusade* saying, in that solemn, knightly voice, "You chose . . . wisely."

All right, so maybe a cute dress wasn't exactly on the level of the Holy Grail or anything, but it was nice to know that my efforts were being appreciated.

"I said wear something that would look gorgeous on the dance floor, babe, not something that would make me not want to let you leave your room."

Heat. Total, instant heat that was so intense, I figured I had to be pretty much the same shade as my dress. I glanced down at the halter top that on most girls wouldn't be all that daring, but on me was cleavage and then some. Since I was more used to downplaying the boobs, it still felt a little odd putting them on such obvious display. Chewing on the pad of my thumb, I asked, "Not too much, is it?"

"For what?" Then he waggled his eyebrows and grinned in a way that made the tension back off—but it wasn't gone. Not completely. This was going to be a good night, baby. I could just tell.

"You look scorching, babe. Just totally amazing."

And there went that heat again. Good night, indeed.

"You ready?"

Nodding, I grabbed my purse, made sure I had my room key and cell phone, and let the door swing closed behind us. As we approached the door to the stairway, my gaze drifted over to Peter's closed door. He said he'd try to stop by, but I doubted he would. Parties really just didn't seem to be his scene, which is why I'd been kind of surprised when he said he'd OD'd on the party thing his freshman year. Then again, maybe that's why they weren't his scene. I suppose it was possible to get partied out. Maybe.

Holding hands, Erik and I made our way down the stairs and to the second-floor walkway leading to the communal rec room. Hard to believe I'd done this for the first time only three weeks ago and totally scared out of my head. Just like then, the floors were throbbing and the walls were shaking—Chamillionaire, not Fall Out Boy, but otherwise, eerily similar. Except I wasn't scared out of my head. Butterflies in the stomach— yeah, those were happening. But they were all about anticipation, not nerves.

A few feet away from the double doors, Erik pulled me aside. At first I thought it was so the loud and well-on-their-way-to-plastered guys who were tromping up behind us could pass, but nope—he was pulling me into that same vending alcove where I'd had my little phone convo with Amy three weeks ago. Where

I had tried to convince her, again, why my taking on the Carolina persona was the right thing to do. Why it was what I *had* to do. Leaning against the wall with Erik staring down at me, brushing a lock of hair from my face, before he lowered his head and touched his lips to mine, just the sweetest, softest kiss, I couldn't imagine *not* having done this. Because would I have really been here if I was plain old Caro? I mean, really. I don't *think* so.

"Last chance," he whispered.

"For?"

"Do you really want to go to this thing?"

"Well, what would we do otherwise?" I teased.

"Come on, babe," he teased right back. "I'm sure we could find *something* entertaining to do."

"But you said to dress for the dance floor. And I bought it just for—" I stopped, staring at a button on his light blue Oxford-cloth shirt and trying not to cringe. Definitely in the giving-too-much-away category.

"Wow." His finger trailed along one side of the halter, making me shiver. "Wow."

Wasn't just for the dance floor that I'd worn it—but I think he knew that. Somehow, without saying anything specific, we'd sort of come to a mutual decision. My dress, my hair, the extra careful application of makeup. Instead of his usual cargo shorts and tee, Erik was wearing a pair of khaki Dockers and the Oxford with the sleeves rolled up, the light blue fabric stark against his tan and making his eyes look even bluer.

Oh yeah, it was way tempting to just bag the party and go back to my room. But part of me wanted to show Carolina off some more. My reflection in the mirror—not to mention, Erik's reaction—were telling me I'd *never* looked better and I wanted to savor it. Revel, even.

He took a deep breath and pulled me back out into the hall. "If I make it one hour, it'll be a damn miracle."

I tilted my head down and shot him a sidelong glance from under my lashes. "I'll make it worth your while."

Breaking away from him, I ran ahead the final few steps to the doors and threw one of them open, letting the music wash over and through me. As I ran onto the dance floor, I heard him calling, "One hour. Not one minute more."

Ha. Never underestimate the power and lure of the dance floor. Way more than an hour later, we were still there and I was still on the floor, still moving, swaying, shimmying, and sending more thanks to the fashion gods that the double-sided fashion tape I'd bought had staying power. So didn't need to be pulling a Tara Reid, exposing myself for the world to see.

I danced with Erik, danced with several of his fraternity brothers, including Nichols, because there were such good vibes in the air that his usual leering wasn't even annoying me. Danced in a big group of all girls, where we took turns in the center of a huge circle with my hips grinding and gyrating in a way that you could only call primal, when the DJ spun the Shakira and I let loose.

"Babe, I've got to take a break."

"Slacker," I shouted over the Better Than Ezra remix pounding through the speakers. He just grinned and shook his head, moving off the dance floor, backing away, like he just couldn't take his eyes off me. Spinning around, I was sure I'd find a new partner and wasn't disappointed, coming face-to-face with the original pair of baby blue eyes I'd met at that first party.

"Hey, Dylan." God, three weeks ago I'd have melted into an incoherent puddle if the dead-sexy RA had asked me to dance; now, I was acting like it was the most natural thing in the world for me to turn and find him waiting. It was intoxicating and crazy and just made me throw my head back and turn again, swiveling my hips, certain that he'd be there to grab my hand when I faced him again.

"Don't know if I should call you Carolina or Dancing Queen."

"You could probably call me the paramedics to cart my ass off the floor."

"No way—you look like you could keep going all night."

"Maybe." Planned to, just not on the dance floor. But much as I'd teased Erik and called him a slacker for needing a break, I was kind of relieved to hear the DJ finally segueing into something slower and of the stand-and-sway variety. Automatically, I turned to look for Erik, spotting him standing with a group of his fraternity brothers, gesturing with a bottle of water and laughing about something. Times like this, when I stood apart and just watched him, it was hard to believe it was me he'd zeroed in on.

"Come on, Carolina. That last dance was too short to count."

Erik was leaning in, listening to something that Nichols was saying. And given how Nichols could go on for days . . .

"Okay." Smiling, I put my hands on Dylan's shoulders while his found a place on my waist and we moved in time to the slow, sweet song. I recognized the vocals—Natasha Bedingfield. And as always, her lyrics were killer, about a girl who didn't think she was quite right for the guy she liked. I glanced over my shoulder again at Erik, found him watching me, even as he continued to lean in, acting like he was listening to Nichols. Winking, he mouthed "*soon*," to which I nodded.

"So, I've been meaning to catch up with you, see how you're settling in and all."

I returned my attention to Dylan, the smile and probably genuinely goony look no doubt still plastered all over my face.

"I guess you're settling in okay, then."

I laughed along with him, because really, it *was* kind of funny.

"Yeah, I'm settling in. Classes are good. Everything's good. I really love Harrison—I'm sorry I won't be here in the fall."

"Where are you going to be?"

"Allegheny." Newer dorm across campus, with suites that had their own bathrooms. I'd been all excited about getting in, it was such a popular dorm, but honestly, I'd kind of developed a soft spot for Harrison. Yeah, it had the world's creakiest elevator and the communal bathroom sitch kind of rotted, but it also had beautiful wood moldings and high ceilings and was intimate and quirky. And as it turned out, I really *liked* quirky.

"That reminds me, make sure you get the name thing situated before then, okay?"

"Name thing?"

"Yeah, I noticed they had a typo on the registration list for the dorm. Caroline, not Carolina. It's not such a big deal during the summer, but with four times as many students living on campus during the fall, the dorm administrators get a lot more militant. Want to make totally sure you are who you say you are."

His voice was mild, the expression in his blue eyes friendly, absolutely nothing about his demeanor to suggest that he'd figured me out for a total faker. As the song came to a close, he smiled and took my hands in his, squeezing gently. "Thanks for the dance. Catch you later."

"Later," I replied, hoping any weakness to my voice could be attributed to all the dancing and not the fact that my heart felt like it was lodged somewhere in my throat and going twice as fast as it had at any point tonight.

"Hey." Erik's voice reverberated quietly in my ear, making me jump and making him put a comforting arm around my waist. "Whoa, babe. Are you all right?"

I turned and smiled. It was no big. No big at all. Dylan was just pointing out what he thought was a typo. Was being a responsible RA. And I was seriously overreacting. "I'm great and so ready to bail. You?"

"I've *been* ready."

So ready, he actually had plans. To my shock, when we got to my room, rather than barrel right on in and get going, he said instead he'd be back in half an hour. Wanted to go back to his dorm and take a shower, since he'd gotten so sweaty on the dance floor.

Given I felt pretty sticky and gross myself, sounded like a fab idea. So I did the same, then freshened up the makeup before donning my new purple kimono robe. Just a Target special, but it was a step up the sophistication ladder from my usual Hello Kitty pink flannel.

When I answered his knock, I was hit with another surprise: a bottle, already chilled, of champagne, two glasses, and candles even. Oh God, he was *amazing*. All I could do was drop down to sit on the edge of my mattress and watch as he lit the candles, turned off the overheads, and uncorked the champagne with such a smooth move, not a single drop even overflowed the lip.

As he handed me a filled glass, I looked up at him and asked, "You knew, didn't you?"

He eased down to sit beside me. "Knew what?"

I looked down at my glass, over at the candles, and back into his eyes, which had gone almost navy in the near dark. "That it would be tonight."

"Hope springs eternal, babe." He clinked his glass against mine. "I've had this chilling for more than a week."

I took a sip, smiling as the bubbles tickled my throat. "You know, that cocky 'tude would be really irritating if you weren't so darn charming."

"If I was that charming, we might have opened this a week

ago," he countered. "You don't really want to finish that, do you?" His fingers toyed over mine on the stem of my glass.

"No, not really."

This was the stuff movies and plays were made of. Romeo and Juliet, Annie Savoy and Crash Davis, and Satine and Christian all wrapped up together in one big sweep-me-off-my-feet package. By now, we were familiar enough with each other that, while it wasn't crazy urgent, it also didn't take all that long for us to be out of our clothes.

Then again, we'd been playing this almost-not-quite game for weeks now, so maybe there *was* some urgency there, as our hands and mouths wandered and skin rubbed against skin, knowing that we were about to take that final step.

"Hang on, babe."

Erik reached over the edge of the mattress and snagged his shorts, pulling a string of condoms from the pocket. Seeing them, I giggled, which made him pause in the act of pulling one loose. "What?"

Leaning over in the same direction, I pulled the bottom drawer of my night table open, revealing the jumbo box of Trojans, still sealed up. Giggling turned into outright laughter as his eyebrows lifted.

"Have some serious faith in my ability, don't you?"

"Going-away gift from my dad, if you can believe that."

"I think I like your dad."

Sliding the drawer closed, I pulled Erik close. "Yeah, I do, too, even if he embarrasses me half to death." I framed his face with both hands and stared up at him. "Erik, it's . . . it's been a while."

"Shh." He brushed my hair back from my face. "I'll be careful, I promise. This is really special to me, Carolina."

My stomach clenched hearing him stumble in his usual endearing way over the name. Maybe this was a good time to at least tell him my nickname, so I could feel like it was really *me* he was with. Then again, the other really anxious and ready for this part of me was screaming, "Are you nuts? Who cares what he calls you?"

No. Time enough for that later. He was with me. He liked me. If he didn't, he wouldn't have been so patient. He wouldn't have gone to such trouble with the champagne and candles. He wouldn't be waiting for me even now, just stroking his hands along my sides and thighs, brushing his chest against mine and dropping small kisses along my neck, the ones he knew made me shiver.

He wouldn't be cringing as my cell phone started playing "Give It Up to Me."

"You are going to let that go—please tell me you're going to let that go?"

But no one *ever* called me this late, especially not—

"It's Ames."

No *way* would she be calling past midnight, especially since she knew I had a date with Erik, unless it was something big. But just as I went to answer, the cell phone went silent. But no sooner did Erik say "thank God" and lower his head back to my neck that it started again.

"Shit."

"Erik, I'm sorry, I *have* to, she wouldn't be calling—" I tried to catch his hand, but he was reaching across me for one of our abandoned glasses of champagne.

Grabbing the phone, I flipped it open. "Are you okay?"

Silence. Well, not complete. I could hear the sound of deep, controlled breathing.

"Amy?"

"I—I'm sorry, Caro. I know you're on a date. I shouldn't have called—I'll call you tomorrow. Maybe."

"Amy, wait—don't hang up. It's okay." Because no way this was good. "Please—what is it?"

"Nothing." Lie. But I could wait her out. And it didn't take long. "Just made the mistake of going out with a customer a few nights ago."

"The cute one you've been telling me about?"

"Yeah, the cute one who brought his brand-spanking-new fiancée in for dinner tonight." Her voice was calm and in control, but now I could hear hoarseness, the rough sound around the edges that I knew meant she'd been crying. A lot.

My grip tightened on the phone. "Oh no . . . oh *no*, Ames . . . you didn't."

"Yeah. I did. I was apparently a last hurrah."

"Oh Amy." It sucked, but it's all I could think of to say. "Oh . . . Ames." I felt the mattress beside me shifting, Erik turning away onto his side.

"I should've known better," she insisted. "But Will's been coming in three, four times a week since the beginning of summer. For lunches and dinners, always when I was working. He seemed so nice and he really acted like he liked me."

As I listened to Amy, I reached out to stroke Erik's shoulders and back. The gesture was really as much to reassure myself as to soothe him and I breathed a sigh of relief as I felt him relax and reach back for my hand, taking it in his and kissing the palm.

"He's an asshole. To not only play you, but to bring the bitch *there*, parade her right under your nose?"

"Best restaurant in greater Summit County," she said with a harsh laugh. "Where else would he bring his intended?" Another laugh that sounded like she was going to break into a million pieces and I felt my heart breaking right along with hers. She was such a good person—she so didn't deserve this.

"Secrets suck, you know?" She sighed and followed it with a quick, "I gotta go. I'll talk to you later," hanging up before I could say another word. When I tried to call back, it went straight to her voice mail. The rest of this was just going to have to wait until tomorrow.

Closing the phone, I set it aside and curved myself around Erik, trying to get warm. As my hand stroked down his front, I was surprised to encounter nothing but skin.

"Erik?"

He caught my hand again, pressed another kiss in the palm. "Are you really in the mood?"

I sighed. And again for good measure. "No." But I really wanted to be. I wanted to lose myself in Erik and what we had— push away the ugly knowledge of what had happened to Amy. "We could try."

He rolled over, taking my face in his hands. "I don't think so, Carolina. When we do this, I want to know that you're with me, all the way, and I can't help but feel that tonight your mind would kind of be somewhere else."

I didn't say anything because, really, what could I say? He was right. Until I talked to Ames again, I'd be worried about her.

"It's okay, babe. Really."

No. It wasn't. As worried as I was for Amy, I was irrationally pissed at her. Her timing absolutely sucked. Or her would-be boyfriend's timing, to be more specific. He couldn't have waited one more night? Or better still, not have been such an amoral dickhead in the first place?

With one final kiss, Erik sat up and started getting dressed.

"You don't have to leave."

After pulling his T-shirt back on, he glanced over his shoulder. "Yeah, I think I should." He turned far enough so he could run his hand down my body. "You're so tempting, babe. I don't know if I can make it another night with you without doing anything. But I swore I wouldn't push myself on you and I won't."

I rose to my knees and hugged him tight. "You're amazing," I whispered. "I—"

No. That could wait, too.

12

My arms loaded down, I just managed to shoulder my door open far enough to drop the full laundry basket on the floor, followed by my overnight bag and backpack. Letting the door swing shut behind me, I flopped onto my bed and kicked off my shoes with a huge sigh, happy to be back even though it had been hard to leave Hampshire.

It'd been an impulse, getting up early yesterday after a mostly sleepless night and deciding to drive the three hours home for the weekend. For Mom and Dad's sake, I used the "I really miss you guys and besides, I seriously need to do laundry" excuse (both of which were true). But it was really for Amy and when I saw her, and she collapsed into my arms and cried for a solid twenty minutes, I knew it had been the right thing to do, even if Erik had sounded a little peeved when I called him from the road and told him I was on my way back home.

"She's a big girl, babe. What happened sucked, but what can you really do to help?"

Well, I could hold her while she cried for twenty minutes and then help her dry her face and pull out the emergency pints of Häagen-Dazs—strawberry cheesecake for her, mayan chocolate for me. I could sit with her and eat ice cream and tell her about studying with Peter and how my history professor was from Massachusetts and wore tweed jackets with leather patches on the elbows, even though it was a million degrees outside. Didn't say much about Erik, given the circs, instead getting her to tell me all the gossip about people we'd graduated with, like Jacey Granger, who'd been the head cheerleader and in the two months since graduation, had pierced her belly button and gotten a tattoo. She'd also put on twenty-five pounds but didn't seem to realize it, since she was still wearing her bikini at the pool to show off the piercing and the tat.

All Amy really said about Will was that as much as her feelings were hurt, her ego was hurt just as much because she hadn't been able to see him for such a player. I'd never met the guy, but I had to wonder, too—I mean, Amy usually had such good instincts, and wasn't the type to just do it with any guy. And you'd think such asshole-ish tendencies would hover over a guy, sort of like a noxious gas.

Anyhow, I left Hampshire feeling like she was going to be okay and that's what mattered. I also left with a belly full of home-cooked food, a few expected comments from Mom about my hair, and clean laundry. By and large, a good weekend. I'd even talked to Erik on the way back to school and he sounded like he wasn't ticked anymore, which was a major relief. And even though I probably needed to study, I was going to see him tonight. I didn't have a morning class tomorrow, so I could study then and I *had* to see him tonight. I owed it to him.

As I rummaged through the clean laundry in the basket, a knock sounded at my door. I checked my watch. If it was Erik, he was a half hour early. Which made me feel good, actually. I'd been anxious to see him, too, but didn't know how to tell him to get his butt over here without sounding like a clingy girlfriend.

Shoving my backpack aside with my foot, I opened the door and said, "Hey, you're early—" the last word dribbling off as I found Nichols and one of the other frat brothers I didn't know very well standing in the doorway.

"Nice to know we were expected." You know, I know that Nichols thought his smile was charming. I suppose it was, if you were into leering. I didn't happen to be. But I could be polite. A little.

"Hey, Nichols. What's up?"

Leaning against the doorjamb, Nichols continued to look me up and down in a way that almost, almost made me reach down for the hoodie zip-up sweatshirt I'd tossed on top of my back-pack when I came in. "Erik sent us to tell you he's going to be a little late."

"Oh. Why didn't he just call? Is my phone not working?" I turned away, partially to reach for the phone, partially so I could escape Nichols's stare.

"I don't have a clue if your phone is working or not. He told us to tell you he'd be late. We're here telling you he's going to be late."

I bit back the snarky commentary on how many frat boys it took to deliver a message, instead concentrating on my phone. "Funny, no messages from him, but the phone seems to be okay." I set it back on my night table.

"He's maybe been too busy to leave you a message, Carolina."

My shoulders tensed at the way he said the name—totally wrong, like it was the state, not the way I introduced myself or even the way that Erik tried to say it. Too close to how "Caroline" was pronounced. Spinning back around, I started to correct him and nearly spun right into his chest, since he and his little buddy had come all the way into my room, the door automatically swinging shut behind them.

Ohhh, something about this was definitely not right. Backing away, I still tried to keep it light. "That's not actually how you say my name, Nichols. It's—"

"Prick tease?" he interrupted. "God, I don't know why he's put up with you the last few weeks, leading him around by the balls like you have. Showing off those tits and ass for anyone to see and then being all touch-me-not."

"Ex*cuse* me?"

"You're going to have to wait to see Erik again, Carolina." He said it wrong again, like he knew it would bother me. "He's out blowing off a little steam with an old friend."

"What the hell are you talking about?"

"What are you, stupid or something? I'm saying he's busy getting what you haven't been giving him." He smirked and spoke slowly, every word coming out in a taunting singsong.

"You know, I don't know what your game is, but I swear, when I tell Erik—"

"He's not gonna give a shit," Nichols broke in, running a finger from my shoulder down over one breast. "God, look at these. I guess I can see why he's put up with you—they're unbelievable. They real?"

Shoving at his chest, I snapped, "Get your hands off me."

"Hey, watch the temper." In one quick move, Nichols grabbed me around the waist, holding on tight. His breath was hot on my face as he leaned in close, one hand coming up to squeeze one of my breasts through my shirt and bra, pinching hard enough that tears came to my eyes. "Damn, they sure feel real. So, what's it gonna take to get *you* to blow off a little steam, huh? Or maybe just blow? I'll bet that mouth can do amazing things."

Oh my God . . . oh my *God* . . . "Get your disgusting hands off me right now." I shoved and squirmed, trying to break free, but for as thin as he was, he was strong and his hold was like a vise.

"Come on, baby. Erik's getting some, why don't you?"

More tears now—maybe because of how he kept mauling

my breasts, maybe because what he'd said about Erik kept echoing. I lowered my head, couldn't look at him as I repeated, "Stop it, stop it, stop it," pulling at his hands.

For a second, I thought he was actually going to ease off, going to stop as he drew back and stared at me, although he kept his arm around my waist, tight enough that I couldn't make a move—not yet.

"You think I'm bullshitting, don't you? That your precious Erik wouldn't do anything like that? Jones?" Nichols called over his shoulder to the other guy, who I'd almost forgotten was even in the room. He stood, back to the door, watching.

"No, sir. No bullshit," Jones said.

"First years don't lie," Nichols explained, as if it was something important. "It's a pretty big offense. Extremely heavy punishment comes with lying. Or not following orders. Tell her exactly where Erik is, Jones."

"He's, uh—"

My gaze met Jones's, silently begging him to help. He started to take a step forward, but Nichols's sharp voice broke through.

"Jones—"

Jones immediately stepped back. "He's with a townie, sir."

"And he's screwing her brains out," Nichols whispered in my ear, his breath hot and wet and reeking of beer. "Because you wouldn't give it to him—because you ran off to be with your little girlfriend this weekend."

"You're lying." Tears were streaming down my face and just wouldn't stop, but from somewhere, I found the strength to push him away.

Nichols laughed and grabbed me again, pulling me close. "I swear to God, I'm not lying. He'd rather screw some townie skank than do the hot little Cuban chick who's been leading him on for weeks. My boy Erik's got some mad ethics, man." Nichols looked over his shoulder again and mentioned almost conversationally to Jones, "He'd never force himself on a woman. Even one who's obviously begging for it."

Turning back to me, he grabbed the front of my shirt, buttons popping as he tore it open. Grabbing my wrists before I could cover myself, he stared at me. "I think he's got you figured wrong. I think force is the way to go—get you hot. I know it does me."

Oh God. I started to scream, but before I could even take a breath in, his mouth was over mine, his tongue thrusting in and out, his breath tasting of stale beer and making me swallow back the bile that was surging up. One of his hands was back on my chest, shoving my bra aside, twisting and pulling—

No, no, *no* . . . this is not what I wanted. This wasn't anyone's idea of an adventure, not anything like what happened to Nana Ellie. Even with Nichols's mouth all over mine, gagging me, I almost laughed at the thought of my sweet nana. She wouldn't have ever gotten herself into such a stupid situation. She chose an adventure with the love of her life, not this, not this, never *this*—

I jerked my knee up, hard, just like James had taught me ages ago, tasting fresh air and feeling the blood rushing back into my wrists as Nichols staggered back.

"Bitch," he wheezed.

"Help me! Please, *help*!" I screamed, loud as I could, at the same time reaching for my cell . . . I needed to call 911, had to call *someone*. "Help!" I screamed again, putting every ounce of air and projection that I could into it, but just as my fingers touched the phone, I felt my head yanked back hard, lightning shafts of pain flashing across my eyes and making me scream again as I was whirled around.

"Goddamn bitch." Intense pain hit from two sides as the back of Nichols's hand cracked against my face, my head jerking against the tight hold he still had in my hair. Blood flooded my mouth, bitter and metallic.

Choking and gasping for air, I couldn't fight as my shorts and underwear were shoved down past my knees and I was pushed down onto my bed. Nichols's body was heavy on mine, one hand snaking between us, the rasp of his zipper the only sound louder than my harsh gasps around the hand he had pressed against my mouth. Then he was pushing against me, forcing my thighs apart, another flash of pain as he shoved himself into me, shoved again, harder, a piercing burn like nothing I'd ever felt before. Tears hot against my skin, I heard whimpering, knew it was me, knew I had to try . . . to fight, because I couldn't—*wouldn't*—go down without a fight, but he kept moving, pressing me harder into the bed. Then—the blinding glare of the overheads and a wash of cold air against my skin.

"You fucking son of a bitch."

Dazed, I sat up, trying to blink away tears and sweat, as Peter shoved Nichols up against a wall, his head landing with a dull thud against my framed print of van Gogh's *Starry Night*. And I laughed. I couldn't help it. Nichols's head had landed right smack against the beautiful golden moon, the glass shattering around him like some sort of unholy halo.

"Never touch her again. *Never*." But just as Peter's left arm came back to finish off Nichols, Jones, who I only just now noticed was sprawled on the floor and rubbing his jaw, got up and lunged toward the wrestling pair.

My "Peter!" came a split second too late as Jones grabbed his arm and wrenched it up hard behind his back, Nichols driving his fist into his stomach at the same time.

God . . . *no*. It was a nightmare—Peter sinking to the floor, the two of them going after him, kicking, Nichols pulling him up by the hair and punching him in the face over and over. I had to do something, *anything*—grabbing my phone, I tried to hit 911 but my fingers were numb and shaking, the phone dropping to the floor where it went skidding off, out of my reach.

Crying, screaming at them to *stop*, to leave him alone, trying to reach for the stupid phone, then the door to my room flew open and people in uniforms burst through, pulling at the tangle of bodies on the floor, yelling for them to stop, and I was part of the yelling, diving off the bed and crawling across the floor to Peter who was lying there, breathing hard, one arm across his midsection, the other, limp at his side in a way that made the bile come rushing back.

"Oh God, oh Peter, are you okay? Please be okay, please, please, oh God . . ."

As I brushed his hair from his face, I gasped. His eyes were narrow and glassy, one of them already purple and swelling. But he still reached up with his good hand to touch my face.

"You . . ." He took a breath, flinching and groaning. "You . . . okay?"

"I'm fine. Help's coming. I promise." I swiped at my streaming face with my hands. Had no clue what was going on, but I'd get him help if it was the last damn thing I did.

"I'm . . . sorry . . . didn't get here . . . faster."

I took his hand in mine, holding on tight. "No, it's okay."

"Miss?" Something was draped over me and, all of a sudden, I realized I was basically nude, my destroyed shirt hanging off my shoulders, my bra torn nearly off. I looked up at the female officer crouching beside me. "He wasn't one of your attackers, was he?"

"No." I jerked my head toward Nichols and Jones, held face-first against the wall, their wrists already in cuffs. "Them. He helped me. He needs help. Get him some help, please."

"It's okay. It's going to be okay." The blanket was wrapped tighter around me, a comforting arm that I really didn't want around my shoulders. "The paramedics are on their way up. We'll take you both in and get you checked out."

I wouldn't let go of Peter's hand, wouldn't stop brushing the hair back from his face, wouldn't let his gaze go. "He saved me. Just get him help. Please."

"This . . ." He coughed, his body jerking, his hand squeezing mine hard. "Doesn't . . . get you . . . off the . . . hook."

"What the hell are you talking about?"

I couldn't believe it. He was smiling. Or, at least, smiling as much as one could with a grossly swollen lip. "Math. We still have a study date tomorrow."

I laughed. And laughed, until I started crying again, hanging on to his hand, hunched over until my head nearly rested on his shoulder.

"Thank you, " I whispered.

"Anytime . . . *amiga*."

13

"**W**e've got another room ready for you to stay in tonight."

"Thanks, Shay, but I want to stay here," I said to the dorm's female RA who'd met us at the hospital, along with Dylan. "They can't get to me. Can they?"

She shook her head. "They're in lockup until someone can post bail for them and, at the very least, they've both been expelled, effective immediately, and aren't allowed back on campus except under escort when they come to get their things. You filed a restraining order, right?"

I nodded, my throat tight as I pushed the door open into my room. Filed the restraining order, submitted to a full exam and a rape kit, answered a lot of questions about my relationship to my attackers, my sexual history, when was the last time I'd had intercourse, all in between the offers for something to eat or drink or someone to talk to.

Felt metal holding me open, cotton swabbing between my legs, antiseptic on the cuts on my face. It was pretty straightforward, actually. Even if Nichols hadn't come, he'd left behind enough evidence to prove without a doubt what he'd done. And the cuts and bruises to prove it'd been by force. He was nailed and I was safe from him tonight.

But scanning the inside of my room, I almost changed my mind. *Starry Night* was on the floor, the frame cracked, shattered glass littering the carpet. My basket of clean laundry was overturned, the stuff that had been so neatly folded by me and Mom earlier today—God, was it only earlier today—lying tumbled and messy, my underwear and bras scattered around like some incriminating red light. My bed was stripped, the clothes I'd been wearing earlier nowhere to be found, since it had all been carted away to spray and scrape and test.

My life, the crime drama. Now wasn't that the definition of irony? The theater major starring in her very own episode of *Law & Order: SVU*? A choked laugh escaped me, except it sounded more like crying.

"Sweetie, I really don't think it's a good idea for you to stay here tonight." Shay's hand rested on my shoulder, her tone social-worker gentle.

"It's my room." I sniffled, wiping away the stray tear that had fought its way out of one eye. "I'll be damned if those assholes will run me off from my own room."

Shay sighed, her expression conveying both worry and a suspicion that I was nuts. "Okay, but you know if you need anything, you can call me, or if you even want to come down and stay in my room, I'm there, all right?"

"Yeah." I held up the piece of paper she'd given me with her phone number. "I know."

She squeezed my shoulder. "Okay, then," she said and turned to go.

"Is Dylan helping Peter?"

Her hand on the doorframe, she turned back to face me. "Yeah. He said he was going to get him settled in his room, make sure he had his pain meds."

I stared down at my feet in the ugly blue hospital-issue slippers they'd given me at the ER. "Good."

"He did a tremendous thing."

"Yeah." *Tremendous* seemed like a tremendously inadequate word, but I just wasn't up for anything more substantial. Wasn't sure there was a single word that could encompass all he'd done for me. Tremendous would have to do.

My gaze followed Shay's shadow as she crossed the threshold. "Good night."

"Night," I replied as the door swung closed, barely missing the strap of my backpack. I stared at it—it was the one thing outside of Peter that had probably done the most to save me, since he told me it was how he managed to get into my room. The door hadn't been closed all the way; the long, nylon strap of my backpack carelessly kicked into just the right place, keeping the automatic lock from engaging. Cracked open just far enough for my screaming to carry down the hall, to his room.

Dropping to my knees, I grabbed onto the backpack and held on as I rocked back and forth, chewing on my lip so hard, I drew blood. That hot, metallic tang trickling into my mouth revived the memory, vivid and sharp—Nichols backhanding me, shoving me onto the bed—

I flung the backpack away and stood, lurching to my closet, grabbing my bathroom basket, some clothes, running down the hall to the bathroom where I tore off the scrubs they'd given me at the hospital because I'd arrived in only my shirt and bra and the blanket the female officer had covered me in. And even those things had been taken as potential evidence. Which was fine. I didn't want them, didn't want the stupid scrubs, didn't want any of it, none of it, *nothing*.

Turning on the water, as hot as I could stand it, I stood there, trying to wash away what it had felt like to leave my room, feeling the stares of the people lining the hallway, watching our bizarre little procession. The cowards who hadn't wanted to get involved, or maybe they simply hadn't cared, who were now openly curious, their stares avid, almost obscene. Staring as Nichols and Jones were led away in cuffs. Checking out Peter lying on the gurney; watching me, wrapped in that blanket and holding on to his hand because I wouldn't let go.

I tried to forget how it felt, being splayed out on that exam table, the lights reminding me of stage lights, bright and hot on me while the rest of the room was freezing cold. Tried like hell not to think of Erik—was it true? Had he been screwing around with someone else?

But most of all, I tried not to think of Nana Ellie—what she would've thought of this mess.

Oh, my impatient Caroline . . .

Forget it. There just wasn't enough hot water in the world to wash away the shame. Not about being attacked. Nichols was clearly a sick bastard and I wasn't going to take on *any* of his guilt for that. No, standing under the spray, the water going from scalding to tepid to cold, my shame—and anger—were all directed right where they needed to be.

Wearing long pajamas and a robe, I finally left the bathroom. On my way back down the hall, though, my steps got slower and slower until finally I turned and headed away from my room. Headed to where I'd known I would end up.

Not that I was sure he would answer. Or want to. But just a few seconds after my first tentative knock, the door swung open. My breath hitched in my chest, seeing him again.

"Is it okay?"

"I was hoping you'd come." His words came out slow, kind of slurred, probably equal parts split lip and painkillers.

Walking past him, I stood in the middle of the room, one hand curled hard around the handle of my toiletries basket, the other twisted in the lapels of my pink flannel robe. Coming here had seemed like the right—the only—thing to do. But now that I was here, I didn't know *what* to do.

"Come on." Carefully, he eased down onto his bed, leaving room for me to sit beside him, propped up against the head-board. Even so, it would be kind of crowded.

"I don't want to hurt you," I said, and tried to choke back another one of those inappropriate laugh/cry sounds. God, how stupid a thing was *that* to say? His chest was wrapped all the way down to his waist, for the three cracked ribs, his left arm in a sling that also had a long band wrapped around his chest to keep it immobile—that was for the dislocated shoulder. His right eye was nearly swollen shut, his lower lip split and bruised and puffy.

"It was a mistake to come. I should go—"

"Caroline."

I froze, my hand suddenly slippery on the doorknob. "You heard."

"Yeah."

At the hospital, when they'd taken my information because, after all, Caroline *was* my name. And it was a small-town hospital, a small ER with only curtains separating the exam areas.

"You're not half-Cuban, are you?"

"No," I barely whispered.

A couple of slow tears escaped, hot and stinging against my lids. I'd cried so much tonight—more than I probably had since I was a little girl. But couldn't deny, either, that among the expected feelings of guilt that he was hurt so badly because of me, that in those tears there was also . . . relief.

"Do you want to talk about it?"

"Yeah."

I gingerly sat down in the space next to him and told him. Told him all about Nana Ellie and her adventures. About taking

Spanish in high school and how I was such a natural, capturing my teacher's attention. How that had led to learning about Nana's past. How exciting it had been compared to how boring and ordinary life in Hampshire was and how everyone there thought they knew me. About wanting more. And how Nana Ellie had had so much more. How she was the only one in my family who wasn't from Hampshire. And how—

"I guess I thought . . . if I took on something of hers. That thing that made her unique. . . . If I cloaked myself in a persona more like hers . . . that I'd finally stand out. Be the kind of person who had—"

I stared down at my folded hands. "No one ever paid attention to me like that before . . . not when I wasn't on the stage. Never just as myself. A guy like Erik—it would've never happened in Hampshire. If I hadn't pretended—"

Oh God. Saying this out loud, to Peter, every word came out slower and slower because with every word I realized just how stupid it all sounded. How stupid it must've sounded to Amy and why she tried over and over to talk me out of it. And in that last word, the whole heart of the matter, right? I'd been pretending. I may have taken to it pretty easily, but in the end, it was just a big, elaborate game of "let's pretend."

Jesus, I might as well have been on a freakin' stage.

"It makes sense now." Peter's voice was still slurred and slow, but when I chanced a glance at him from under my lashes, he looked pretty lucid.

"What does?"

"There were things about you that just didn't seem to fit. Like the speaking Spanish with a little bit of a weird accent, but just . . . I don't know. It was more than that. But it was little stuff and I figured I was being stupid—that if there were things that were different, it was because you were brought up in Ohio and not Miami where you totally drown in the culture. But every now and again . . . " He began to shrug, then cringed and reached for his bad shoulder.

Just add one more blow to the ego, not that that mattered worth a damn anymore. But there it was: I hadn't faked Peter out as much as I thought. Yet, like when he'd said my real name, there was a combination of embarrassment and relief at war inside me. I drew my knees up, careful not to jostle the mattress too much, and dropped my head down, flinching, then relaxing, as his hand rested on my back.

"How much of the girl I've gotten to know is the real Caro?"

Turning my head so my cheek rested on my knees, I met his gaze. "You're the only one here I told my nickname."

There was a lot more to it than that. I think he knew that, but was fine with leaving it where it was for the moment. All he did was rub my back while I turned my head back and closed my eyes.

We stayed like that for a long time—no need to talk. There never was, with Peter. He was easy to be quiet with.

"What about Erik?"

"Tomorrow," I sighed into my knees. "I'll deal with that tomorrow."

14

I sat straight up, my heart pounding, dazed and disori-
ented. A loud "Ow!" made me jerk sideways and into something.

"Caro, *stop.*"

"Oh Peter, I'm so sorry." Instinctively, I started to reach out
but found my wrist trapped in a strong grip.

"Don't touch. Please."

Blinking, trying to clear the fog of sleep from my brain, I
slowly withdrew my hand. "Are you okay?" I asked quietly.

"Just need more meds." Sweat beaded along his forehead as
he rubbed his shoulder before he moved his hand to the mattress, struggling to a more upright position. I knew if I tried to
help, he'd probably be a total guy about it, but at least I could
get his meds without hurting him or offending his guyness. I
found the bottles on the night table—anti-inflammatory in one,
painkiller in the other.

"You due for both?"

Gritting his teeth, he nodded. I shook out the dosages and
got a bottle of water out of his minifridge, loosening the cap for
him. After he swallowed the pills, he eased back onto his pillows
and looked up at me.

"Thanks."

"I should be saying that to you. Again." Last thing I'd meant
to do was spend the night. I'd wanted to be all tough and
independent—secure in the knowledge that those jerks hadn't

scared me out of my room. And God knows the last thing Peter needed was to be babysitting me. But I'd just been so wrung out that I had drifted off with my head on my knees, his hand on my back feeling secure and—yeah—safe. Then later, a vague memory of a soft voice, encouraging me to lie down, before drifting back off.

"I'm sorry if I hurt you."

"*You* didn't hurt me. You startled me." A half smile curved the corner of his mouth. "Trying to sit up in a hurry, *that's* what hurt."

Typical guy, trying to make a joke, brush it off, like no big deal.

"Did you have a nightmare?" he asked.

Did I? I tried to remember. "No," I said, slowly shaking my head. "I don't think so . . . but something definitely woke me up." I jerked my head up, listening.

"Carolina, open up, come on, babe, *please.*" The sound of pounding against wood was louder, not quite as faint or polite.

"*That's* what woke me up." I was out the door and down the hall before Peter could say anything—try to stop me. Anyway, I'd said I would deal with this tomorrow, and it *was* tomorrow.

"I'm here."

Erik spun around, and apparently his night hadn't been that great, either, judging by the wrinkled clothes and dark circles beneath those blue eyes I'd once thought were the most gorgeous eyes I'd ever seen. Now, red-rimmed and bloodshot, they weren't any big deal.

"Oh God—there you are. I was so damn worried but you weren't answering your cell and there were cops and campus officials and regional reps from the fraternity all over the dorm and we couldn't go anywhere. I got over here as soon as I—" He started to reach for me—I took a step back.

"Don't touch me."

"Babe?"

He looked genuinely confused. "Don't call me that," I said, with a glance over my shoulder, noticing a few doors cracked open. Vultures, I swear. "Come on, let's get this over with." Pulling my key card from my pocket, I jerked it through the lock and punched in my combination. I didn't particularly want to be alone with him in my room, but then again—let him see. I held the door open and gestured for him to go in. I wanted him to go first because I wanted to see his face—hear his reaction.

He turned in a slow circle, taking in the wrecked interior as he scrubbed a hand over his face, like he couldn't believe what he was seeing. "Jesus Christ, it's really true . . ."

All of a sudden, I went from the cold and calm that I'd some-how pulled from somewhere deep inside to really, really angry. "What? Did you think it was made up? That these bruises and cuts are some twisted figment of your imagination?"

"I kept hoping it was a mistake . . . the cops wouldn't say who the girl was, but some of the other brothers, they said they'd heard it was you." His face went dark and his fists clenched. "I'll kill the son of a bitch, I swear."

"Oh, save it." The anger drained away as quickly as it had shown up. I was just too tired for it and besides, cold and emo-tionless was so much easier to maintain.

Erik's face went from angry to confused again.

"Babe?" he repeated.

"I told you not to call me that." I let the door swing closed and leaned against it, crossing my arms. "Were you fucking some-one else?"

He didn't need to answer. That dark, dull red sweeping up from the collar of his shirt and across his face was enough of an answer. And a little pinprick of hurt pierced my detachment. I needed to get this over with—fast—before I totally dissolved into self-pity, which I had a feeling was even easier than the cold-and-emotionless gig.

"I can't believe this," I said, my voice shaking a little on the last word.

He reached a hand out, but didn't touch me. "It didn't mean anything and—thing is—I sort of did it for us."

My jaw dropped. "For *us*? Are you kidding me? Seems to me you're the only one who scored all the benefits. Well, you and—" I waved my hand around. "Whoever."

"She's a bartender at Buff's," he explained, even though I hadn't asked. And really, didn't want to know. "She's just someone I've hooked up with a few times—"

"At Buff's?" Great. The favored off-campus bar for the frat boys and one of the places I knew he'd hung out when I hadn't been able to spend time with him because I was busy studying.

Seeing my eyebrows go up, he shook his head hard. "No, no, babe, not since we've been going out—I swear. It's just been this casual thing every once in a while, the past couple of years. No feelings."

"Oh, that makes me feel so much better." I hit him with a hard stare. "Why, Erik? Why *now*?"

"It was for *us*," he insisted, although he shifted his weight from side to side as he said it, looking away, then down, anywhere but at me. "And . . . I was pissed," he finally admitted, his voice low. "I didn't see why you had to go back home to babysit your friend."

"Okay, pissed I get, though it doesn't make you any less of an ass, but I'm having a hell of a time wrapping my brain around this theory of 'for us' that you keep spouting. So, seeing as how I'm only an innocent freshie and you're the big, smart psych major—" I gestured with my hand again. "Please, explain."

He looked at me, kind of helpless, kind of like he wanted to take a step closer, to hold me, but to his credit, he stayed right where he was. "I—I wanted you so bad, but I *promised* I wouldn't push. And I just . . . wasn't sure how much this was going to set us back. Your buddy probably being all pissed because of what happened to her and you maybe holding out longer because of it and I just didn't want to pressure you—"

"Are you serious?" My hands were clutching my elbows, desperate for something to hold on to. "What do you think, that Amy and I are attached at the hip or something? Yeah, she's my best friend and I was upset for her and wanted to help her, but God, Erik, how stupid are you? If anything, I was *more* grateful for you—or so I thought. I couldn't wait to get back here. To be with you. I opened the door without even thinking because I thought it was you . . . I wanted to be with *you* and you were off screwing someone else, and then Nichols—"

My voice was shaking, fury storming back in a big, crashing wave. "Do you want me to tell you all about it, Erik? About how while you were getting your rocks off *'for us'* with your bartender, he had his hands all over me—" I jerked my robe and my pajama top aside, revealing one of the many bruises on my breasts. "Doing *this*. Shoving his hand down my pants and telling me you weren't going to show? Because he knew what you were doing. You told him you were going to fuck someone else, so he thought I was fair game, Erik. Because you *told* him!"

Now he was looking sick and I honestly didn't care.

"I'm so sorry. I'm so, so sorry. Please, Carolina, let me help. Let's try to get past this. I—I love you so much—"

Twenty-four hours ago, I would've killed to have heard that. Twenty-four hours ago, I thought I felt the same way. "If you really loved me, Erik, you wouldn't have done this. You would've talked to me, told me how you were feeling, maybe we might have even had a fight, but there's no way you would have done this."

God, that hurt. That realization.

"I could've screwed you that night you were so wasted and I didn't. I knew you were special and I wanted to wait. Doesn't that count for anything?"

Thankfully, hurt and anger were backing off again, so I was able to reply fairly calmly, "Yeah, not screwing someone who's totally incapacitated really qualifies you as noble. Nichols made a point of mentioning that strong ethical streak of yours."

"Carolina—"

"Forget it, Erik. It's done. We're done." I opened the door, somehow not surprised to find Peter leaning against the opposite wall, his ankles crossed in a casual sort of way, but the expression in his eyes wary—and concerned. I smiled—as much of one as I could manage at any rate—and turned back to Erik.

"And by the way, my name's Caroline."

ENTR'ACTE

15

After sliding the last box into the back of the Forester, I slammed the hatch shut and wiped my hands down the sides of my jeans. It was drizzly and gloomy and cool, not more than sixty-five. Even though it was only August, fall was definitely on its way.

"Are you all set to go?"

"Yeah."

I leaned back against the car, my anorak providing a barrier between myself and the wet car. "How about you?"

Peter shoved his hands into his jacket pockets. After three weeks, he'd finally been freed from the shoulder immobilizer and had been given permission to do light stuff. Which meant, of course, he tried to help me load my car, the fool. I let him carry my laundry bag.

"My dad and uncle are on their way up here in the U-Haul with my stuff. They're going to help me move into my apartment, then we'll drive back to Miami in my car."

"I didn't think your place was going to be ready until the beginning of September."

He shrugged, then winced. "I called the manager and explained my situation. Most of the apartments are done, so they said I could move my stuff in, just can't legally live there until the first."

"That's good." I bit my lip, watching as his hand came up to rub his bad shoulder. Guess the damp and cold weren't helping. "You'll be careful?"

He smiled. "My family knows my shoulder's been hurt. And Dad and *Tío* Benny know if I come back home even the slightest bit more sore than I should be, they'll catch all manner of shit from my mom." His smile faded.

"Did the prosecutor call you?"

I nodded. "Yeah, just to keep me updated since I don't actually have to do anything." Thank God for the legal system taking over—wouldn't even have to make so much as a single court appearance. "You?"

"Yeah. I had to give my statement again. But it's a slam dunk. That Jones kid totally rolled on Nichols. It's over."

Yes. And no. Maybe not ever.

"Are you going to talk to your parents, Caro?"

"I don't know."

The counselor I'd been seeing at student health services thought I should. Shay thought I should. Dylan thought I should. Peter *definitely* thought I should. I wished I could ask Amy's opinion, but for the first time in my life, I couldn't tell her something.

I *had* told her a couple days after the attack that Erik and I broke up—mostly because I didn't want her to keep bringing him up in conversation. Reason I gave was that I'd confessed to being Caroline, not Carolina. Wasn't entirely untrue, after all. Which had prompted one "I warned you," followed by a ten-minute rant on what a self-centered, insensitive jerk he was. But that had been it. Like a good best friend, she never brought him up again.

But if I told her the *whole* story—Erik's cheating and Nichols coming after me—there was no question she'd put two and two together and then she'd feel tortured and guilty and I honestly couldn't deal with what I knew would come after the guilt. The talking.

As it was, I was barely holding it together, trying to deal with nightmares where Nichols was on top of me, pushing into me, laughing as he told me Erik was with someone else. Four straight nights of waking up on the floor, huddled against the wall, holding a pillow as I cried into it was what had finally driven me to finding a counselor at student health. There was no way she could possibly understand what that was like and I didn't *ever* want her to understand. But I knew Amy. She'd want to talk it out—thinking that lots of earnest, endless dissection would help, just like in all her books, but I had news for her. This wasn't like a book. And it couldn't be resolved in two or three chapters. And I just couldn't go through what it would take for her to figure that out.

Yet at the same time, I never thought in my life I'd have to keep something so major from Amy. Another thing to hate about this miserable experience.

"Are you going to come back?"

I looked up at him, the light of the streetlamp above us cutting through the gloom and making the fine drops of rain misting his dark hair appear silver. Reminded me of a stage spot just before it faded out on the final scene. "Don't know that, either," I finally said.

We stood there for a few more minutes, a sort of uncomfortable silence encompassing us. We knew it was time to say good-bye—at least for the time being—and, well, maybe for good. That's probably what had me hesitating. I didn't *want* to have to say good-bye. As great as Shay and Dylan had been the last few weeks, so incredibly supportive, it hadn't been like it was with Peter. He'd been my real saving grace. Just by being there.

Just as the rain started getting heavier, sending cold trickles down my neck, he leaned in and put both arms around me in a hard hug. "Take care, Caro."

It was over and done so fast, he was already halfway back up the path to Harrison before I even reacted. Before I could say good-bye. Swiping the moisture from my face, I watched until he disappeared into the dorm, then got in the car and slowly drove off campus. But I wasn't headed home—not just yet. I had one more errand to take care of before I could go back to Hampshire. Pulling into the shopping center closest to the highway, I drove through the parking lot until I found the storefront I wanted. Grabbing my purse, I headed into the salon and up to the reservations desk where a pretty redhead was sitting.

"Hi, can I help you?"

"Yeah, I have an appointment. Caroline Darcy."

She tapped the keyboard and studied the computer screen. "Yeah, here you are. In fact, you're mine." Glancing up from the screen, she cocked her head and took me in again. "We're doing a cut and color, right?"

"Yeah." I reached into my purse and pulled out a picture of me, pre–Havana Brown hair. "I'd like to get it back to something like this."

16

A few days later, I was in the back room of the pharmacy with Dad, putting the labels on prescriptions as he filled them while Mom sat at the desk and worked at the computer. It was early, about an hour before we opened, but that had always been my favorite time to be here—as a little kid, it was like having my own playground, checking out the new magazines and the toys and games we kept stocked for the tourists to buy when the occasional rainy day drove them indoors. As I got older and actually started helping out, it was just a nice, quiet time before it got crazy with customers, coming in to pick up stuff or grab a Coke float at the long counter, sharing gossip over who was doing what and with whom.

Hampshire really was stuck in perpetual *Leave It to Beaver* land, like it or lump it. But hanging at the pharmacy? That I'd always loved.

"Here's Sam Newall's Ritalin, Caro." Dad handed me the filled amber plastic bottle.

I studied the sheet of computer-printed labels, locating the one I needed. Peeling it off, I carefully stuck one edge down, then wound it around the bottle, smoothing out the wrinkles with my fingertip. "I don't remember Sam being all that hyper," I commented. Nice little kid I used to babysit. I'd helped him learn how to read by having him run lines from plays with me.

"No, he doesn't seem to be," Dad commented mildly. Too

mildly. That was his "I've got an opinion I really can't share because of my responsibility as a pharmacist" voice. Told me pretty much all I needed to know.

"Oh brother, another Lynette," I groaned, referring to the *Desperate Housewives* character who bogarted her kids' Ritalin.

"It's an epidemic," Mom commented without taking her eyes from the screen. She didn't have the same restrictions Dad did, but she was still pretty discreet. Small towns and all that. But they knew I wouldn't blab. "Parents looking for shortcuts—for their kids or themselves. No such animal, unfortunately."

As I stuck a label onto another bottle, I glanced over my shoulder at her. She had her glasses sliding down her nose, like always, a pen stuck behind her ear, pretty much like always, with about five different windows open on the computer screen—a serious improvement over the stacks of notes and neon Post-its she used to have. She was an accountant by training (and why couldn't I have inherited some of *her* math skills?), but around here, she did a little bit of everything, basically running everything *but* the pharmacy proper, which was strictly Dad's domain. He'd have to share with James eventually, but that was a few years down the road, when James got through with grad school—good thing. Mom said Dad was going to have to be eased gently into that whole sharing concept. Or hit upside the head with a two-by-four.

"Mom, did you always know you'd live in Hampshire for good?"

Whoa. Well, that came out of nowhere. Apparently to Mom, too, since she took her glasses off and turned her chair to face me. "Why, Caro?"

I stared down at the bottle I'd just stuck a label on, smoothing out an air bubble with my thumb. "Just curious."

She ran her fingers through her wavy hair, still a natural light blond, even though these days there were more than a few silver strands mixed in. "Well, I'd been crazy about Dad since I was fifteen and I knew if I wanted to be with him, I'd pretty much have to come back here."

"You didn't want something . . . more? Bigger?" Boy, that was some air bubble, the way I kept smoothing it down, although I snuck looks at Mom as I did.

"Sure. Who doesn't?" She was leaning back in her chair, cradling her coffee mug in her hands, one of her thumbs smoothing the ceramic edge in the same way I was smoothing the label. "But that's why I went to UCLA for school. I figured I should have the big, huge college experience so I didn't come back with any regrets over missing out on stuff. Grammy agreed," she added with a wicked grin. "Granddad wasn't happy about the tuition, but she leaned on him."

I dropped my head into my hands and giggled, imagining my tiny grammy putting the screws to my retired fire chief grandfather.

Turning on the old-fashioned wooden stool, I looked at Dad, who was busy counting out and measuring more pills, but I knew he was paying attention. He was Mr. Multitasker. "What about you, Dad? I mean, it was expected you'd take over the pharmacy, right? But didn't you ever at least *think* about living anywhere else?"

"I *wanted* to take over the pharmacy." The tip of his tongue stuck out between his teeth as he carefully slid a new batch of pills into a bottle. "Mrs. Lavello's celecoxib. And I lived somewhere else."

I rolled my eyes as I searched out the label for Mrs. Lavello's arthritis meds. "Columbus hardly counts." For undergrad *and* grad school. And so many people from here went to OSU, it was nicknamed Hampshire West. Part of the reason I'd chosen Southern Ohio—hardly anyone from Hampshire went there.

He set down the bottle he'd been about to fill and turned to look at me, his expression thoughtful, like he was weighing what he was about to say. "I lived in Los Angeles for two years, Caro."

"You did? When? You never said anything about . . . oh." I swiveled on my stool, looking between him and Mom, who was . . . blushing? Dude, Mom *never* blushed. She'd overheard James bragging about a cheerleader going down on him behind the bleachers after a Hampshire High football game and hadn't even batted an eyelash (although she gave him an earful about discretion, respect, and safe sex), but *this* was making her blush?

"It was after he got his bachelor's degree, Caro. I still had two years to go. So he put off grad school for a while."

"It was Nana Ellie's idea," Dad said, crossing to the coffeemaker and pouring himself a mug, refreshing Mom's automatically, Mom's fingers brushing across his wrist as he did. "She didn't want me just settling into some predestined path without making sure it was what I really wanted. And she knew I missed your mom."

"And then he didn't even let me know he was there for nearly four months."

My fingers curled around the edge of the stool. "Are you for real, Dad? You go all the way out there because you missed Mom and then you didn't even let her know you were there?"

"It was going to be a surprise." His smile was kind of sheepish as he ran his hand through his light brown hair. "After I got there, though, I realized maybe she wouldn't be as happy for me to be there as I was. That she might see it as me honing in on her freedom—her adventure. It could've been possible she'd changed her mind about coming home—about wanting to be with me. So I figured it was enough just for me to be closer."

Adventure. My fingernails dug into the soft pine underside of the stool at the word. "So how'd you find out, Mom?"

"He got impatient—finally let me know he was there and wasn't going anywhere unless I wanted him to." She grinned at Dad and he grinned back, big goofs the two of them. It should've been embarrassing having parents who were clearly still so hot for each other, but honestly? It was kind of cool.

After they got done exchanging goony grins, they both turned to me, both with the same expression on their faces. Uh-oh. Should've known they'd figure this conversation was meant as more than just a trip down the Parental Memory Lane.

"What's up, baby?" Mom asked. "Why the sudden interest?"

My fingers dug harder into the stool, my knuckles turning white. "I—I'm kind of thinking of not going back to Southern Ohio. I think I want to stay home."

"What?"

"Why?"

Their voices blended together in this combination of shock and immediate concern that had my throat closing up, but after a few deep breaths I was finally able to say, "I have something I need to tell you guys. Something that happened at school."

17

"**H**ey, Sleeping Beauty, you ever gonna get your ass up out of bed?"

No. Not if I could help it.

But I wouldn't say that. Not out loud, anyway. So I settled for rolling over and sitting up, shoving my fingers through my hair as Amy flopped down across the end of my bed.

"Man, if summer session wiped you out like this, I'm wondering if you should do any more of them."

"What time is it?" My voice sounded rusty, like it hadn't been used much. Or used too much. Mom and Dad had found a therapist for me to go to who was over in Aurora, so I wouldn't have to deal with any questions. God knows, if the locals caught me wandering into the Hampshire medical center on a regular basis, there'd be questions aplenty. Because the only reasons to do that were if you were a) pregnant, or b) batshit crazy.

"Would you believe, three-thirty and I have officially finished my last lunch shift."

I noticed then that she was in a cute skirt and top. "Congrats," I said, reaching for the bottle of Tazo I'd been nursing since lunch. Or rather, the half bag of microwave popcorn that had passed for lunch before I went back to bed.

"Now a week of relative freedom and then I go up to Ann Arbor for Orientation and then, after that, classes begin."

"That'll be fun." God. Felt so far removed from that.

"Yeah, it will." She rolled to a sitting position, crossing her legs. "What about you? When do you go back?"

She'd been working a lot, the couple of weeks I'd been home. Wanted to save as much money as possible for school. So the deepest any of our conversations had gotten was, "You decided to go back to blond, huh?"

"Um, couple of weeks. I can skip orientation."

"Oh, that's cool."

"Actually, Ames—" I took another gulp of warm tea. "I'm not going back."

"What?" Her head jerked up from studying the purple nail polish on her toes. "Are you kidding?"

"No, I'm not." I set the empty bottle aside. "I'm going to register at Summit Community, get some general requirements out of the way, work at the pharmacy—earn some cash. Go back for the spring." Or not.

"Are you *kidding*?" she repeated, hazel eyes getting rounder and more enormous until they looked like they were dominating her face. "Please don't tell me this is because of that Erik jerk."

"No, not really." Well, it wasn't except in the most peripheral of ways. That had been the last session—coming to that conclusion. Yay, me.

"It *is* about him. God, Caro, this is so unbelievably stupid."

Oh Jesus. She was about to go off on another rant. And I couldn't deal. "Amy, it's not about him, okay?" I twisted my fists in the sheets. "It's not." Oh God . . . my breath was coming a little faster, my heartbeat accelerating. Gail, my therapist, had said they were classic anxiety symptoms and would probably ease up with time. She didn't say how *much* time, though, and that's what I wanted to know—*needed* to know. I couldn't keep doing this. I just—

"Caro, are you all right?"

I blinked, trying to bring Amy's face into focus. Amy's very worried face. Suddenly very horrified face.

"You're not pregnant, are you?"

My breath came whooshing out of me in one harsh laugh. "Oh God, *no.*" Most definitely not. And I still had the six different tests I'd taken to prove it. And the blood work results. "Look Ames, I've been fighting a summer flu bug since before I came home and Mom's just worried about me taking care of myself. You know how she is. It's no big deal, really. And it's not like it's set in stone. If I get to feeling better, I'll go back."

At this point, I'd say almost anything to keep her from delving any deeper. But luckily, my explanation seemed to make sense. "You have seemed really rundown since you came home." She fidgeted with the pleats in her skirt. "I'm sorry I haven't been around more."

Finally, I was able to breathe again. Untwisting my fingers from the sheet, I leaned back against my pillows. "It's okay. You've been busy with work and getting ready for school—and honestly, there's not much that can fix this other than a lot of rest." Maybe not twenty hours of sleep a day, but did it count as sleep if it was just lying in bed, staring up at the ceiling?

Guess I'd tackle that at my next session.

It was really quiet in the kitchen, considering the four of us, Mom, Dad, me, and James—who was home from Northwestern on his break from grad school—were together. A normal dinner for all four of us was usually noisy, full of conversation and good-natured arguments. It wasn't as if we weren't trying either—going for a bit of that forced gaiety. Someone, usually Mom, would try to start a conversation and there'd be a halfhearted attempt to respond and keep it going, but after a sentence or two, it would dribble off into silence as we went back to staring down at our plates, pushing around mashed potatoes and green beans and meatloaf. Well, I was pushing around. So was Mom. Dad was at least making an attempt at eating and James was grabbing his third helping. A sure sign of the apocalypse would be if James ever lost his appetite.

Sitting down at the table, he asked me, "Did Amy leave yet?"

"Yesterday."

"Michigan, right?"

"Right."

"You'll have to give me her e-mail so I can harass her when OSU plays those losers."

Mom broke in, probably not wanting to dwell any further on the "going *off* to college" tangent, since, you know, I wasn't. "Have you got what you need for tomorrow, baby?"

I glanced up from my fourth attempt at making a roadway through the pile of mashed potatoes I hadn't touched otherwise. The gravy had almost, *almost* gone from pretty swirly patterns through creamy white to mud. I probably had one more pass left before that happened.

"Yeah, Mom. I've got my schedule printed out and downloaded the list of books I'll need to buy. I'll go in early tomorrow and go to the bookstore before my first class."

"Are the clothes you want clean? Do you need me to wash anything?"

"I'm good, Mom, thanks."

"Have you got gas in your car?" Dad asked. "Do you need me to check the oil?"

"Yes and no." I managed a smile. "I just took it in for a checkup last week. Everything's good."

I loved them so much for trying to make everything as normal as possible. And in a way, it was. Mom and Dad totally supported me and I think Mom, especially, was just as happy to have me sticking close where she could do her protective mama-hawk thing. But, really, it wasn't okay and we all knew it.

"Oh, for the love of—" James's fork landed on his plate with a sound that echoed like a shot. "I can't believe you're actually going through with this."

Dead silence dropped over the kitchen as we all stared at him.

"This is bullshit, Caro. I've never known you to be a coward."

The grip I had on my fork tightened until my knuckles turned white as I continued staring across the table at him.

"James," Dad growled, his hands flat on either side of his plate. Oh boy. James had better watch it. I mean, Dad had a long fuse and hardly ever lost his temper, but he'd been so on edge since I told him and Mom about the rape. The night after I told them, I'd walked in on them, right here in the kitchen, to find them holding each other, his head resting on top of hers. They hadn't seen me, not right away, and even though the kitchen had been dark and shadowed, I'd seen the wet sheen on Dad's face. Then, barely louder than a whisper, I'd heard, "I couldn't protect her, Nancy."

And it was in that moment I realized that parents could lose their innocence, too.

So I don't think James really realized he was treading on such thin ice, but I was also getting the feeling that even if he did know, he didn't much care.

"Look, Dad, I haven't said anything before now because I promised you and honestly, I thought she'd change her mind about this. But I can't stay quiet anymore." He looked around the table at each of us in turn, his gaze locking with mine the longest before he looked at Dad again. "We all know it should never have happened—and it wasn't anyone's fault except for that sick bastard's. And believe me, I know exactly how you feel. I swear, if I ever get my hands on him . . ."

I lowered my fork to the plate, stunned by the ferocious note in his voice. When he turned back to me, his voice was softer, but with a different kind of fierce in it. "If Caro caves and stays home, she's not healing—she's hiding. No matter how many therapy sessions she goes to."

The jerk. The big know-it-all jerk. He *knew* I could never back off from a dare. Especially from him. And eyeballing me across the kitchen table with that insufferable, smug big brother look on his stupid face—that's exactly what it was.

"And how did that make you feel?"

"How did it make me feel?" I shook my head at my reflection in the window. "Like stabbing his eyes out with my fork."

"Okay, fair enough." Behind me, Gail laughed. "But after you got done with the predictable little sister reaction, how did you feel?"

With a sigh, I turned away from the window and flopped down into the squishy leather beanbag that was one of Gail's alternatives to the typical shrink couch. "Angry, I guess."

"Why?"

"He doesn't know what it's like—what I've been dealing with."

"No, and he probably never will and you already know that. Let's move along, okay?"

Busted. Damn, but my therapist was too smart.

With another sigh, I said, "I don't know, Gail—it made me think. And I don't want to think anymore. I thought I was done with that kind of thinking. I made my choice and I was cool with it and Mom and Dad were cool with it and along comes James, just like always, mucking everything up. Just like when he broke his arm on my tenth birthday."

Gail smiled at me from her big leather chair, her angular, black-rimmed glasses perched on the end of her nose. Other than the superhip eyeglasses, she looked like someone's grand-mother, with her short, silver-white hair, the khakis and tiny floral-print button-downs that were her outfit of choice, and the warm voice that sounded like it was about to invite you in for milk and cookies. All of which meant that when she went hard-ass, it came as that much more of a shocker.

"I hardly think he did that on purpose, Caroline."

"He was trying to swing from the tree in our backyard on a rope." My voice was dry. "He thought it would be a fun way to de-liver my present. He wound up crashing into the table with my cake and I wound up having an ice-cream sandwich with a match stuck in it, hanging out in the waiting room of Akron Chil-dren's Hospital."

"So his timing and methods aren't great."

"Oh, *really*?"

She tilted her head. "However, it sounds as if his intentions are."

Busted again. Because I knew that. I'd known it when I was ten, even if I'd been completely ticked off that he'd ruined my party, not to mention my chocolate cake from DaVinci's. Admit-tedly, it *had* taken Mom and Dad a while to convince me that he wasn't trying to ruin my life. But then, the fact that he spent his allowance—without any prompting from Mom or Dad—to get me a new chocolate cake went pretty far in convincing me that he meant well.

"His timing and methods still suck," I grumbled, crossing my arms and sinking farther into the beanbag.

"Yet, you know his intentions are good."

"Yeah."

I turned my head on the beanbag and stared out through the window at leaves that were just beginning to show a hint of gold. Things were quiet then, for how long, I'm not sure. Gail wasn't one to rush things. But she knew I had something to say. It's why I was here, after all.

"You know, I never really gave college a chance."

"How so?"

I watched as a cardinal landed on the branch nearest to the window, the late-morning sunlight turning him a blazing red. "Well . . . before the rape, it was all about the Carolina thing and Erik, and then after . . . it was more about existing, I guess, until the session was over."

The next round of quiet was surprisingly broken by Gail. First time she'd ever done that in the month I'd been seeing her.

"I've been curious about that, actually."

As the cardinal flew off, I looked away from the window. "About what?"

"Why you didn't come home right after it happened."

I shrugged. "I wasn't ready."

"Even to come home? Where there are people who love you and would protect you?"

"There were people *there* who protected me." And I couldn't desert Peter. Not after he'd risked so much for me. No way was I about to turn tail and leave him there by himself after everything he'd done. Even if getting through every day of those last three weeks had been hell. By the end of it, I'd felt this overwhelming sense of relief that it was finally over. And . . . kind of proud of myself, too.

"I learned a lot about myself in those three weeks. Made me really appreciate home, for one thing." I pushed myself up from the beanbag and leaned against the windowsill. "And don't get me wrong—it's been good to be here. I needed it. More than I even realized, I think."

"But . . ."

I sighed. "But I *really* hate it when James is right."

ACT II

18

A light breeze lifted my hair away from my neck, the sun warm on my skin. *This* was perfect Indian summer weather. The beginnings of the season I lived for, all golden light and crisp air and a vibe that brought to mind football and comfort foods like stews and hot cocoa and warm pies with ice cream. An orange-tinged leaf drifted down into my lap—no doubt from one of the tree branches that hung over my spot on the patio. Picking it up, I twirled it around on its stem, studying the shadings and tracings of the veins before setting it aside and returning my attention to my laptop.

A second later, it went airborne again, twirling much the way it had when I held it.

"This is going to be so weird, seeing leaves change for the first time."

I smiled at Peter's reflection in the screen as he studied the leaf. Then his reflection smiled back.

"May I?"

I practically knocked my chair over, standing to give him the hug I'd had in reserve for more than a month.

"Hi."

"You came back."

I let him go and dropped back into my chair while he took the one across from me. He set his backpack on one of the free chairs and opened his bag from the Organic Llama. Just like always.

"It was a near thing, to the point where I was literally on my way to my first class at Summit before I changed my mind, but yeah, I came back."

His head was down as he rummaged around in the bag, making his "I wasn't sure you were going to" come out quiet.

My voice was just as quiet as I replied, "Obviously, neither was I."

"So what tipped the scales?"

I couldn't help but smile. "My brother being a jerk."

Peter looked up from unwrapping his sandwich. "I thought he was up in Illinois."

"He was home on break and didn't have anything better to do with his time than accuse me of hiding out. Basically dared me to come back to school. Insufferable twerp knows I never back down from dares."

Behind the rims of his sunglasses I could see his brows drawing together. "Caro, after what you went through, no one could possibly blame you—"

"He was right," I broke in. "God, but I hate admitting when James is right." I ran my thumb along the edge of the bottled Tazo Peter had handed to me as soon as he sat down. Like he knew I'd be right here, just like always. Glancing up with a smile, I added, "Not that it happens that often."

Peter snorted and shook his head. "Sisters. You're all alike." But his face relaxed into a smile as he pushed half his sandwich toward me.

"Yeah, yeah." Closing my laptop, I slid it to one side and pulled the sandwich closer. "Like you brothers are any better."

"Smoked turkey and Havarti," he mumbled around a mouthful as I lifted the sandwich and started to peek under the bread.

"You're a god, Peter." Especially since my stomach was audibly growling now that it sensed food was in the immediate vicinity. And I was only just now realizing how much time had elapsed since I first sat down to work.

"You know, I was going to take offense at the insult to brothers, strictly on principle, but for the god comment—" A pile of Terra Chips landed on the wrapper beside the sandwich.

"Jeez. Have you got dessert?"

An eyebrow rose. "Why?"

"Because if you do, I'll have to think of a compliment that trumps 'god.' "

Setting his sandwich down, he reached into the bag and pulled out—oh *man*—one of the Llama's enormous chocolate macadamia nut cookies. He really *was* a god.

"Just so you have time to think about it." He slipped the cookie back into the bag with a smug grin.

I grinned back and bit into my sandwich. Guess we were both hungry, since we left conversation alone in favor of eating. Or maybe it was just our ability to be quiet together, which I realized was as welcome as lunch had been. So it wasn't until I cleared away our trash and he split the cookie in half that either of us felt any need to say anything. At the same time, of course.

"How's your shoul—"

"Your hair—"

I laughed and accepted my cookie half. "You first."

"Nah, ladies first," he countered.

I broke a piece of cookie off but just held it, feeling the chocolate dough getting warm and soft between my fingers. "How's your shoulder?"

Of course he just shrugged, the total guy. "It's fine. Only acts up when the weather's nasty." Mirroring my actions, he broke off a piece of his cookie, but didn't eat it right away. "Your hair looks nice."

I automatically started to reach up for the self-conscious touch, remembering only at the last second that I had a handful of cookie. "Yeah, well—" I popped the cookie piece into my mouth. "This is me. More or less." More, actually, since my cheerful hairstylist had added some tawny lowlights that took it from blah-beige to something warm and caramel-y. Different, but at the same time, still me.

"Suits you."

"Thanks."

Another couple minutes of peaceful quiet as the crowds ebbed and flowed along the union's enormous patio and the paths beyond. Definitely more action than there'd been during the summer, more energy, almost as if there was this subtle charge in the air, propelling the bodies along. But even so, some of the people had this sort of lost expression on their faces, clutching shiny, new backpacks and loaded bags with the university bookstore logo on them as they stared down at already-battered campus maps. Freshmen. It was kind of hard to believe I was one of them, too. Felt so far removed from that lost-in-the-woods feeling and into a whole different kind of lost. Amazing what six weeks' worth of the college experience could do for a girl.

"So what were you working on?" Peter tapped my closed laptop. "I know it couldn't have been homework—classes don't start for another two days."

I opened the computer and turned it so we could both see the screen. "I was planning my future."

He rummaged in a pocket of his backpack, pulling out a hard-sided eyeglass case. Taking off his sunglasses, he slipped his familiar wire-rims on and studied the open window.

"Union went wireless while we were on break," I said casually. "Cool, huh? Can browse the 'Net, check e-mail—register for classes, all from the comfort of a patio table, latte in hand."

Peter looked from the screen to me. "This says your major's undecided."

"Yeah, well—" I shrugged and glanced away. Boy, needed a manicure, didn't I? "I can't quite decide between history or cultural anthropology and really, I've got time until I have to declare. So I'm just going to take courses in both while I fulfill my general requirements—see which way I lean. But I have my minor set. See?" I pointed at the screen where "Spanish" was in the box beside "minor."

"I see that." His voice didn't give a thing away, other than maybe a mild curiosity. "What about majoring in theater, Caro?"

I turned the computer and hid my face behind the screen as I logged off and powered down. Finally, I closed the machine and put it away in my backpack. "I think I've kind of had enough of acting for a while."

He propped a foot up on one of the unoccupied chairs. "Okay."

"And just because I don't major in it doesn't mean I can't go back to it at some point." There was always community theater, after all.

"Makes sense."

I was starting to get antsy, fidgeting in my chair like a five-year-old doing the potty dance. "So aren't you going to ask?"

"About?"

"Why history? Or anthropology?"

"I would if it didn't make such perfect sense." He drained his Coke, then replaced the cap on the bottle. "Whenever you talked about theater, you talked more about how much you enjoyed preparing for a part, about a character's background and motivation, than you did about actually being on a stage. Given how much you love history and how observant you are, either major seems like a natural."

"Guess that makes me kind of a dork, huh?' I followed the path of the empty plastic bottle as it arced through the air and into the garbage can a few feet away.

"Makes you more interesting than your average bear." He stood and hefted his backpack to his shoulder, exchanging his reading glasses for his shades. "Are you staying?"

"Here—" I gestured at the table. "Or here?" I swept my arm in a broad gesture, encompassing, well, pretty much everything.

He lifted a shoulder. "I meant more here, as in the union, but yeah, the other, too, I guess."

"Here," I put my hands to the table and stood. "I'm done, but the other here—" I lifted my backpack to my shoulder and slipped on my sunglasses. "Yeah, I'm definitely staying."

Nodding, he fell into step beside me. "So where's your dorm?"

"This way." I weaved my way through the tables, filled with chattering students and some parents who were clearly finding it difficult to let their little darlings go. Luckily, for all that Dad and Mom were nervous about my return to USO, they'd been pretty good about not doing the clinging thing. Although Mom made me swear to call at least three times a week. And to continue seeing the student health counselor.

At a fork in one of the many spiderweb paths leading away from the union, we paused. "My dorm's this way." I nodded in the direction of one of the paths.

"My parking lot's this way." Peter cocked his head in a slightly different direction. "The downside of living off campus is you have to park in Outer Mongolia."

Hm. Something to note if I decided to do the off-campus living thing. Dad had actually offered to see if one of the gated apartment complexes had any availability—thought maybe I'd feel safer in one of them rather than a dorm. Given the circumstances behind what had happened, I wasn't sure it would make a difference. But I loved him for the gesture, nevertheless.

"Speaking of which—"

I snapped back, realizing that Peter was studying me with kind of a funny expression on his face. "Of what?"

"Off-campus housing. You want to come by and see my apartment?" Even from behind the dark lenses of my shades *and* his, I could see his eyes closing as he cringed. "And please tell me that didn't sound as cheesy and 'hey baby' come-on-ish as I'm afraid it did."

"Maybe from anyone else. But not from you." Smiling, I reached out and patted his arm. "I'd love to see your place. Is later on okay? My roommate is supposed to be showing up this afternoon and I suppose I ought to do the meet-and-greet thing."

"Later on is fine—just call my cell when you're done. We can go get something to eat and you can tell me all about Bambi, the psychotic cheerleader."

For a second, I was confused—as far as I knew, my roommate's name was supposed to be Zoë. Then I burst out laughing. "My God, I can't believe you remembered that." The crack I'd made when I first found out he was going to be living by himself in an apartment and had nearly died from the jealousy. "You must have a memory like a steel trap."

Struggling to bring his own laughter under control, he said, "You have to admit, it brings to mind a pretty singular vision, Caro."

"I suppose it does."

We grinned at each other for a few more seconds, then he

surprised me by reaching out and touching my hair. "It really does suit you better."

My fingers brushed his as my hand rose to touch it, as well. "I think so, too."

He nodded and turned to head down his path as I went to do the same. Hadn't taken more than five steps, though, when I heard him call out, "Hey, Caro?"

I glanced back over my shoulder to find him standing in the same place. "Yeah?"

"I'm glad you don't back down from dares."

Looking up into the trees and bits of cloudless blue sky showing between the branches, I slowly nodded my head. "Me, too."

19

"In and of itself, genealogy is a fascinating discipline, but it can also be considered an integral component to anthropology."

In and of itself, genealogy is a fascinating discipline, but it can also be considered an integral component to anthropology.

Yep. I'd heard my professor right. Wrote it down, word for word and everything.

Good God, you know, there were times, like now, that I wondered how it was I managed to walk upright and breathe at the same time.

In and of itself, genealogy is a fascinating discipline, but it can also be considered an integral component to anthropology.

"You okay?"

I lifted my head from where I'd dropped it to my notebook and looked into the concerned face of the guy who'd asked. "Yeah, just feeling really stupid."

Triple-pierced eyebrows lowered. "Dude, no kidding. It's a rough class."

Actually, it really wasn't. But Punk Boy was being nice, so I didn't burst his little bubble, just nodded and gathered up my stuff, shoving it into my backpack.

"Don't forget to pick up your papers on your way out," the professor called. "Nice job, most of you."

Making my way up to the desk, I shuffled through the thin

notebooks, finally finding the one with my name on it. I flipped open the cover, breathing a sigh of relief at the 96% scrawled across the top.

"Very nice job, Ms. Darcy."

I glanced up from skimming the written comments on the first page. "Thank you, ma'am."

Behind me, I heard a slightly awed, "Duuuuude." Turning, I found Punk Boy peering over my shoulder. "Don't know why you feel stupid, man. That's a seriously epic grade." My gaze shifted to his open folder, a totally respectable 85% on his front page.

Dr. Germaine glanced up from sliding her notes into her leather portfolio. "Stupid, Caroline? Why?"

"Oh, not because of this, Dr. Germaine." I moved out of the way of the rest of the students who were waiting to retrieve their reports. Sliding my backpack from my shoulder, I zipped it open and slipped the notebook in. "Just something you just said in lecture—it was kind of an aha sort of moment for me."

She laughed, sliding her glasses off and slipping them into her purse. "I love those aha moments—as much as they can be frustrating because they seem so obvious, they can lead you to some pretty amazing places."

"Exactly."

"Anything I can help with?"

My stomach tightened as all the possibilities began running through my head. "I don't know yet. If my gut instinct is right, then yeah, I'll definitely need some help."

Because if my gut instinct was right, this could be "aha" on a big freakin' scale. I was so psyched by the idea, I practically ran across campus to the library, anxious to get started—to start testing my theories. Commandeering a small study carrel, I immediately got lost in Internet searches, yanking book after book from the shelves and piling them on the floor by my feet when the carrel's surface got too crowded. Jeez . . . *why* hadn't I thought of this before? I was so deep into what I was doing that when my cell phone rang, I was shocked to see that three hours had passed. Returning the hugely dirty look I got from the grad student stationed behind the library's reference desk with an apologetic one of my own, I quickly shut the phone off and returned to the book spread open in front of me. The call could wait—especially once I explained.

Only after my back and eyes started threatening to strike in protest did I finally give up. Probably a good thing, since who knows how long I might've stayed, lost in my discoveries, otherwise?

Standing on the library steps, I zipped my hoodie up against the chill. Still shivered, though, because what had been enough for unseasonably warm October midday wasn't quite doing it for late-afternoon chill. I started walking, fished my phone out of my bag, and glanced at the screen. Three calls in addition to the one I'd cut off—two more from Peter, one from Zoë. I called Zoë first.

"Hey, what's up?"

"Girl, where've you been?"

"Library."

"Well, that explains why your phone was off. But listen, next time you plan on disappearing for hours, you want to tell your boyfriend first so he doesn't make himself crazy calling all over the place, looking for you?"

I sighed loud enough so that she would be sure to hear that whole put-upon thing. "I've told you a million times, Zo, he's my friend. *Not* my boyfriend."

"Right." Her tone made it clear she didn't care how high a dose of put-upon I gave her. "I *know* you say he's not your boyfriend and I know *he* says he's not your boyfriend, but the aura? She says something totally different."

"You and your auras. You didn't do a spread again, did you?"

"Who needs to, with that aura?" she singsonged all taunty-like before adding, "Now call the boy, would you?"

Ending the call, I made a face at the phone—like she could really see me. Wouldn't you know I'd get a roomie who read tarot cards the way other people read their horoscopes? And was all about yoga and healthy eating. We wouldn't even go into the fact that she was a disgustingly brilliant bio-chem major. Luckily, she was also unbelievably nice, or I'd have had to kill her in her sleep before the first week was out.

I pressed the autodial digit for Peter's cell, barely having time to raise it to my ear before I heard, "Where the hell have you been?"

"Hello to you, too, and *so* not my mother."

"Sorry." At least he sounded sheepish. "But I got worried when you blew me off."

"Blew you—" My eyebrows drew together, trying to remember. "Oh no. Oh *no*, Peter, I'm so sorry."

"Hey, it's okay."

"No, it's not. I'm a worm."

"Ease up, Caro. It was just hanging the stuff—not the actual opening of the exhibit."

Of course, that was part of why he'd wanted me there—moral support. He already knew he was going to be part of the student art exhibit, just hadn't known how many pieces or which ones. "How many did they end up hanging?"

There was a long pause, long enough that I wondered if I'd lost the signal. Nope—a quick glance at the screen showed four little signal bars glowing. "Peter?"

"Four." He sounded sheepish again, but of a whole different brand of wool.

"Four? Oh my God, that's unbelievable!" He'd *hoped* for two. "Which ones?"

"You'll just have to come see for yourself." He laughed, then mock-scolded, "And if you blow off the exhibit, I'll be the first to call you a worm."

"You'd have to get in line."

"Okay, so now that we've established you're not a worm, nor are you in any danger of becoming one, where've you been, anyway?"

"The library, which is why I couldn't answer your calls. But listen, Peter, it's the most amazing thing."

"Libraries? I've always thought so."

"Jerk." I swear, the people walking past me were going to start thinking I was a psycho or something, all the faces I was making at my phone. "No, seriously—I had a big, lightbulb-going-off-over-my-head moment in class today." I glanced at my phone's screen again, noticing the time. "Which I will tell you all about later, because right now I've got to motor—have an art exhibit to get ready for."

Another pause, then he asked, carefully, it sounded, "Do you want me to pick you up?"

"I'm going to walk over to the gallery with Zoë." A pause of my own, then I said just as carefully as he had, "The dark doesn't scare me, Peter. Not any more than it ever did, at any rate."

"I know that Caro." He sighed. "I'm just being that jerk you accused me of being."

I smiled into the phone. "You're being a friend. It's cool."

"Look at all these people, trying to pretend they understand what they're staring at."

"Shh." I giggled and elbowed Zoë. "Behave yourself."

"Honestly, you take all the fun out of everything."

All of a sudden, a small, pale guy in ripped jeans and an artistically paint-spattered button-down left open over an iconic Bob Marley T-shirt appeared in front of us, staring at Zo with this intense, slightly maniacal expression in his eyes. He held his hands up in a frame, thumbs together as he prowled around her.

"What the *hell* do you think you're doing?" she snapped, turning half a step behind him, trying to keep him in her line of sight.

He ran his fingers through the beads at the ends of her waist-length cornrows, making them swing and click gently together. And pulled his hand back in time—if she could've bitten him without fear of contracting some disease, she just might have.

"Your skin, it's flawless, like bronze silk," he muttered, acting as if he hadn't heard her.

"Bronze *what*? Are you high?"

He completed his circle and stopped in front of us again, the stare toned down a notch, from manic to just shrewd and assessing. And lust. *This* could be interesting.

"You'll pose for me—nude, of course."

"Boy, now I *know* you're insane—" But before she had a chance to finish verbally shredding him to little bloody ribbons, a pair of hands grabbed the wannabe Picasso's shoulders and turned him away.

"Generally helps if you *ask*, Walter. Maybe introduce yourself, even."

"But Peter, look at her—"

"Forget it." He shoved him a few feet down the hall. "Seriously. If you value your life, forget it."

"The two of you really do your best to take away my fun, you know that?" Zoë complained.

"Bloodshed at an art exhibit only works if it's one of the actual exhibits, don't you think?" Peter asked me.

I nodded, biting my lip to keep from laughing outright. "Totally." We both turned pseudo-innocent glances toward Zoë, who just snorted.

"Like I said, no fun." Crossing her arms, she leveled a stare at Peter. "So?"

He pointed behind himself. "Down the hall and to the right. They're grouped together."

"All right then. See you guys in a bit."

We'd been so distracted by the semisurreal mad artist experience that only now did I get my first good look at Peter. "Wow."

"What?"

"You clean up good." Really good. Wow.

He pushed back the edge of the black blazer and shoved a hand in his charcoal slacks, his skin starting to take on that telltale flush. "My mom made me swear to dress nice or else she'd haunt me until I was eighty. Otherwise, I might've just worn jeans. Maybe a nice shirt."

"This is an occasion. You *should* dress nice." I reached out and picked a piece of fluff off the front of his dark red turtleneck.

"I'm glad I did now." His skin was close to the same color as his sweater. "Since you went to the effort."

"It's an occasion." I shrugged, although okay, *yeah*, I was glad he'd noticed. Maybe he wasn't my boyfriend or anything, but still, he was my friend and he *was* a guy and, well, it just felt nice to be noticed again. "Besides, I like getting dressed up."

Nothing major, just a dark amber rib-knit sweater dress that I wore with a leather belt and stacked-heel Frye boots. Big gold hoop earrings that were holdovers from the hot tamale wardrobe, a touch of makeup, and color me dressed up.

"So both our mothers can be proud of us."

"Should we call and tell them?" I held up my cell phone.

"I don't know about your mom, but I don't *have* to tell mine. Cuban moms just *know things*." He shot this pseudo-paranoid glance up over his shoulder, like he was looking for the bugs and secret cameras. While I giggled at the image of some nice Mom type parked in front of a panel of high-tech spying devices, he put his hand to my back, leading me through the gallery.

The exhibit was called "Images from the Twenty-first Century" and had all sorts of media, from computer images, printed out and mounted, like what Peter had submitted, to really freaky-looking abstract stuff made out of what looked like trash from the union. And wouldn't you know, that was the stuff people were staring at thoughtfully and making all sorts of deep commentary about "how the artist's vision had a vibrancy and uniqueness unlike any other."

What*ever*. I shouldn't have stopped Zoë from mocking. People were such total sheep, thinking that just because something was hanging on a wall it was worthy of adulation. Or else I was severely art-impaired. Because, you know? Looked like trash from the union.

"It's a stunning example in the neo-Cubist mode, don't you think?"

The *what*? I stared at Peter as if he'd grown a second head, then, as he cocked his head and tapped a finger against his pursed lips, mimicking the guy who stood about three ugly paintings down, I had to turn away to keep from busting out into laughter. And felt the urge to laugh shrivel and die.

"Oh God."

"Caro?"

I turned back, closing my eyes and ordering myself to breathe. I'd known it was going to happen eventually. Even with thirteen thousand students, it was bound to happen at some point, right? That's what I'd told myself—tried to prepare myself for the inevitability. But now, faced with Inevitability up close and personal, I understood that what I'd really been telling myself for the past two months was, "Hey, there are thirteen thousand students and he's a senior. You'll make it through the whole year without having to see him, then he'll graduate and go off to law school and you'll be done with him forever."

Inevitability can go suck red-hot monkey ass, you know?

"Come on, Caro, let's go."

Opening my eyes, I found Peter staring past my shoulder, his mouth pressed into a tight line. Obviously, he was seeing what I'd just seen. Or rather, who.

"Your pictures—the exhibit."

"The pictures will be here tomorrow. We'll come back tomorrow."

"I'm being a big baby," I protested. "I should be able to handle this. This is your night. And Zoë—"

"*Dios mío*, Caroline, just shut up and let's go. You can call Zoë's cell after we get out of here and let her know we've left. She'll be cool with it. It'll give her a chance to kill Walter in peace or something."

Forget it. I'd done my big, brave thing—all ten seconds of it. I was more than happy to let Peter put his hand to my back again and lead me away. Especially when a final glance back over my shoulder revealed Erik still standing there, studying a painting before leaning down to kiss the girl next to him.

20

"**D**o you miss him?"

I looked up from the blob of whipped cream floating in the giant hot chocolate Peter had bought me. I'd thought after we blew out of the gallery that he might just take me back to my dorm or maybe over to his apartment, for the big decompression. For whatever reason, though, after helping me into his car, he'd turned and driven off campus and toward a nearby Panera.

It worked. Something about the bright lights, the smells of roasted coffee and fresh-baked muffins, the chatter of the crowd—college students, high schoolers, families with little kids—underscored by the KT Tunstall playing in the background, all served to settle me down. Being somewhere quiet, I might have thought about it too much.

"Honestly? No, I don't."

Honestly? After I'd gotten over the main part of the hurt—which was big, don't get me wrong—I couldn't deny what was left was this pretty huge sense of relief. That I didn't have to be *on* all the time, didn't have to remember what I might've said about my family background or how I might've said it. That I didn't have to put on that stupid tinted moisturizer anymore.

"But I also haven't seen him since—" I drew a finger through the melting whipped cream and licked it off. "Well, it just sort of came as a surprise." Lifting my mug, I glanced at Peter over the rim. "And frankly, an art exhibit's sort of the last place I would've expected to see him."

"And with a girlfriend."

Peter had that artist's sensitivity thing going for him—he wouldn't say something like that if he thought it would really hurt my feelings. At the same time, though, he also worked in the clinical, measurable medium of computers, where every little flaw could be revealed and magnified to scary proportions. So maybe even more than artistic, he was analytical—and honest.

"Yeah."

He nodded. Curling his hands around his mug, he leaned forward. "Much as I hate to give the son of a bitch any kind of credit, maybe he's trying to grow up some, Caro. An art exhibit's pretty far removed from a kegger."

"Maybe." I lifted my shoulder and took another sip of cocoa. "She was pretty—looked Asian. Guess he's going for an exotic you can't fake so easy."

"And she could also be third generation from Shaker Heights. Is it possible he just likes her?"

See? Analytical and honest. "Anything's possible." I set my mug down and pushed it away. "And if that's the case, then I really *was* stupid. You know, I really wanted him to like me for who I am. But I never gave him the chance. So he liked who he *thought* I was." I stared down at the amber rib knit that, while fairly heavy, still clung. "And my tits." I sighed.

"You know, there is just some shit you need to quit boo-hooing about, Caroline. Get over it, already."

"*Excuse* me?"

My jaw feeling like it was about to hit the table, I stared at Peter. His mouth was pressed back into that same tight line as it was back at the gallery, and even though he was looking away from me, out over the happy, chattering crowd, I could still see that his eyes had gone all narrow and dark.

"Excuse me?" I repeated, feeling stupid, but what else could I say?

"You think you're the only person on the planet who's ever done something so stupid? Jesus, you remind me of some of my baby cousins who think when they skin their knees, they're the only ones it's ever happened to."

Shoving his chair back so hard the legs screeched against the floor, he grabbed his blazer off the nearby coatrack and handed me my leather coat. Without another word, we pulled on our coats, got in his car, and drove back to campus. Longest freakin' ten minutes of my life, it seemed. He was so angry, it practically vibrated around him and I was near tears because I had no idea what he was so angry about except that it had to do with me. Then about eight minutes into the ride, *I* started getting angry, too. I mean, what the hell? He was acting like a toddler throwing a tantrum, unable to say what he was so pissed about and he was accusing *me* of acting like a baby?

There was so much tension in that car, the windows should've been fogged with it. When he finally jerked to a stop in front of my dorm, I couldn't unlock the door fast enough, but just as I started to pull the handle, the locks engaged again.

"Stop it, Peter." I tried to hit the button, but got nothing except an empty clicking sound and the locks staying put. I could *not* believe him—first, he couldn't get me home fast enough, now he'd engaged the stupid switch where he had control of the locks. And wouldn't you know, the damn things were flush with the doorframe, so I couldn't even pull them up manually. "Let me out, dammit."

"You want to know why I don't party?"

What? Slowly, I eased the handle back into place, although I kept my hand curled tight around it. And I wouldn't look at him.

"You did it your freshman year. You got over it."

"Yeah. I did it my freshman year. Every weekend." His voice was dry . . . cold, almost. Involuntarily, I shivered as he kept talking. "Got together with a bunch of guys from my old high school and we'd get totally ripped. Because it was fun, right? Booze, pot—Ecstasy or blow a few times, when we could put enough money together."

My fingers went limp, slid from the handle as I turned to stare at him, but he wouldn't look at me. Instead, he seemed to be studying his hands, clenched tight around the steering wheel.

"Only on the weekends—that was my rule. And the grades couldn't slip, because I did have my plan in place. That wasn't bullshit." Now he chanced a glance over at me, something sort of pleading in it.

Shaking my head, I said, "I never thought it was."

Nodding, he turned to stare at his hands again. "Girls always hung with us, too. They liked partying, we liked them." His voice dropped. "*I* liked them. A lot."

My stomach was knotting up, because obviously, this was incredibly hard for him. And he had to have a good reason for telling me.

"When you're eighteen and have that first taste of adult freedom, you don't tend to think of consequences, *tú sabes*?" As he continued to speak, his voice lost the dry-and-cold edge in favor of a slight, oddly familiar lilt. "Using rubbers? Sometimes I did—most times, I didn't."

He finally unclenched his hands from the wheel and turned to face me completely. "One of the girls I partied with? Found out, after we hadn't seen her around for a while, that she was sick—had hepatitis."

I shook my head, not completely understanding.

"It's nasty, Caro. It can be cured, but the treatment's a bitch. And sometimes, depending on what strain it is, it doesn't respond well to treatment at all and you're sort of stuck with it." His teeth dragged across his lower lip for a brief second, then he very quietly said, "It's the kind of disease that can be transferred through unprotected sex. I could remember that I'd had sex with her—whether or not it was protected . . ." He dropped his gaze to his hands, fisted against his thighs. "Not so much."

"Oh."

"Scared the shit right out of me, Caroline. She'd been with most of us. And God only knows who that we didn't know about. So who knows what else she might've had?"

"Oh my God." A sick, raw sensation began clawing at the insides of my chest.

"I got lucky. Every test came back clean. And every test for two years after that." The breath he took was so deep that when he blew it out, I could feel it ruffling the hair around my face. "And I became the straightest damn arrow in Miami."

Next thing I knew, his hand was on my chin, turning my head so our gazes met directly, holding it so I couldn't look away. Unbelievably, a smile started curling up one side of his mouth. "On the stupidity scale, *m'ija*—trust me, you're pretty far down."

"Oh man." I groaned, pulling away and dropping my face into my hands. "I feel so unbelievably—"

"*Don't* say it." He pulled me against him, half hugging, half muzzling me, I think. My cheek pressed tight against the scratchy wool of his blazer, I listened to him say, "What happened with Erik? It wasn't because you faked being Cuban and it sure as hell shouldn't have been because he didn't know you. The *real* you, the important stuff, was there the whole time. What he did had *nothing* to do with you."

Okay, *now* I cried. Enough so that I sniffled against his jacket, "Oh man, I'm going to have to pay your dry cleaning bill."

"That's disgusting, Caro."

"Your fault, Peter." I took another deep, shuddering breath. "How'd you know?"

"Because I know you get that Nichols wasn't your fault. But Erik? Obviously something still there, even if you don't miss him." His hand was stroking my hair and my back. Outside of those two brief hugs we'd shared—one good-bye, one hello—this was the closest we'd been physically since the night of the rape. "Okay, yeah, you both lied, but they're two completely different beasts. You were trying to figure out stuff about yourself, trying on a different persona. Hell, everyone does that to a certain extent when they go off to college. He was just a selfish, immature prick. So you think you can try cutting yourself some slack? Trust me, I know it's a bitch, but it's doable."

"Yeah . . ." I said slowly. "I think I could try." I mean, if he could—what kind of sad, self-pitying brat would I be if I didn't even *try*? Amazing how Peter had known, that the one thing that had kept bugging me about Erik was the "why." That I'd kept looking for excuses and justifications and kept trying to put it on myself instead of just accepting the simple fact that he'd been selfish, and nothing more.

Groping in my pockets, I found a couple of napkins from Panera and used one to swipe at the gooey spot on Peter's jacket and the other on my eyes and nose. "You know . . . the Carolina thing. I've been thinking about it."

Taking the napkin from me, he swiped at his jacket some more, then shrugged it off as a lost cause, tossing it in the backseat. "Oh?

"Yeah. Remember earlier today, when I told you I had a big lightbulb moment?"

He crossed his arms and lifted that one expressive eyebrow. "Why do I have a bad feeling about this?"

"It's not that bad."

"You know, whenever my sisters say that, it turns out to be that bad and worse."

"Oh, relax."

"And when they say *that*, that's the last thing I should do."

21

"*Now switch off your phone and tell me exactly how long it is that you've been working here?*"

"*Two years, seven months, three days, and I suppose, what—two hours.*"

"*And how long have you been in love with Karl, our enigmatic chief designer?*"

I pointed the remote at the TV and jabbed the pause button, halting one of the great exchanges of all time between Alan Rickman and Laura Linney. "Enigmatic. *That's* the perfect word for Peter."

"You *really* think so?" Amy asked, chasing down a handful of caramel popcorn with a swig of eggnog.

"Oh please. That boy's not the least bit enigmatic." Zoë leaned down from her perch on my bed and grabbed a handful of the caramel corn from the enormous bowl on the floor.

"Then how would you guys describe him?" I demanded, draining my mug of hot spiced cider.

The only sound was the hum of the DVD player. Turning my head to the left, I saw Amy just staring at me; tilting my head back, I saw the same "oh please" expression, albeit in a really abstract, upside-down sort of way, on Zoë's face as she loomed over me.

"Augh." I fell over sideways and buried my head in my giant floor pillow. "Why did I ask you guys to spend New Year's with me again?"

"Because Peter's at home in Miami?"

Blindly reaching up to my bed, I found one of my throw pillows and threw it toward the sound of Zo's voice. Then threw another in Amy's general direction even as she protested, "Is she *wrong*?"

Which made me stop. And think. Would I be hanging out in my bedroom in Hampshire with Amy and Zo on New Year's Eve, watching *Love Actually*, eating junk food and waiting for Ryan Seacrest to do his best Dick Clark if Peter had been around?

Well . . . oh, forget it. Why was I even considering this? "It's a totally moot point. It *is*," I protested when twin sets of doubtful eyebrows rose in my direction.

Peter was back home for the monthlong Christmas break—I'd dropped him off at Akron-Canton airport myself on my way back to Hampshire—and I was spending New Year's Eve like I had for the past million years, watching movies with Amy and waiting for the ball to drop. The only difference from any other old New Year's was the addition of Zoë, who'd driven down from Lakewood to spend a couple of days hanging with us so, as she put it, "I don't kill my little sisters because that would so mess with my karma."

"But if it wasn't a moot point?" Zoë asked.

"I don't know . . . he'd maybe be hanging with us, I guess."
"Us?"

Amazing how, despite having only met each other yesterday, Amy and Zoë had the synchronized responses and eye rolls down. But you know, the chicks were completely delusional. Thinking . . . that he. . . . *Nah* . . . I sighed into the floor pillow.

"I just wish I understood."

Reaching over, Amy skated her finger along the silver charm bracelet I was wearing. "How hard is it to understand that, at the very least, he likes you a lot?"

"Okay, yeah, I do get that," I agreed. "And I like him a lot, too—I mean, I think it's safe to say he's my best friend outside of you guys."

"Friend, schmend," Zoë chimed in. "Girl, he doesn't just like you, he *gets* you."

Okay, no doubt on that one, either. Especially now. We'd exchanged gifts—or so I thought—before we left school. Partially because what I'd gotten him was kind of big and was meant for his apartment anyway.

"This is awesome, Caro," he'd said, staring down at the framed print of *A Sunday on La Grande Jatte*. "I've always loved this painting."

"The way he did the dots of colors made me think of pixels."

"Exactly." He looked up from studying the print, one of those enormous smiles lighting up his whole face and wiping out the exhausted vibe pretty much everyone on campus had going after finals. "It's a style called pointillism—man, if Seurat was alive today, he'd be such a kick-ass graphic artist."

Giggling, I nodded my head. "That's exactly what I thought, too."

The idea had come to me when I caught a rerun of *Ferris Bueller's Day Off* while pulling an all-nighter. That scene where Ferris's best friend did nothing but stand in front of this same painting and completely zone out, staring at it, the camera zooming in, tighter and tighter, until all you could see were individual dots of color. That stunned expression, the complete absorption, reminded me of the expression on Peter's face when he was deep into working on a project.

For his part, he'd given me a book—the most amazing book—*Cubans in America*, that was an accounting of the entire Cuban immigration and exile experience since the dawn of time, practically. I'd nearly cried when I tore off the wrapping paper and read the title. Maybe to some people, it would seem like a totally dry gift—a book that's just this side of an academic text. But coming from Peter, after the last couple of months and what I'd been doing? Call it a nice, reassuring dose of validation.

Because my big lightbulb moment that had begun in Dr. Germaine's anthropology class back in October was to start researching Nana Ellie's family. Even if the passing myself off as a Cuban girl was dead like a dead thing, even if I knew I'd never *be* a Cuban girl, no matter how much an affinity I still felt for that part of my background, I couldn't help but feel that there was something left . . . I don't know, unresolved, I guess. Something that kept nagging at me.

Then it hit me. Nana Ellie had obviously never talked about her family, except with Papa Joseph, maybe—but did she have any clue what had happened to them? Did anyone have *any* idea what had happened to *her*?

And given how many Cubans had come over to this country— could some of her family be in the United States? Could I actually have family that wasn't of the sixth-generation-Hampshire-born-and-bred variety out there?

Initially, Peter thought I was nuts. Told me what a risk it was, that I might not like what I found, if anything. Dr. Germaine, after rubbing her hands together in glee, had said more or less the same thing to me when I asked her help in getting started. Warning me that any search worth its salt carried a measure of risk in discovery equal to, if not exceeding, the potential payoff. So yeah, I got that. But even so . . . I *had* to.

So the fact that Peter gave me the book—what it signified meant a whole lot more than the book itself, you know?

We gave each other a couple of other little things, too. I gave him a CD of tunes I burned for him, stuff I knew he'd like; he gave me one of his prints from the gallery exhibit.

"I'm giving one each to my parents and my sisters. That left me with one more and, well . . . you never replaced *Starry Night*, did you?" The entire time he spoke, my stare kept going from the small, framed print to his face, which was surprisingly serious— maybe even a little sad.

"No, I didn't." I had it fixed and tried hanging it back up, but took it down because all I could see was Nichols's face superimposed over the dreamy blue background—jarring and totally nasty and bringing back every horrible feeling from that night. Hadn't bothered to look for anything to replace it with.

That familiar wash of red started creeping up from his collar. "Not that I'm comparing myself to Vincent or anything, you understand."

"But . . . don't you want to keep one?"

"I've got them all burned to disc, Caro, so I still have them. Besides, how big would my ego have to be to hang my own stuff?" Shoving his hands in his jeans pockets, he nodded at the one I held. "Bad enough my ego's big enough to give 'em as gifts."

I couldn't stop looking at it—at first glance, it was nothing more than a tawny-colored expanse overlaid with thin, black criss-crossed lines and squiggles of black and burgundy. But because I'd been there while he was working on it, I knew this was a flamenco dancer, the ruffles of her dress cascading down the length of one fishnet-stockinged leg, blown up to those scary huge proportions he was so fond of, and set at an angle to create a really cool abstract piece.

"Hey, for my part, I'm glad your ego's at least that big."

So that was the gift exchange—or so I thought. Come Christmas day, there I'd been, as tradition dictated, totally crashed in my room. It was post presents under the tree, cranberry-orange muffins and cider for breakfast, and the enormous midday orgy known as Christmas dinner with as much of my extended family as we could fit in my maternal grandparents' house. Given that whole "sixth generation, Hampshire born-and-bred" thing, you can imagine how many bodies comprised "extended."

Anyhow, there I was, near-stupor, flipping channels on the television, when my cell rang. Figuring it was Ames, calling to see if I'd be sufficiently recovered enough for us to do the gift comparison later, I didn't even bother looking at the screen before answering.

"Hey—I am so dead, you have no idea."

"That would be a real shame. Seems like Christmas is a lot more fun when you're among the living."

I sat straight up, holding the phone tighter. "Peter, *hi*—Merry Christmas!" And color me surprised—and really, really pleased.

"Merry Christmas, Caro. You having a good day?"

"Yeah, as much as anyone can have when you have to deal with a million family members getting tanked on eggnog that's more rum than nog, and trading embarrassing stories, many of them starring yours truly."

"Oh yeah, like what?"

"Well, without fail, someone always manages to mention the Fourth of July picnic on the Green when I was four and decided it would be a good idea to strip naked as the community band launched into 'The Stars and Stripes Forever.' "

While he choked with laughter, I protested, "Come on, I was *four*, you know? You'd think they'd let it go already."

"Hey, I peed in the punch at a family barbecue when I was three and they've never let me forget that, either, so I totally sympathize."

"Oh Peter, that's truly gross."

I could almost see him shrugging as he said, "Look, it wasn't completely my fault. I'd only just mastered the whole potty-training thing, you know? And it was some sort of nasty-ass punch that was apparently the same blue as that Ty-D-Bol stuff my mom used to use in the toilets."

Oh . . . oh God. I could just imagine a little tiny Peter, checking out the punch bowl and assessing it with that analytical stare of his. I was laughing so hard, I barely heard him start speaking again.

"What? I'm sorry, I didn't get what you said."

"I *said*, I'll bet you haven't even opened your backpack once since we left school, have you?"

Still giggling and wiping my eyes, I replied, "Dude, of *course* not. Hello? Vacation—remember?" Please—if he told me he'd been studying, I'd have to hurt him.

That's not what he told me.

"Thought as much. Go look inside."

"What? Why?"

He sighed, but somehow sounded like he was smiling, too. "Just do it, Caro. Please."

"What's with the mystery boy routine?" I muttered as I leaned down from my bed and snagged my backpack, dislodging a dust bunny that had already started gathering underneath the dark green canvas. "I take it I'm supposed to be looking for something?"

"Main compartment."

"*Ew.*"

"What?"

"Funky sweatshirt."

"Oh yeah, you really haven't looked in there since we left, have you? That thing was headed toward funk two weeks ago."

Sticking my tongue out at the phone, I pulled out the sweatshirt and tossed it in the general direction of my hamper. The phone lodged between my shoulder and ear, I started groping around the books and notebooks that were still in there, only slightly nervous over what else I might find.

"It's not gonna bite, is it?" I joked as I shifted a couple of books aside and my fingers collided with something long and narrow, tucked in along the side. "What—?"

A long, narrow, gift-wrapped box. "Peter?"

"Open it, Caro."

Having a hard time coordinating functions like untying ribbon and tearing paper with breathing, it took a few tries, but soon enough I had the box on my lap, the lid off, staring down at the contents, lying in soft white cotton.

His voice was soft. "Do you like it?"

"Peter, it's—" I lifted the silver bracelet, laying it across my thigh, the charms bright against my black sweatpants. A state of Ohio, an Eiffel Tower, an itty-bitty folded map, a box of cigars, a windmill. "It's amazing." I was sniffling, trying not to cry outright, but *God.* As perfect as the book had been, as much as it showed that he got it—this was more . . . personal. He didn't just get what I was trying to do. He got *me.* Because each of these charms, they signified something special. The Ohio and Eiffel Tower for Nana and Papa, obviously, because those were the two places they'd been happiest, and the map because of all the traveling, natch. The box of cigars because that's what her family's business had been, in Cuba—and that had been the first piece of really important information I'd been able to uncover.

"What's the windmill for, though?" I asked, holding the bracelet up and watching the mellow late-afternoon sunshine play off the silver charms. "Nana and Papa didn't go to Holland. Not that I know of, at any rate."

"No. That one's for you. For your quest." His voice was still quiet, but that smile was back in it.

"Think I'm tilting at windmills, do you?" My turn to smile into the phone as I lowered the bracelet to drape it across my wrist, loving how it looked. "Chasing some impossible dream?"

"The world needs dreamers, Caro. And at least you're nowhere near as nuts as Don Quixote."

"Gee, thanks, I think," I said with a laugh. The bracelet fastened, I held my wrist up, turning it back and forth, listening to the music the charms made, clinking against the links.

"There's plenty of room to add more charms. The closer you get. Merry Christmas, Caro."

"Merry Christmas, Peter."

A week later, and I'd only taken the bracelet off when I showered. And I was still confused as all get out.

"I just wish I knew what it meant," I said, hugging the pillow even tighter.

"That he really likes you, Caro," Amy repeated.

"And that he gets you," Zoë added. "Isn't that enough for right now?"

22

"**Y**es." I stared from my laptop's screen to the printed pages I had spread around me, to the legal pad I'd been scribbling on, to the books I had open and overlapping each other, and back to the laptop's screen. "Oh, abso-freakin'-lutely *yes*." My favorite grad student reference librarian shot me the obligatory dirty look—guess I was gushing above a whisper again.

You'd think he'd be used to it. My aha moments were getting to be pretty commonplace these days. Didn't take the thrill away, however. Sending the command to the nearby printer for the pages I wanted copied, I set about returning some of the books to the shelving cart, setting others aside to check out, and slipping my already well-used copy of *Cubans in America*, along with my legal pad, into my backpack.

After I checked out the books I wanted and paid for my copies, I ran from the library to the parking lot. A short run, thank God, because it was beyond cold and getting colder by the second, a nasty, sleet/snow mix spitting down from iron gray skies. March, my *ass*. Felt more like January. In the freakin' Arctic Circle. Thank God I'd had the foresight to drive to the library from my dorm because I would've hated hiking back there in this mess just to get my car.

A few minutes later, I pulled into the guest spot in front of the town-house-style apartment where I spent almost as much time as I did my dorm room.

"Peter, open up." I pounded on the door again, feeling the icy tingles vibrating through my fist and up my arm, even through layers of gloves, sweater, turtleneck, and parka. "It's *cold* out here!" Bouncing from one foot to the other, I drew my arm back to pound even louder, the force of my swing carrying me across the suddenly open doorway.

"Why don't you just use the key?"

Catching myself on his outstretched arm and pulling myself upright, I replied, " 'Cause you gave me that for emergencies." I tossed my gloves and backpack onto the sofa. "This isn't an emergency."

"The way you were pounding the freakin' door—"

"Jeez, you're in a foul mood." Looked pretty foul, too, his hair standing on end, a few days' worth of stubble taking him from fashionably scruffy to borderline hobo and scary bags under his eyes.

"Have you slept?" Pulling off my scarf and unzipping my parka, I tossed them on top of the gloves and backpack.

"Couple hours."

"When? Two days ago? Moron." I unlaced my boots and left them on the grooved rubber Southern Ohio Cougars mat just to the side of the front door. He'd laughed like a loon when I got that for him as a housewarming gift back in September. Miami Boy didn't laugh so hard after the first snowstorm in November.

"Did you come over just to call me names or is there some specific reason?"

Okay, admittedly midterms *were* a bitch and I knew a big chunk of one of his grades depended on this project he was losing sleep over. And adding to the stress factor, he'd just taken on a new web design client who made Lindsay Lohan look meek and submissive, but enough was enough already.

He was supposedly the older more mature one, so why was he the one acting like he didn't have the sense God gave a cabbage?

"Calling you names because you're acting like a fool isn't reason enough?"

"You know, if I want this kind of abuse, I'll just call home." He waved one hand as he shoved the other through his hair, making it stand up even more.

Ducking under his arm, I took off my heavy fisherman's knit sweater and pulled at the collar of my navy blue turtleneck, trying to get some cooler air to my skin because, as usual, he had the thermostat set to just below sauna, no matter how often I tried to drill sixty-eight degrees and layers as the Ohio way. Trying to cool off—*period*—and not strangle him for excessive weenieness because I actually *had* come over with a purpose that wasn't pissing him off.

"When did you last eat?" Not the purpose I'd come over with—not exactly—but it was as good a place as any to start.

He eyes were predictably blank behind his glasses while I tried to stifle a sigh. Such a total *guy*.

"I had coffee?"

Wasn't even gonna ask when. Probably better that way. "How about some spaghetti?"

He still looked fairly blank. "I'm not sure I have—"

"I stopped at Kroger on my way over," I cut him off, crossing to the sofa where I picked up the bag I'd tossed, along with my backpack. "Pasta, sauce, bread, a bagged salad so we can pretend to be healthy. I even remembered the Parmesan." If I'd gone big guns, I might've brought the ingredients to make something like *arroz con pollo*, just like Nana taught me, but that was more labor intensive. Definitely special-occasion material. Spaghetti was the universal college student's meal, quick, filling, and cheap, something we'd done plenty of times—enough to not rouse suspicion.

"Do you want help?"

"Doesn't take much to set water to boil and dump salad into a bowl." Taking the bag of supplies into the kitchen I traded him for the big pot he'd already gotten out and started filling it with water. "I need to do some more studying anyway, so I'll just do that while stuff heats up."

"Do you need help with calc?"

"After we eat, maybe. I can't deal with math on a seriously empty stomach."

"Seriously empty stomach?" That infuriating eyebrow went up. "When was the last time *you* ate?"

"I had coffee." I crossed my arms and stared right back. Couldn't help but laugh—albeit quietly—as he stomped off up the stairs grumbling something under his breath in Spanish along the lines of "insufferable pain in the ass." It was funny when he forgot I was fluent. Or maybe he didn't. One way or another—it was funny.

Just as the beeper went off, signaling that the pasta had hit that nice al dente stage, he reappeared, having changed from his shorts and ratty Nickelback T-shirt into a long-sleeved henley and sweats, his hair damp and combed into submission.

"You showered? For me? Aw, you shouldn't have," I teased.

"Shut up and let me get that." He shot me a dirty look as he grabbed the heavy pot and carried it to the sink, dumping the contents into the colander I had waiting while I tried not to laugh outright. *Tried* being the operative word.

"Pain in the ass," he muttered again, this time in English. "Back on the burner?"

Stifling a few more giggles, I replied, "As always." Another Nana Ellie trick, learned forever ago about taking pasta from good to awesome. Put the pasta back on the warm burner and add in a little olive oil before serving. Kept it from getting all sticky and clumpy. She learned that in Venice. Of course.

Oh, Nana Ellie. Any time I cooked, I thought of her. And missed her. Still.

"You thinking about Nana Ellie again?"

Funny, I couldn't remember when Peter had quit putting the "your" qualifier in front of the word "Nana." He just referred to her as Nana Ellie, same way I did. And it felt good sharing her—the Nana Ellie who I'd always thought of as mine—with him.

"Yeah." Serving pasta onto the warmed plates, I poured the sauce over and sprinkled shredded Parmesan with a nice bit of flair. Then reconsidered and unceremoniously dumped another giant handful on his.

"Thought so." He was fishing the bread out of the oven, without the benefit of mitts, juggling the hot baguette from one hand to the other before dropping it onto another plate. "You get this really distant but happy expression on your face. And it's almost always when you're cooking."

"I guess Nana and cooking are forever linked in my brain." I carried the plates to the breakfast bar. "And thank you again, for allowing me to satisfy my cooking jonesin' in your kitchen. Beats fighting for time in the dorm kitchen."

He didn't look up from pouring two glasses of red wine. "Like I'm gonna say *no*? You think I'm crazy, *m'ija*?"

I grinned and shook my head. *Such* a guy.

Slipping onto the bar stool beside mine, he put one of the glasses in front of my plate, and no, this wasn't some backslide into partying for either of us. It was just that Peter looked at having a glass of wine with dinner as a normal fact of life—something he'd been doing since he was a little kid.

And now I saw it as a normal fact of life whenever I had dinner with Peter.

Despite our somewhat cranky prelude, dinner was surprisingly relaxing. We talked about maybe catching a movie later in the week with Zoë and a couple other friends after we were done with midterms and about how Walter, the crazed art student from the gallery opening, had somehow wound up in Zo's English class and was following her around like some pathetic, paint-spattered lovesick puppy. And laughed like crazy when I told Peter she was seriously considering trading in yoga and incense for Krav Maga and pepper spray.

Really, I was way proud over how I was able to keep my end of the conversation going even though I had major-league butterflies—although why should I? It wasn't like I needed his permission or even his approval. Nope. Not at all. This was strictly for announcement purposes. Although a little emotional propping up wouldn't go amiss here. Because he was my friend. And because while it was inevitable—it was scary, too.

"I'm going to Miami for spring break."

He paused in the middle of scooping up a third helping of spaghetti, the long strands dangling from the tongs, waving slightly, almost like they were mocking me.

Dropping the tongs and pasta back into the pot, he brought his plate over to the sink, which put him right across the breakfast bar from where I sat. But rather than look at me, he kept his head down as he ran water over the plate, muttering, "*Dios mío*, this happened faster than I expected."

Shredding a piece of bread, I stared at the top of his head. Noticed that his hair had gotten really long—long enough so that it fell over his forehead and I couldn't even catch a glimpse of his expression.

"What happened faster than you expected, Peter?"

He looked up, his expression still not giving away a thing. "You wanting to take the chase from the abstract to concrete. That you'd find something that would send you . . . wherever." He shrugged and ducked out of view, putting his plate in the dishwasher.

"Why do you say that?" Down to nothing but crust, I began torturing a new piece of bread. "It's not like there were ever any absolutes about this—any certainty that I'd find much of anything. You warned me about that from the beginning and I accepted it. Tilting at windmills, remember?"

He straightened and leaned on the counter, studying me. "Yeah, but I *knew* you'd find some clue or other that you'd want to follow. Just not so fast—" He stopped short, taking a deep breath and walking around the counter. Leaning over, I placed my plate in the sink before following him to the sofa where he was waiting. I shoved my backpack and parka to the floor and settled in at the opposite end.

"You did find something, right?"

"Yes and no." Watching him stretch his legs out, prop them on the coffee table, like he was settling in, was all I needed to keep going. "I think I've found all I'm going to using the resources I have available here."

"Even with the Internet?"

I nodded.

"So what did you find that would take you down to Miami?"

"Nothing specific. It's more like I have all these dots, and I keep finding more and more dots, that should connect, I just can't figure *how* they connect."

"Okay." He nodded, clearly mulling that over. "But why—"

"The University of Miami's library," I answered before he could even get the whole question out. "They've got a monster collection of documents in their archives. Correspondence, flight manifests, posters, business documents, books, magazines—you name it, they've got it. Some of it's online, but not all . . ." My voice drifted off, but I didn't need to finish. He was sighing and shaking his head and smiling all at the same time.

"And you want to go look."

"Right." I nodded so hard, my ponytail slid, coming loose. Yanking the elastic off, I ran my fingers through my hair. "Getting to dig through those archives—it's the best place I can think of to start figuring out how to connect the dots."

"But will they even let you? I'd think most of that stuff would be reserved for hotshot scholars." He didn't even blink at my raised eyebrows and crossed arms. "Hey, face it, a freshman from a state school in Ohio versus a Ph.D. candidate or postdoc from, say, Stanford? Who do *you* think they're going to let look at the rare, fragile, irreplaceable materials?"

Damn, I hated when he was right almost as much as when James was. Except I had an ace in the hole I hadn't gotten around to telling his smug ass about yet. "Dr. Germaine is arranging a sponsorship with one of her colleagues down there—a sponsorship that'll grant me library privileges." Feeling my cheeks heating up, I stared down at my fingers, twisting the black elastic band I'd pulled from my hair so tight, the tips went numb and turned a dark, angry red. "And I know I'm not a hotshot scholar, but she thinks if I choose to stick with anthropology, I might just have the framework for a possible dissertation here."

Carefully untwisting the elastic from my fingers, Peter took my hands in his. "I'm sorry. That was a shitty thing for me to say."

"But not totally wrong."

"A lot of people would've given up before now, Caro. You haven't. Indiana Jones couldn't be more tenacious."

Smiling down at our hands, I joked, "He's an archaeologist, fool."

"*And* an academic." The tightening of his fingers made me look up and into his eyes, dark and serious.

"Are you telling your parents?"

"That I'm going to Miami for spring break? Sure. I mean, I had to ask them if it was okay, after all." I shrugged, tossed my hair over my shoulder as I tried for a carefree smile. "They're concerned, of course, their baby in the big, bad city, but at the same time, they're trying not to hover and Mom even mentioned that she thought it might make a nice change for me and . . ."

My voice faded as my gaze fell away, from that expression on his face that said he clearly hadn't bought "carefree" for a second.

"Caro—"

"No. I'm not ready to tell them about this yet, Peter."

"Why?"

I shrugged again. "I don't know . . . after . . . after everything that happened this summer—that it all sort of started because of Nana Ellie and wanting to be more like her. I just don't want them to worry that maybe . . ."

"What?" His voice was so gentle, like I could tell him anything, including the one worry I'd had through all of this. The one thing I hadn't been able to shake.

"That maybe . . . I'm a little crazy. Because I haven't been able to let this go." Now I looked up, straight into his face, hoping he, at least, understood. I thought he did, but still—

"It's totally not the same. It's not about being *like* Nana . . . not at all. Not ever again. It's just—it's about finding out who she really was and—"

"Caro, it's okay," he broke in. "You *know* I don't think you're crazy. I get it." His thumb slid beneath the edge of my sleeve and brushed against my bracelet. "I get it," he repeated while I breathed out a sigh of relief. Deep down, I'd known he got it. But still, it was kind of reassuring to hear him say it.

"So—are you going alone?"

And *this* was where we got to the part that had had the butterflies going haywire earlier. "If I have to." I took another deep breath and added really softly, "But I don't want to."

Because I got how much of a total crap shoot this all was. It could be a dead end—it could be a whole lot more. And a little emotional support definitely wouldn't go amiss here.

No words, not even so much as a sigh. Just another squeeze around my fingers.

It was good enough.

23

I had never, in my life, experienced *chewy* air before.

No, seriously.

I mean, I know that northeast Ohio has that whole Rust Belt image issue and, of course, you couldn't mention you lived anywhere near Cleveland without some smart-ass bringing up the Cuyahoga going up in flames, but really—that was like way back in the sixties and it was much better now. Or so we were told. I wasn't about to get close enough to find out.

But this—this air wrapping around us as we waited—was air with *texture*. It wasn't that it was polluted, although there was definite car-exhaust action going on. It was more than that. It was the exhaust and the dense humidity that had sweat beading along my hairline after less than two minutes outside. It was the honking of car horns and whistles from the cops trying to guide traffic and the shouts echoing around us in more languages than I could even begin to recognize.

It was vibrant and alive and so unbelievably *real*, I felt as if I could reach out and take a bite.

It was my introduction to Miami.

It was also, after the forty-degree temperatures we'd left behind in Middlebury, hot as the proverbial Hades.

"Tell me again why we're waiting out here and not inside where there's air-conditioning?" I shouted at Peter. Had to shout because it was so loud in the breezeway outside the terminal.

He laughed. "First lesson in visiting a Miami native. We *never* park at MIA because it's a futile endeavor—by the time you've fought for a space that's practically in the Everglades and hiked up to the terminal, whoever you're meeting already has their luggage and is wandering around looking for you." Leaning forward on the handle of his small rolling suitcase, he grinned. "The way to do it is wait until you get the phone call, probably the nanosecond the plane has landed, then, depending on where you live, wait to leave so you can time driving past the terminal with the retrieval of luggage. If you've got it *just* right, you only have to drive around twice, max."

So that's why he'd pulled his cell out the nanosecond we'd landed. He wasn't really serious, though? But like it was the Bat Signal, his phone rang.

Sending me a smug grin, Peter answered. *"Sí, Papi, ya te estamos esperando. Delta, sí."* Clipping the phone back onto his belt, he said, "He'll be here in about two minutes."

This flaky system actually worked?

"One minute, if he doesn't hit any more traffic lights."

No lie. About a minute later, Peter started waving as a dark blue Nissan Maxima edged up to the curb, trunk popping open, hazards flashing, and with a tall gray-haired man in a knit shirt and jeans rounding the front—all at the same time, it seemed.

"Hola m'ijo, ¿cómo anda?"

"Hey Dad—I'm good, how're you?"

I watched as Peter's huge smile lit up his face and he reached for his dad, first for a typical guy handshake that went right into a bear hug and kiss, no hesitation, no embarrassment. I tried to remember the last time I'd seen James kiss our dad. I couldn't. Not that they weren't affectionate, but it was more in that "shake hands, clap each other on the shoulder in a manly man" sort of way.

Drawing back, Peter's dad patted his cheek before reaching for one of the suitcases. "*Regular* . . . more or less same as always."

Helping load our stuff, Peter asked, "Why'd you bring Mom's car?"

"She wouldn't let me bring my truck. Said it's a mess, with all my tools and equipment in the back, that it would make a bad impression on your friend."

"Oh God—excuse me." Tossing his backpack into the trunk and slamming it shut, Peter turned to me. "Dad, this is my friend, Caroline Darcy."

"*Mucho gusto, Señor Agosto.*" I held out my hand, which was grasped in a brief shake, then felt the air whoosh out of my lungs as I was yanked in for a hug and kiss on the cheek of my own.

"*Ay m'ija, no, el placer es mío.* Peter talks about you so often, we feel like we already know you. And call me Jorge. 'Señor Agosto' makes me sound like an old man."

I must have looked some kind of shocked if the laugh that exploded out of Peter was any indication. "Welcome to Miami, €aro." He chuckled as his dad let me go and whapped him across the back of the head. Go, Dad.

"*Tranquilate.*" Holding the passenger door open, he put a hand to my back—so that's where Peter got that habit—and guided me in, saying to Peter, "You sit in the back and count yourself lucky I don't stuff you in the trunk, *sinvergüenza.*"

I ducked my head as I fastened my seat belt.

"I can see you, by the way."

Shifting in my seat, I glanced back at Peter, then followed his pointing finger to the rearview mirror. I shrugged, smiled again, and turned back. "What can I say, I like your dad."

"You would," he grumbled as his dad slipped behind the wheel and edged back out into traffic.

"So this is your first visit to Miami, Caroline?"

"Yes, sir."

He nodded, keeping an eye on what looked like, to my Ohio eyes, absolutely insane traffic. And this was still the terminal. God, what were the actual roads like?

"Peter told us about your search—about your *abuelita*. *Cómo es el apellido de la familia otra vez*—¿Sevilla, *sí?*"

"Yes, Sevilla y Tabares," I replied, automatically adding the maiden name of Nana's mother.

"Of course, that's right. My parents are familiar with the name, of course, since the Sevilla family was very well known in Cuba, but they're asking around to see if anyone knows if any of them came over. See if we could make the search go a little easier." He spared a glance away from traffic and winked at me. "That way you have more time to go to the beach. Right, *m'ija*?"

"Right," I answered, kind of weakly. I glanced back over my shoulder again—this time in surprise. Peter leaned forward between the seats, his hand brushing my shoulder. "Welcome to Miami, Caro," he said again, his voice soft below the roar of the air conditioner and the Spanish rock his dad had going on the radio.

Even with the psycho traffic, it wasn't that long before we were pulling into the driveway of a white ranch house with a white tile roof and an insane garden of palm trees and bright pink and red tropical flowers all over the front yard. Everything seemed brighter, more colorful—even the grass was the most brilliant green I think I'd ever seen. Pretty amazing contrast with the Ohio we'd left this morning, which was still brown and gray and barren, with only the barest hints of spring beginning to make an appearance.

"Peter, this is amazing," I whispered to him as we walked up to the front door, having been shooed away from getting the luggage by Jorge.

He glanced around as he pulled a set of keys from his pocket. "I suppose it would be to you." Fitting the key into the lock, he said, "Same way that the changing leaves were amazing to me."

"Yeah, exactly." As we exchanged smiles, I couldn't help but think, again, how cool it was that someone could be so different—yet not. I cocked my head toward the next-door neighbor's house, which was painted, no *lie*, orange. With a red tile roof. "I'm trying to envision that in Hampshire." Among the staid Colonials and early Victorians painted their nice, muted blues and grays or, if someone was feeling *really* daring, maybe pale yellow.

Pausing with his hand on the doorknob he looked over, raised his eyebrows. "And?"

"Failing miserably."

Laughing, we crossed the threshold and I stopped cold. The wave of smells assaulting me—the cumin and olive oil and onions and garlic—I could almost *feel* myself hurtling back. Back to Hampshire, back in time . . . back to Nana's kitchen.

"Oh . . ." I put my hand to my mouth, biting my lip and blinking hard. "Oh man."

"Caro?"

My gaze darted between Peter and the kitchen, half expecting to see Nana emerging instead of the dark-haired woman who looked exactly like Peter.

"Peter, don't just stand there *cómo un bobo, m'ijo. Vamos, mi vida, pasa, pasa* . . ."

Still half-stunned, I let myself be led toward the kitchen and a chair at the table.

"Caro, are you okay?"

Heat rushed over my face and down my neck as I stared at Peter, who was down on one knee beside my chair. "I'm sorry . . . just . . . it just reminded me so much of Nana's . . . of when she used to cook . . . how she taught me . . ."

Let's listen to the babbling fool some more, right? Shaking my head, trying to dislodge the eerie sense of déjà vu, I was sure I was making absolutely no sense, but Peter's mother was nodding. "It's tremendous, how a smell or a sound can trigger such a powerful memory, *verdad*?" Putting a glass of cold water on the table in front of me, she slipped into the chair next to mine.

"Sometimes I'll be at the grocery and I'll hear music, something from when I was a girl, and I'm no longer in an aisle pushing a cart, but on a street in Habana, listening to the musicians playing, watching the people sitting on their steps or dancing." Just like Peter's dad, she winked. "You know, grocery carts make fairly passable dance partners."

Standing, Peter crossed to the fridge. "You have *any* idea how embarrassing it was to go to Sedano's with her?"

"*Descarado*." But she was smiling and rising to give him a hug as she said it. "So, *papito*, are you going to act as if you have manners?"

Papito? Oh, I was so going to have to ask him about *that* one later. And judging by the eye rolling going on, he knew it, too. "Mom, this is Caroline Darcy; Caro, this is my mom, Ileana."

Just like Jorge, Ileana gave me a kiss and a hug, but by now I was getting the hang of it, so I was able to stand and return it without so much as a passing chuckle from Peter.

"*¿Oye, qué huele tan rico, mama?*" Jorge blew into the kitchen, hugging Ileana from behind while sneaking looks in the various pots and pans on the stove. "You can smell it all the way out to the driveway—it was driving me crazy."

"Jorge, *por favor*—" Ileana slapped at his hands and scolded, but she was laughing, too, and the looks they exchanged—not to mention the look on Peter's face.

"Don't worry," I murmured to him. "My parents act like that, too."

"Honestly, you'd think they'd tone it down for visitors," he whispered back, his face turning that familiar shade of red.

"Peter, why don't you show Caroline to Natasha's old room?" Ileana suggested, still smacking at her husband's hands but not really, if you know what I mean. "Let her have a chance to settle in before dinner?"

"Settle in, my ass," he continued in a whisper as we burned rubber out of the kitchen and grabbed our stuff from the living room. "They just want a few minutes alone."

I sympathized, really I did, but he sounded so outraged, I couldn't help but giggle a little. "Peter, really, it's okay. I swear, I know exactly how you feel. But at the same time, think about it. How cool is it that they still feel that way about each other?"

"I suppose," he admitted on a long sigh, but he still looked pretty pained about it, poor guy. We stopped in front of a door that he pushed open. "This'll be your room while you're here, bathroom's through that door. I'm across the hall."

I looked in the room that had been his oldest sister's when she still lived at home. "It really is awfully nice of your parents to let me stay here." With its pale gray walls and double bed covered in a dark rose bedspread, it sure beat any hotel I might've been able to score on my budget. "It was totally unnecessary."

"Caro, I *told* you. If my parents had found out we'd come down here and you were staying in a hotel, I'd be dead. Even if it was the Fountainbleau. Think of it as saving me from a royal ass-whipping."

"Wouldn't want that to happen." And it was just the nature of his last comment that I even glanced down in the direction of said ass, right? Thank God he had already turned away from me and was headed across the hall, but almost like he felt my glance, he turned back just before going into his room.

"Take your time—we don't eat at any set time and I'll lay money my sisters will both just happen to 'show up.' "

Oh no. "Peter, everyone knows we're just friends, right?" I gestured between us, feeling kind of stupid for even asking.

"Oh yeah—they know. Doesn't mean that they're not curious. They're family. Come on, what would you do if your mom told you James was bringing home a girl from school—even if she was just a friend?"

Seeing as that had happened precisely *never*? "Uh, trot my butt back home in a hurry." Or at least be on the phone 24/7.

"See?" He held his hands up and shrugged. "Same thing, except I have *two* sisters to deal with and they're older *and* they're Cuban. But don't worry." Poking his head back around the edge of his door, he smiled. "It'll be okay."

The phrase "famous last words" did come to mind here, you understand.

24

Okay, understanding the sister thing and knowing I'd probably be doing the exact same thing if it was James didn't make it any easier to deal with the knowledge that *I* was about to be on the receiving end of the sister thing. I'd never *been* on the receiving end of the sister thing. What did one wear to something like this? Had to be something that didn't scream "bimbo out to snag your baby brother," but I didn't want to come off as a total bookwormish mouse, either. And why it mattered either way—I mean, we were just friends. This was *not* a big deal.

Augh.

"Amy, help."

"Are you down there? Is it tropical and gorgeous and I hate you, you understand that, right? It's thirty-eight degrees and raining here."

I'm down here to work, you know that, and I need help."

"Yeah, of course, work, and you need help? With what?"

Tucking my bath towel tighter around myself, I clutched the cell phone to my ear and kept rummaging through my suitcase, willing the perfect outfit to, I don't know, jump out and bite me or something. "Peter's sisters are in all likelihood on their way over for dinner and I don't know what to wear."

"Why does it matter? I thought you were down there to work."

Oh, if I could reach through the phone and strangle her—

Settling for tightening my grip on it, I snarled, "Amy, *now* is not the time to play stupid." I swear, I could almost hear her smiling. "Ames, come on," I whined, pulling stuff out and dumping it out on the bed.

"Right," she sighed, then asked, "Did you bring the black and pink tank tops?"

Remnants of the hot tamale wardrobe, but downright conservative if what I'd seen at the airport alone was any clue, so good for meeting sisters. "Yeah."

"The turquoise zip-up hoodie?"

I dug through my suitcase—yep, there it was. Thank goodness. "Yeah."

"Black denim skirt?"

"A skirt? You think?"

"Either that or plain old jeans and your black, sparkly flip-flops. So you look nice, but casual enough to go barefoot if the occasion demands."

Damn, but she was good. It *was* the perfect outfit. "You're a genius."

"Of course." *Now* I could practically see her blowing on her fingernails and buffing them against her shirt. "Did you bring your bracelet?"

As a matter of fact, I had, but . . . more as a good luck token. "I'm not so sure I should wear it, Ames."

"Why not? You wear it all the time, right?"

"Yeah."

"He sees you wear it all the time, right?"

"Yeah."

"How do you think he'd feel if you didn't wear it now?" Now she was beyond her usual English professor sound and more like a kindergarten teacher talking to the little kid who didn't quite get it. "Like you're embarrassed or something?"

More like I didn't want *to* embarrass him, actually. I mean, I didn't know if his family knew he'd given it to me and if they happened to notice it and asked about it, I didn't know what I'd say and as usual, Amy knew what I was thinking before I said a word. "He's a big boy, Caro. I'm pretty sure he can handle it. Just wear it. You know you want to."

Bitch. I stared at the phone and said nasty things at it for a few seconds before tossing it to the bed and pulling on the prescribed outfit with jeans, not the skirt, I decided, after trying on both. After an Ohio winter, my legs were the disgusting white of a fish belly and I so wasn't dealing with tinted moisturizer. Ever. Again.

Earrings that were dangly and cute, but *not* gaudy, and the bracelet, of course, although the hoodie's sleeves covered most of it. But the weight of it on my wrist was familiar and kind of comforting and what do you want to bet Amy knew that? Honestly, I think her gifts were wasted as an English major.

Pulling my hair back into a low ponytail, I brushed a light dusting of powder over my face for makeup. Anything more felt like too much.

After straightening up the avalanche of clothes into neat piles, I decided to head into the kitchen. If it was anything like the households I'd grown up around, it was the center of all the action anyway. And again, crossing the threshold into the kitchen, that eerie sense of déjà vu tingled down my spine and gave me goose bumps. Not so much the smells this time, but the sight of Ileana, seated at the table, with a cutting board and a pile of plantains in front of her, so ripe the skins were almost black.

"Can I help with the *platanos*?"

Ileana glanced up. "You know *maduros, m'ija*?"

Smiling at the memory, I nodded. "Nana used to make them

for me all the time. She'd let me help her." I accepted the knife and cutting board Ileana handed me and took a seat at the table, falling into the rhythms of peeling, slicing, sliding them off the board and onto the waiting plate.

"And yet—she never told you. At least not directly," Ileana said almost more to herself, it seemed, her voice rising and falling with that soft, oddly familiar lilt. The one I heard in Peter's voice sometimes, when he was tired or thinking something through out loud. But maybe because this time I was hearing it in a woman's voice I suddenly recognized it.

God. All this time, I'd thought that Nana didn't have an accent. But she did. It was really, really slight and it was more of a lilt, but clearly, Nana had spoken English with a trace of what appeared to be a Cuban accent, just like Ileana and Jorge and, well, Peter.

Smiling to myself, I continued slicing the plantains while Ileana asked me about school and my family—universal mom stuff, until Peter reappeared. He'd obviously showered and changed, too, trading in his jeans and flannel shirt for a T-shirt and shorts and bagging shoes altogether.

"What?" He dropped into the chair next to mine and began peeling the skin from a plantain.

"Nothing."

"Bull, it's nothing. You look like you're about to crack up."

Taking the peeled plantain from him, I started slicing. "I was just thinking how nice it must be for you not to have to crank the temperatures up to sauna level just so you can wander around barefoot and in shorts."

"You're never gonna let that go, are you?"

"Hey, your electric bills, dude."

Shaking his head, he set another peeled plantain at the edge of the cutting board. "You are such a—"

"Hey, where's everyone?"

"Kitchen, *m'ija*," Ileana called out.

"That's Natasha," Peter said, grabbing a dish towel and wiping off his hands, then handing it to me so I could do the same. Following him out of the kitchen, I found him hugging a small woman wearing pink scrub pants and a top printed with suns and palm trees. She was a pediatric nurse, Peter had told me, while Sara, his other sister, was an assistant bank manager.

"Tasha, this is my friend Caroline Darcy."

"Pleasure to meet you, Caroline."

"Call me Caro, please." I took a deep breath—shook her outstretched hand, smiled as we both leaned in at the same time for a kiss on the cheek. And tried not to stare too obviously. I'd seen pictures of her, of course, but in person—wow. Dark red, curly hair and huge cat eyes that were almost the same shade of turquoise as my hoodie. But what really got me was that she had one of the sweetest smiles I'd ever seen in my life, giving her this incredibly gentle air. Her patients probably adored her on sight.

"And this is my fiancé, Damario Lopez." Holy cow. Sisters and fiancés, too? More smiling and shaking the hand of the tall, dark guy in the EMT uniform while exchanging what I hoped weren't panicked glances with Peter. He, clearly, was taking it all in stride, grinning at me while he shook Damario's hand and did that shoulder-slapping guy thing, while Jorge appeared from somewhere and went around asking everyone if they wanted beer, wine, soda, and Ileana came in with cheese and crackers and some tiny pastries that were absolutely to *die* for. There was so much nice, genial, *loud* chaos that I totally missed the door opening again. But at the touch on my shoulder, I turned to find Peter standing there with another woman. Small, like Tasha, but with short, dark hair and deep brown eyes.

"Caroline, this is my other sister, Sara."

"Hi, nice to meet you," I said automatically, although I couldn't stop glancing over at Peter, who was looking decidedly green.

"Nice to meet you, too, Caroline. We've heard a lot about you."

"Yeah—we sure have," drawled another voice from behind Sara.

Okay, now I was certain. He was definitely green. "And this is Sara's best friend—" Pausing, he took a deep breath. "Josie."

Well, no wonder he looked so sick. I had no idea that Josie was his sister's best friend. But I knew who she *had* been.

So . . . sisters and fiancés and . . . exes. Oh freakin' my.

And he'd said it was going to be okay and they all realized we were just friends. *Right.* At least one person in the suddenly quiet living room clearly thought otherwise. And for some perverse reason, made me kind of glad I'd gone to at least some effort with the outfit.

"Hi, *mi amor*, how're you doing?"

I *know* my eyebrows were headed high-rise as I watched her arms slide around his neck, going for the Cuban hug and kiss, but this wasn't some "hey, maybe we broke up but we're grown-ups, nice to see you again" peck on the cheek. No, she was clearly going full frontal, aiming to plant one right on his mouth. But Peter wasn't that easy, turning his head so her lips just brushed his cheek; a split second later, he pulled her arms from around his neck, going from green to annoyed just that fast.

"I'm doing fine, thanks." The step he took away from her brought him close enough to me that I could practically feel him shaking. Oh boy. He was good and mad. Josie realized it, too, but it didn't seem to faze her much as she just crossed her arms and tossed perfect J. Lo–streaked layers, brown eyes looking him up and down.

"You look good, baby. Your hair's getting so long—it's . . . nice."

He self-consciously shoved a hand through it, muttering, "Uh, thanks."

Wow.

And here I thought this kind of melodrama was reserved for the *telenovelas* I'd OD'd on back when prepping to do my Carolina thing. Because this chick was all about making a scene—first, trying to mark Peter as hers, like a cat peeing in the corner, while at the same time tossing out those compliments that really weren't. How very passive-aggressive of her.

Speaking of which, what was up with the comment about the hair, anyway? Maybe she dug the short preppy look better, but honestly, how could anyone think his hair didn't look nice? So he probably hadn't had it trimmed since Christmas, but it still looked good; thick wavy layers that ended just past his collar, yet tapered enough along the sides to show off his earring. Empirically speaking, a pretty hot look overall.

"And how's school going?"

Even though he was still giving off definite anger vibes, I could sense him trying to relax—to get through this with some shred of dignity. "It's fine. Really good, actually. I'm really enjoying it."

"So I've been hearing." Another smile, another look up and down, with the added bonus of a glance in my direction from under perfectly mascaraed lashes. *"Y lo veo—¿Ahora estás estudiando gringas rubia y tetona?"*

Ex*cuse* me? I know I couldn't have possibly *heard* the phrase "big-boobed blondes." That she was accusing Peter of studying . . . of . . . of— Because if I had . . .

Right that second, I sent up a silent prayer to every acting god I could think of, from Aristophanes to Meryl Streep, thankful for all those years of classes—especially in improv. Because seriously, it's the only way I managed to keep from glancing down at my boobs. Or touching my hair. Or just reaching out and decking her. I mean, how *dare* she? Not so much the nasty commentary about me. But to act that way toward Peter—to deliberately try to embarrass him in front of his whole family? Even if he had hurt her, it had never been meant as a malicious thing, whereas what she was doing? Bitchtastic. With a capital B.

See, *now* I had my crank on. But before I got the chance to do something that would no doubt be even more embarrassing to the poor guy, a Higher Authority stepped in.

"Caro, Peter." Every head in the room swiveled toward Ileana who smiled, pleasant as anything, and said to us in Spanish, "Could you two please come help me finish up in the kitchen and set the table?" And then, shifting her stare to me, she arched one eyebrow, just like Peter tended to do. Oh, I *really* liked her.

"*Sí, seguro,* Ileana. *Vamos ahora,*" I replied. Glancing back over my shoulder, I saw Peter standing there, a sort of bemused expression on his face, like he got what was happening but his brain was having a hard time processing. And Josie, just beyond him, slowly turning a choice shade of red as she realized if Ileana had spoken to me in Spanish and *I* was responding in Spanish, then . . .

Just about then, I felt a little devil poke its tiny sharp pitchfork into my ass and propel me to do something—well, I don't know. On the scale of wicked, fairly low-grade, but even so, there'd probably be hell to pay later. That was fine. I'd deal later.

"Come on, Peter." I brushed my fingers across his cheek to get his attention, then grabbed his hand to guide him out of the living room, my steps only stuttering the slightest bit when I felt his arm go around my waist, pulling me tight against him.

"Will you be staying for dinner, Josie?" Ileana asked, her voice still pleasant but with a definite undercurrent of "If you do, you'd better be prepared to behave." I think all moms had that.

"No . . . *gracias*, Ileana, but I don't think so."

Call me a big wuss, but you know—I couldn't help but feel a little sorry at the note I heard in her voice.

25

"**Y**ou okay?"

Peter looked up as I handed him a Coke. Kicking off my flip-flops, I dropped into the chaise lounge next to his with my Diet Coke.

"Yeah, I'm okay." He stared down at the plastic bottle, turning it around in his hands. "I'm so unbelievably sorry, Caro. I had no idea—" And there you had the most words he'd spoken at once since the predinner festivities.

"Of course, you didn't. She blindsided both of us—or you, I suppose I should say." I grinned, even though it was probably too dark for him to really see. "I was just a bonus."

"No kidding."

We fell into our customary quiet, sitting there, drinking our pop while I tried to wrap my brain around the fact that I was lounging outside, barefoot, in mid-*March*. Getting all goose bumpy, not because my hoodie was unzipped and slipping off one shoulder, but because I was hearing for the first time the unique music palm trees made, rustling in the breeze.

"And I'm *really* sorry I didn't say anything—when she said that crap about you."

"Honest, it's okay," I reassured him. "I could've said something, too, you know. Just didn't think it was polite to get into a massive bitchfest on my first night."

"It was just so—"

"Peter, forget it. I have." Well, no. Not really. I'd kind of felt like a total cow when Josie stared at my chest while crossing her arms under what were no doubt perfect B-cups. But that was *not* a conversation meant for Peter. Amy and Zoë, maybe. Or not. I could only imagine what *they'd* have to say.

Behind us, the glass doors slid open. "Hey, I'm going to take off."

Peter didn't look up at Sara's comment. "Okay."

"You guys are going over to the university tomorrow?"

"Yeah."

"All right, I'll probably come by on Sunday then."

"Fine."

Jeez. Now *he* was being a jerk. Clearly, Sara felt bad about this, too, and unless I was totally wrong—

"*Mira, papito,* I'm really sorry. I honestly had no clue she was going to come over."

Nope, wasn't wrong. Chalk her up as another one on the blindsided scorecard.

"When I told her I couldn't go clubbing tonight because you'd come home for spring break, she didn't act like it was any big deal. Next thing I know, she's pulling up behind me in the driveway. That's when I told her you'd brought a friend down and maybe it wasn't such a good idea for her to come in, but she said I was being stupid, she just wanted to say hi." Coming up behind our chairs, she looked down at me, her brows tight. "I really am sorry, Caroline. She's my best friend and I love her and I understand that she might not be completely over Peter, but it was totally wrong how she acted with you. Whatever's between you guys, it's none of her business."

And there it was. *Hell to pay, Caro.* "It's okay, Sara." I cleared my throat and shifted in the chaise. "Not your fault."

But still—talk about relief. I tried to imagine how I'd feel if

James hooked up with Amy and then broke her heart—God *forbid*—then brought some other chick home. As a friend or what*ever*. But Sara had been nothing but nice, asking me about school and the search for Nana's family over dinner, and now apologizing because the Josie Show had inadvertently been her fault? She was *definitely* cool. And if Peter didn't get that, I was gonna have to slap him. A lot.

He got it—no slapping necessary. "No, it wasn't your fault." Looking up, he smiled at his sister. "But next time, tell her I've run away to join the circus or something, *por favor*?"

Sara's worried expression cleared and she leaned down to drop a kiss on Peter's head before whapping it gently. Touching my hand, she said, "Good night, Caro. And if he drives you too crazy this week, just call me—Tasha and I will take you shopping or something."

"Thanks—good night." And count me thankful for the night-time hiding the heat I could feel creeping over my face. More payback. Since Sara's offer was *so* obviously sister code for "Call us because we're going to completely pump you for info and see what you and our little brother are really about."

After the door slid shut behind her, I settled back into my chair, drawing my feet up under me and staring up at the stars. "You never told me Josie was older than you."

"Three years—same as Sara."

Well, the whole wanting-to-settle-down-and-pop-out-babies thing made a little more sense now. Not much, considering Peter wouldn't even turn twenty-two until May. But a little.

"She was safe, you know?"

I kept staring up at the sky, idly wondering if what I was seeing was a shooting star or just a plane.

"After all those tests came back clean and I quit partying . . . I was still so scared and so, I don't know, lost. And

I'd known Josie forever and she was familiar and there and well . . . safe."

"I get it."

"Do you get that I was a total jerk, too?"

Turning my head, I saw that he was wasn't staring at the sky, but was looking right at me. "How's that?"

"What we had—it never felt like this big, true-love-forever thing. It was good, for what it was, and I thought she felt the same. Guess I figured that when the time came, we'd both real-ize it had been a nice ride and that would be it. Freaked me right out when I finally understood how serious she was."

"Can I ask you something?"

We didn't have a whole lot of light—just what was filtering out from somewhere inside the house. Even so, I could see the famil-iar half smile, what little light there was, flashing off his eyes.

"Yeah, sure."

Turning all the way onto my side, I propped my head on my hand. "When *did* she let on how serious she was about you? The whole marriage-and-babies thing?"

"Not until I started talking about applying to schools that weren't in South Florida." He shifted onto his side, as well, mir-roring my position.

"So, basically . . . you assumed she knew you weren't think-ing forever and she didn't let on that she *was* until there was a possibility you might leave."

Man, I couldn't believe what I was about to say. "In other words, you were maybe both a little less than honest with each other?"

Nope, the irony didn't escape him. He just laughed quietly, the sound drifting off into the warm March night, followed by the release of a long breath—like it was one he'd been holding in for a long, long time.

"I know all the jokes about getting tied down and everything, Caro, but I swear to God, she started talking like that, and it felt like a noose dropped around my neck. All I could see were the plans and dreams I'd been working on for years being shaped and altered by someone else to fit *their* idea of what those dreams should be. I just . . . I couldn't. I hated hurting her, but I couldn't pretend that it was okay."

"I really do get that. And you know, for someone who's had as much practice with that cutting yourself some slack scenario, you're kind of sucking at it, in this case."

"You honestly think so?"

"Think about it Peter—yeah, you hurt her and it sucked, but how much worse could it have been if you hadn't?"

After a few seconds, he quietly said, "Much."

"All right, then."

When he held out his hand, it seemed like just the most natural thing in the world to take it in mine.

After a few seconds, he asked, "Are you nervous about getting started tomorrow?"

"A little." More than a little. And excited. And scared. His hand felt so warm, I let my fingers tighten around his, trying to get more of that warmth.

"Don't worry. It'll be okay."

"Yeah? Well, that's what you said about tonight."

After we both quit laughing, he said. "It really will be, Caro."

"I sure hope so."

26

To: CaroDarcy@uso.allegheny.edu
From: AMac@hampshire.net
Subject: How's it going?

Any inroads? You sounded kind of discouraged on the phone yesterday—had my fingers crossed that maybe you'd get a big breakthrough today. Listen, even if you don't find anything this trip, hang in there. There'll be others.

Tell Peter I said hi.

A.

To: AMac@hampshire.net
From: CaroDarcy@uso.allegheny.edu
Subject: Re: How's it going?

Nothing yet. At least, nothing major. I have found some really cool stuff on the Sevilla family, dating back to the mid-nineteenth century. Kind of hard to wrap my brain around the idea I have roots that run as deep as the Hampshire ones somewhere else. But about Nana's immediate family, nothing more than what I already have. So yeah, kind of discouraged. I don't know. Maybe I thought, with the resources I'd have here, the information

I needed would just jump from the archives and say, "Here I am! Let's party!"

I know . . . stupid to think it would be so easy. Dr. Germaine told me before I came down that what I'd managed to accomplish in such a short amount of time was nothing short of remarkable and to not be surprised if the rest of it was lot more needle in a haystack. Dr. Machado said pretty much the same thing, so I came down here ready to come up empty.

And I know there will be other trips, either here or maybe to other universities or libraries. I guess the one thing that's really come out of this is I've discovered I'm even a bigger geek than I thought. Being allowed access to all this archival stuff—handling all these materials from another era, another way of life? It's so unbelievably cool, Ames.

See? Big übergeek.

Peter says hi back. I'll call you later tonight.

C.

To: CaroDarcy@uso.allegheny.edu
From: ZWarfield@uso.allegheny.edu
Subject: So?

How's everything? Please don't tell me that you've spent all your time cooped up in a library and haven't so much as touched a grain of sand with the dainty soles of your feet. How's Peter ever going to get the chance to make his move?

Can't wait to hear all about it. And I mean the search for your Nana, girl. And anything else, of course.

Remember . . . auras.
Zo

To: ZWarfield@uso.allegheny.edu
From: CaroDarcy@uso.allegheny.edu
Subject: Re: So?

Not so much to tell about the Nana sitch. At least, nothing new. About your auras and anything else?
Bite me.
Caro

"*¿Cómo va,* Caro?"

"Not so great." I kept shuffling through the items spread all along the long library table. Actually, the better word was *sorting*, ever so carefully, since some of these materials were headed toward the century mark and my career as an academic would be cut tragically short if I damaged so much as a corner of fragile newsprint. Shuffling, sorting, inspecting with a fine-toothed comb, whatever. It didn't much matter. Another day of searching, another day of dead ends.

While I started rearranging some things, prepping to return them, Dr. Machado sat down in a nearby chair and started scanning my notes.

"So, nothing new then?" he asked.

"Nope," I sighed.

I glanced over to find him flipping through the legal pad, looking at the questions, the diagrams, the arrows I'd drawn, trying to connect all those dots I'd been so excited about not that long ago. He would check in on me a couple times a day, offer comments, insights, and always give my notes a quick scan because "Who knows what might jump out at me, *m'ija*? A fresh eye is always good." Otherwise, he let me know he was available and left me to it, trusting I had some clue what the hell I was doing.

He'd been an unexpected surprise. Relatively young, for one thing—I mean, for a guy who had two Ph.D's Totally hip, for another, *especially* for a guy with two Ph.D's, with his shaved head and faded jeans and raunchy *Family Guy* T-shirts that just showed off a couple of tats, including one on a still-massive bicep that read "National Champs" across a football. Dude, I'd hate to be in Dr. Machado's class and piss him off—he might revert back to Rodrigo Machado, bad-ass Canes linebacker and just smack your butt into submission without even breaking a sweat.

But most importantly, he was sharp as hell and knew what he was about, especially in Latin American history, his specialty.

"I think the biggest problem is that Nana Ellie didn't have any brothers whose trails might be easier to follow. Just her two sisters and I haven't found anything new on them."

"Well," he said, tapping one of the pages, "at least you know their names—that's huge."

No kidding. When she'd told the family her story, she'd mentioned that she had sisters, but not their names, unfortunately. Probably only so much she could stand to reveal, especially after so many years of silence.

"Yeah, actually, the birth announcements were one of the first things I found." Pulling my laptop toward me, I opened the file with the family names. "Older sister, Maria Carmen Estelita Guadalupe, and her younger sister was Lourdes Sebastiana." I looked up and grinned. "Only two names for her. I guess they started running out."

"Smart-ass," he said with a laugh as he continued to flip through the legal pad. "And you said you found them in the *New York Times*?"

"Yeah, with one Google search and a lot of stupid luck." I reached across the table again, this time for a leather binder where I had every photocopied and printed-out item I'd been able to find carefully arranged by date. Flipping through, I found the three announcements and handed them to Dr. Machado, who read through them, rubbing his lower lip with his thumb.

"I assume you searched the *Times* archive again to see if there were any wedding announcements?"

"Yep. Nothing. Weird that they would've announced the births but no weddings."

"Maybe, maybe not. Timing's everything, in some ways. Your nana, for example, got married right at the height of the Depression in this country. I'm guessing a fancy wedding announcement might've been considered just a bit crass." Grinning, he added, "Cubans, for all our flamboyance, have very strong opinions on decorum. Just ask my *abuelita*. She'll put a serious hurt on if she thinks you're being tacky." He looked down and flipped through each of the announcements once again. "Hm."

"What?"

"Look at these announcements. Tell me what jumps out at you about them."

I took them from him and spread them out side by side. Nothing really out of the ordinary. Your standard-issue birth announcements, if a bit with the flowery language of the time.

Time.

Timing's everything.

Wait a second.

Nana Ellie had been born in 1915. Maria Carmen was two years older. But—

"Lourdes wasn't born until 1926," I said, still staring down at the pages. "I never paid attention to how much younger she was."

"Right. Now, do the math, Caro. Even if she got married at seventeen, like your Nana did, when would that have been?"

"Nineteen forty-three." I slumped back in my chair and stared at Dr. Machado, feeling like the world's biggest dope. "I'm guessing that printing fancy wedding announcements from Cuba might've been considered pretty crass, what with a world war raging."

"I'm guessing a fancy wedding, period, wouldn't have been a real high priority." He rubbed a hand over his head, the overheads gleaming off his smooth skin. "And given the changing dynamics of the times, it's possible she didn't marry within her social class or even within the culture."

The horror of what he was suggesting hit me. "You're saying she could've married someone who wasn't Cuban?"

"Cuba declared itself part of the Allied forces a couple days after Pearl Harbor, *m'ija*. Lot of soldiers went through there at some point or another. And that's assuming she married at all."

Oh, they weren't supposed to do this to me. Nana Ellie had been the family rebel, dammit. The other two were supposed to behave and do what was expected and make my life easier.

I groaned and rubbed my eyes. I'd already been at this for five straight days, nine hours today alone, and now *this*?

I was seeing that freakin' haystack getting bigger and bigger and that needle getting tinier and tinier.

"Unless . . ."

The little hairs on the back of my neck stood up at the note in Dr. Machado's voice.

"There's no way—that would just be way too easy."

Too easy? At this point, I'd kneel at the altar of "too easy." Please God, let it be too easy. "What is it?" I asked.

"Jesus, Mary, and Joseph—"

"What?"

Rather than actually answer, the big jerk, he rose and crossed to the computer terminal in the corner, typing way faster than anyone with hands that huge should be able to. Opened another window . . . typed some more, lather, rinse, repeat, until it looked like my mother's computer at home, with five or six open windows.

"Jesus, Mary—"

"And Joseph, yeah, yeah, I get it. *What*?"

"*Mira*, Caro." One long finger pointed at the screen, the window showing an article from the *St. Louis Post-Dispatch*, circa 1951. A story about a Cuban baseball player—a pitcher—signing to play for the Cardinals. Thrilled to be playing major league baseball, was excited to be in his new country, et cetera, et cetera.

"Okay, yeah. So? Lots of Cubans came to this country to play baseball." Couldn't see what had his jock strap in such a twist.

"Starting as far back as 1911. Rafael Almeida and Armando Marsans. Cincinnati Reds," he muttered in this absentminded monotone while minimizing that window and bringing another one forward.

"What are you, like the Rain Man of Cuban trivia?" I demanded. "And what does a Cuban baseball player signing with the Cards in '51 have anything to do with this?"

"Did you happen to catch his name?"

Reaching over his shoulder, I grabbed the mouse and brought the window up again. "Cando Sebastián." It was when I said it out loud that what he was hinting at slapped me upside the head. "You aren't suggesting what I think you're suggesting? Are you? Come *on*—it's ridiculous."

He leaned back in his chair and studied me. "Sebastiana's an unusual middle name for a girl and Sebastián's not a common Cuban surname. Now, take another look at him, Caro."

I took another look at the photographs and even in the grainy black-and-white resolution of the midcentury newspaper, I thought I saw what he was talking about. "He wasn't white?"

He nodded. "In all likelihood a light-skinned *mulato*."

"Okay, so assuming that Lourdes was . . . his wife—this is what we're assuming, right?" I waited for his nod. "Why take her name? Her middle name, at that? He must've had his own."

"Not if he was born out of wedlock or was an orphan—which, if he was *mulato*, at that time, fairly probable. If that was the case, he might've gone through the *Casa de Beneficencia*—the national orphanage. All male children raised there were given Valdes as a surname. Given that the orphanage was founded in the eighteenth century, we're talkin' a whole lot of Valdeses. Maybe he wanted something to set him apart."

This felt like riding a train going nowhere. And my head hurt. "Dr. Machado, I'm totally digging the pure knowledge, believe me, but you said it would be too easy and right now, I'm not seeing the too easy—just a bunch of what ifs. Some of them pretty far out, you know?"

"I know, *mi vida*, and I get where you're coming from. But remember your analogy about connecting dots?"

I nodded.

"I'm establishing more dots for you right now—but they're all going to connect, I promise. *Ven aquí.*" He pulled a chair next to his. "*Sientate.*"

I dropped down into the chair as he kept shifting through the different windows he had open. "Okay, so Sebastián had a nice solid career, played several years with the Cards, another couple with the Mets, before retiring." He turned and looked at me. "To Miami."

The little hairs on the back of my neck that had gone all limp and disappointed started perking up again. "Okay," I said slowly.

Then I noticed the last of the windows he had open: an article from the *Miami Herald*, from 1962 that announced the opening of a new car dealership in Little Havana, owned by retired baseball star Cando Sebastián and aiming to serve the increasing Cuban population in Miami by offering the best in bilingual sales and service. And just like these articles tended to have, there was a big, cheesy picture of the grand opening, complete with Cando and his family, a couple of little boys, a little girl, and his wife—Lola. Which even *I* knew was a common nickname for Lourdes.

"Holy—"

"She looks just like you, girl."

The hair was in a short, old-fashioned poofy 'do, fairly light in color—maybe even blond, and her face—

No way . . . it just wasn't possible. Yet . . . there she was. There *I* was, in a way, right there, on that screen. We'd done *Bye Bye Birdie* senior year. I'd worn a poofy sixties-style wig. This picture on the screen I couldn't stop staring at could've almost been in the show program under my name.

Wow. And wow again. Although she would've been in her thirties by then, it was still looking-in-a-mirror scary. Damn, I was gonna look pretty good when I hit my thirties.

"But how could you have possibly known?"

"Stupid luck, Caro. Just sheer, stupid luck meeting a fleeting memory in a wet, sloppy kiss. That's half the battle in academic investigation—not that some of my blowhard colleagues will ever admit that." He laughed, making me look away from the screen to see him shaking his head, rubbing his hand over the smooth surface again.

"We started talking about the names and something just clicked. I all of a sudden remembered it from when I was a kid—could see the sign for that dealership plain as day. Can't tell you how many of my *abuelos'* friends got their cars there. Probably even knew people who worked there. They were big on employing from within the community."

A sudden, sharp pain down in my chest reminded me to breathe. It was difficult—like a metal band was wound tight around my ribs. I kept looking from the picture to Dr. Machado and back again, the understanding slowly starting to sink in . . . this was my family. *Nana's* family. Her little sister. "Is—" I was having trouble getting the words out around the tightness, my fingers clutching the computer mouse. "Is the business still around?"

His voice was very quiet as he looked at my hand resting on the mouse. "I haven't looked yet."

Okay. I got it. He was letting me connect this last dot on my own. Guiding the mouse up to the Google search window, I started typing slowly, then faster: "Sebastián Autos Miami." My heart pounding so hard, I could hear it in my ears, I hit return.

"Hey, how'd it go today?" Peter called out the window as he pulled up in front of Richter Library in Ileana's car. She'd given Peter use of it this week, insisting it was no trouble for Jorge to drive her to and from the beauty salon she co-owned.

Not answering his question, I opened the back door, set my backpack on the floor behind his seat, then rounded the back of the car and dropped into the passenger seat. Leaning my head back on the seat rest, I closed my eyes and heaved out a long, tired sigh. *What* a day. What a freakin' weird-ass day, full of as many twists and turns as some of the more nauseating Cedar Point coasters.

"Caro, what's up? What's the matter?"

Turning my head, I opened my eyes. "I found Lourdes."

"Nana's sister?"

"Yeah."

Peter's eyes got absolutely huge in his face. "And?"

I felt a huge grin starting to spread across *my* face. "They're here, Peter. The family's here in Miami."

Good thing I hadn't had a chance to fasten my seat belt yet. Might've gotten strangled as hard as Peter hugged me.

"You did it, Caro. *Dios mío*, you really did it."

Wasn't gonna cry. No way. Even if he was only wearing a cotton T-shirt that could be thrown in the wash, I wasn't going to cry all over Peter again. Besides, this was happy stuff. Good stuff. Even so, couldn't help the few tears that did manage to escape and soak into his shoulder. Smiling against his chest, I said, "Couldn't have done it without you."

The air conditioner blew cool air against my overheated face as he pushed me back far enough to look at me, his smile gone. "No way, Caro. This one's all yours." His hands stroked from my shoulders to my elbows and back. "I didn't do a thing except stay out of your way."

"No." I shook my head. "No. You may have thought I was nuts at the beginning of all of this, but never *once* did you question why it was so important or any of a million things you could've said and with all sorts of good reason. You came down here with me, for God's sake." Resting my hands on his shoulders, I looked up into his face. "I couldn't ask for a better friend to go through this with, Peter."

Part of me wanted to look away, to say this last bit with some sort of anonymity, but his gaze wouldn't let mine go and honestly—I *did* want him to see, as much as hear, what this meant to me.

"As important as this search has become to me—it means even more, being able to share it with you."

His hands were warm on my shoulders, one finger drifting

over to stroke the curve of my neck. "Caro—" The deep breath he released teased my cheek, slow and warm, faintly scented with the vanilla peppermint gum he loved. "Thank you."

We just stared at each other for a long moment. . . . But then, whatever was there was gone as his hands slid from my shoulders and he turned back to the steering wheel. With a deep breath of my own, I settled back into my seat, fastening my seat belt and willing my stomach to unclench as Peter drove us off the campus. Other than asking if I was up for a quick ride over to South Beach where we could grab some dinner and maybe cruise around Lincoln Road Mall, he didn't say much of anything else until after we parked the car. I was just as happy that way anyhow—was still processing well . . . everything.

"So—"

I looked over at him as we strolled along the busy open-air mall. "So?"

"You *are* gonna go meet them, right?"

Stopping so suddenly I nearly got flattened by a couple of guys blowing past on Rollerblades, I grabbed his hand. "You'll go with me?"

He cocked his head. "Of course. If that's what you want."

"It's what I want."

"Okay." We resumed walking—my hand still in his, since he didn't seem to be in any hurry to let it go. "So we're going to meet the family."

"Yeah." *Really* deep breath time. "We're going to meet the family."

27

Limp. Utterly limp. That was me. With a side of dish rag thrown in for good measure. I made my way into the kitchen—slowly and ever so gingerly, since every muscle I owned was screaming at me after my power shopping expedition with Sara. Because after all the emotional build-up, the big family meeting had to be put off until tomorrow because that's when Dr. Machado could come along and I seriously wanted him there. He was moral support—Peter was emotional. And I was a basket case.

But when Sara heard that I was taking a break, she'd declared I needed a new outfit for meeting the long-lost family and decided to take a day off to take me shopping. "Girls only," she warned Peter. "You better not be showing up, dogging us, *papito*, or I will slap you halfway to next Thursday, you hear me?"

His sisters really did have him trained well. Not so much as one cell phone peep from the boy as Sara and I bonded over cute shoes, jeans that did amazing things to my ass, and green tea frappuccinos. And surprise, surprise, no third degree over Peter. So I was able to relax and have a good time when I wasn't freaking over tomorrow.

"Did Sara leave?" I asked as I grabbed a soda from the fridge and groaned my way into a chair.

Ileana nodded as she stirred the *sofrito*, the combination of olive oil, green pepper, onion, and garlic that was the basis for tons of Cuban dishes. "She has a date." She let loose with a long mom sigh. "She's actually seen this one more than three times, so maybe we'll have a prayer of eventually meeting him."

I grinned. Sara was the family player, cheerfully flitting from guy to guy. Terrified me, the idea of that many different first dates, but she seemed to dig it. However, she also seemed to *really* dig Mr. "More Than Three Times" if the outfit she bought today was any clue.

"Did you find something nice for tomorrow?"

"Yeah, Sara's got great taste." I was still smiling as I said it, but now my stomach was churning again, blending that frappuccino in a way Starbucks never intended. God, I wished it could've been today. The shopping and bonding had been nice, but I *really* wished it had been today. I mean, it *seemed* like a slam dunk, but until I talked to them—*saw* them—I couldn't be completely positive.

And I used to think the unexpected was fun. Ha.

"*¿Ayudame,* Caro?"

I straightened in my chair, rolling my shoulders. "Yeah, sure. What do you need me to do?"

She was holding a cutting board with several large chunks of cooked meat on it. "You know how to do *ropa vieja*?"

"The shredding?" At her nod, I said, "Of course," taking the cutting board and two large forks she handed me and getting to work, pulling the tender beef apart into the long, ragged strips that gave the dish its name: "old clothes." Had to love the names Cuban dishes had. Had to love the food period—although I think I'd been loving it a little too much this week, judging by the sizes of the jeans I'd tried on. Still did great things to my ass—there was just more of my ass for the jeans to do great things to.

As she set a large bowl next to me, she said quietly, "Caro, I want to talk to you about tomorrow."

Not a surprise. Ever since we'd come in last night and I'd announced, right in the middle of the third quarter of the Heat game, that I'd found Lourdes, Ileana had acted . . . I don't know . . . a little off. While I could tell she was happy—kisses and hugs and asking for all the details—there was definitely something also weighing on her mind.

You know what it was? It was her eyes. She and Peter had the same eyes—same color, same shape, same thick fringe of lashes that were totally wasted on a guy. And I knew Peter's eyes. I knew when he was in a bad mood or something was bugging him without his ever having to say a word because his eyes would go dark and the lids would drop over them, just like Ileana's were now as she stared down at the table.

"*M'ija*, I don't want you to think I'm trying to discourage you—" She stopped and looked around—I got the feeling it wasn't simply looking around at the kitchen or the house, but . . . sort of everything.

I set the forks aside. "What is it, Ileana?"

She came back from wherever it was she'd been in her head, her expression clearing. "*Bueno*, I'll just say it. You're a smart girl and I know that you, especially, understand how surface appearances can hide much, *verdad*?"

Yeah, you might say that.

"I have a good life, a life I would never have imagined as a little girl. Peter's told you I came over during Mariel, right?"

I nodded. He'd explained while both his parents were Cuban-born, his dad had come over as a very little boy and really couldn't remember Cuba, while his mother had come over during the enormous boatlift in 1980. She'd been on a boat with a cousin of Jorge's and that's how they wound up meeting. And yeah, it sounded all romantic and fated, but at the same time, I'd done enough research to know that "romantic" wouldn't be the first word anyone involved would think of.

"I'm sure you've wondered, too, how it is that Natasha looks so different from the rest of the family?" She cocked a knowing eyebrow my direction.

"I—" Well, *yeah*, but recessive genetics, maybe . . .

"It's okay, *m'ija*. Like I said, I know you're a smart girl. Tasha was three when we came over." *Okay* then. Hadn't even occurred to me that she could be that much older than Peter. She sure didn't look it and typical guy, he'd never mentioned it.

Ileana's gaze took on this faraway look and her voice got dreamy, like she was telling a bedtime story, her accent intensifying to a degree I hadn't heard from her. "My parents planned to come over in '59, but my mother was pregnant with me—the doctor wouldn't let her travel. So my father came over by himself, to 'make preparations', he told her. She never heard from him again."

At my audible gasp, she came back enough to look at me again, a sad half smile curving her mouth. "Like so many women of that time, she'd been raised to do little more than keep a home but after I was born, she had to find some way to support us. She was an only child, her parents were dead, his parents had emigrated to South America years before—there was no one. But she was attractive and educated, fluent in several languages, so she did better than most, finding a job as a receptionist in one of the few hotels that remained open."

Fidgeting with one of the forks I'd abandoned, she continued, her voice steady and calm. "We were able to live in the hotel, but even so, it was very, very difficult, Caro. Then when the Freedom Flights began, we thought we might be able to leave, but the government told Mami that her multiple languages made her a skilled worker, therefore ineligible, so we had to stay."

It seemed like sitting still any more was just too hard for her—leaving the table, she went to the stove where she stirred the bubbling pot of *frijoles negros*.

"In a way, I was lucky—living in the hotel allowed me to meet people from all over the world. Even with what *ese diablo* has done to my beautiful island—there are still very few places that can begin to touch it, *tú sabes*? And our hotel hosted many guests—and sometimes even served as living quarters for visiting professors to the university."

My hands curled into fists, my nails trying to find purchase on the Formica surface at how her voice dropped. Because, by now . . . yeah, I was young and this was totally beyond any experience I'd ever had, but—I got the idea.

"He was a very nice young man—a bit shy, really—and so lonely, since his appointment to the university was going to be for two years. Two years where he would be away from home . . . from his family. He was very nice, how he asked my mother about it."

Even from my vantage point at the table, I could see how white Ileana's knuckles were, holding on to the edge of the counter. "She did ask me how I felt about it, but she also made it clear how much easier it would make our lives. Even though he was sending money home, what he had left over—well, to us, it was a fortune. And Cuban women—*mira*, we're really very practical, when it comes down to it. The idea of having enough money for decent meals and maybe some clothes that weren't total rags?"

She turned and looked at the meat I'd been shredding into the "old clothes," shaking her head—whether it was because back then she couldn't have imagined that much food or simply because of the irony, I couldn't tell you. "How could I say no?"

"How—how old were you?" My God, I couldn't believe I'd just asked that. But . . . but—

Ileana lifted her head, her gaze meeting mine. "I was fifteen. Seventeen when Tasha was born, two months before he had to leave. He asked if I would mind naming her for his mother, since he already had two little boys. It seemed right, since she had his hair and eyes."

All I could do was sit there, hand over my mouth, slowly shaking my head back and forth.

"When we first heard about Mariel, I didn't think much of it. We didn't have anyone in Miami who would come for us, and I wasn't about to fight to try to get on a boat with strangers, crazy to get off the island, not with having to deal with a baby and my mother. Anything else required money we simply didn't have— I thought. But Mami surprised me. She somehow had just enough to bribe some soldiers to put me and Tasha on a decent boat."

"But not her?"

Ileana nodded. "She said she'd try to come over on another boat, that it would be easier for her to try to come by herself, but I don't think she ever really intended to." She sighed. "And deep down, I knew that, which was why she practically had to force us onto the damn boat."

My eyes widened. Ileana gave me a smile that trembled around the edges. "Oh yes, forced. Even though I had been wanting to come to the U.S. as long as I could remember, at the same time, I was terrified of leaving what I knew—the only family I knew—for something so completely *un*known. But she told me I had to do it for Tasha—so I'd never be forced to do to her what she'd done to me. *Te lo juro, m'ija*, my daughter was the only reason I got on *La Aventura*."

"Excuse me?"

"That was the name of the boat. You know what it means, yes?"

"Uh, yeah . . . I know." *The Adventure.* Because it would be. Somewhere, Nana was probably shaking her head at me.

"It was some adventure, all right." She sighed, the sound harsh and ragged. "Jorge's cousin, who owned the boat," she explained, "saved me from being raped by a soldier while we were waiting to board. With people watching, too scared to jeopardize themselves by doing anything, and Natasha right there, for God's sake— But Pedro wouldn't let him, even though the other soldiers punished him by detaining the relatives he'd come there for. Said they wouldn't allow them to leave. They lied, of course. They put them on another boat and just didn't tell him."

I swallowed, my stomach knotting hard at my own flood of memories . . . Nichols . . . Jones, standing there, waiting . . . no one doing a damn thing, except for Peter.

"Caro." Looking up, I saw that Ileana had resumed her seat, her hands reaching for mine. "*Mi vida*, like I said—I have a wonderful life, *una vida envidiable* that I thank *la virgen* for every day. But—" For the first time since she'd first sat down, her eyes brightened, the brown going almost translucent. "No one looking at the surface of my life now—including my own children—could even begin to imagine what I came from or what I went through to get here. Your family—it *looks* like everything turned out fine. But I want you to be prepared to hear anything."

I nodded slowly. "I understand, Ileana. I'll remember."

Her hands released mine to cup my face, wiping away the tears I hadn't even realized were streaming from my eyes, soaking my cheeks.

"Ileana?"

"*¿Qué, mi amor?*"

"You said the cousin who saved you was named Pedro?"

"Yes." Reaching across the table, she grabbed a couple of napkins from the holder, wiping my face like I was two, not eighteen.

"You named Peter for him, didn't you?"

Her smile was very soft and sweet. "Yes."

Staring down at my fingers twisting the hem of my T-shirt, I asked in a soft voice, "Did Peter ever tell you exactly how he hurt his shoulder last summer?"

28

"**A**re you ready, *m'ija*?"

"Define 'ready.' " I glanced over at Dr. Machado in the driver's seat and pressed down hard on my knees, trying to stop the nervous bouncing action. "If by 'ready' you mean, hurl my guts out, yeah, I'm more than ready to do that. If you mean verify that this is my long-lost family . . ." My voice drifted off. I was ready, I wasn't ready, how could I ever be ready, I was out of my mind to be doing this, I was scared shitless . . . I tensed, then relaxed as warm hands landed on my shoulders from behind.

"You're ready." Peter's voice was calm and steady and everything I wasn't. "You haven't come this far to not see it through to the final act, Caro." The dare was implicit. Twisting around in the seat, I met his raised-eyebrow stare with one of my own.

"You suck as bad as my brother, you know?"

He leaned back, his hands sliding from my shoulders. "What I know is that you'll hate yourself if you punk out now and I'm the one who's gonna have to listen to you bitch about it." He crossed his arms and cocked his head.

My mouth opened, closed, opened again, but honest to God, *nothing* came out. Not even a decent squeak. I settled for huffing out a huge sigh and flopping back into the passenger seat of Dr. Machado's Escalade and pretending that I didn't know Peter was in the backseat smirking like a monkey. Jackass—even if I was so scared I felt like there was a black pit where my stomach used to be, there was no way I wasn't going to go through with . . . go through with . . .

Oh God. The red light changed and there it was—a final half block and into the parking lot of the dealership, now in South Miami instead of Little Havana. This big, modern, steel-and-glass behemoth set in the middle of a lot that seemed to go on for miles, but the important thing was the sign set at the edge of the road that read "Sebastián Motors." Fords and Volvos. Practical cars. Weirdly reassuring.

"What do you think?"

I tore my stare away from the sign to find Dr. Machado pulling something from the center console—a silver tie with small dark blue dots that he held up. "Tie or no tie?"

For a second, I was able to forget why we were here as I considered his question. "It's a nice tie and I'm sure it'll look good . . ."

"But?"

I wrinkled my nose and shook my head. "Totally not you. As it is, the rest of the outfit's almost too much for my brain to process." Only black slacks and a dark green dress shirt with the sleeves rolled up, but it was genuine culture shock after the ripped jeans and "Whose leg do I have to hump to get a dry martini around here?" T-shirt that was the last outfit I'd seen him in. Had to wonder—when *was* the last time the man wore a tie? Probably his wedding.

"*Oye, fresca*—" he warned, tossing the tie back in the console and slamming the lid down. "My wife made me bring the tie, okay? Says it would be nice if every now and again I dressed like the professional she seems to think I am."

Okay, yeah—*definitely* his wedding. But Dr. Machado wasn't the only one who'd gone to the effort, natch. Sliding from the passenger seat to the pavement, I smoothed the skirt of the pale blue sundress that had been Sara's recommendation as the "perfect family meeting outfit." The rest was just as simple: flat sandals, my hair back in a long ponytail, small silver hoop earrings—and my bracelet. As I held my skirt down against the hot breeze that was trying to make me flash all of South Dixie Highway, I heard Peter say, "Buttoned or unbuttoned?"

"What?" Turning my head, I saw him standing next to me, a smart-ass grin on his face as he fiddled with the buttons on his navy blue polo, making me giggle.

"Stop that." Still laughing, I swatted at his hand.

Dr. Machado rounded the front of the truck, shooting a death stare in Peter's direction that made it clear he'd heard his riff, but it was me he spoke to, saying, "You got your material?"

I clutched my trusty binder even tighter, no doubt leaving sweaty handprints on what was once nice black leather. But it held all the evidence I'd collected, so it was necessary. Hand-prints or not. "Got it."

"How do you want to play this, Caro?"

He was asking *me*? "I think you should go first. For one thing, I'm not sure what's liable to come flying out of my mouth—" Improv classes or not, this wasn't some play, it was the real deal. "And second, you're the professional—even with-out the tie." Things couldn't be that bad, I guessed, if I could still crack a joke that had him shooting me a death glare and mutter-ing under his breath as he held the showroom door open.

"*Buenos días*, welcome to Sebastián Motors. What can we help you with? A car for the young couple maybe?"

Young couple? I blinked at the coy, hot-pink smile of the saleswoman who was staring from me to my right and back again, large gold hoops swaying. Out of the corner of my eye, I spotted a familiar wash of red rising from the unbuttoned collar of Peter's shirt. Felt a matching wave of heat rushing across my chest and up my neck. Oh Lord, to be back in turtleneck weather.

"Ah, no, señora, we're actually not here looking for a car . . . for the young couple. Maybe another day." Dr. Machado's glance in our direction was brief, but I still caught how his eyes glittered. Smug bastard. "I'm Dr. Rodrigo Machado—a history professor at UM—and the young lady is a student of mine conducting a research project. We were wondering if Señor Sebastián might be available?"

"Señor Sebastián? I think he's supposed to be on a conference call . . ." I swear, even the frosted tips of her hair seemed to droop as she realized—no commission today—at least not from us. "*Déme un momento*—I'll have the receptionist check."

As she turned away to speak to the impossibly perfect-looking blond chick behind a curved glass counter, my grip tightened on the binder.

"Relax," I heard in my ear, felt a familiar touch on my back.

"He's just finishing up with the call—he'll be right out." Some of the perk returned to our would-be saleslady as she noticed where Peter's hand was. "Are you sure—"

"Thank you so much for waiting."

Thank you so much for saving our asses from more potential humiliation.

"How can I help you?"

Vaguely I heard Dr. Machado repeat his "I'm a professor at UM" shtick while I studied the man in front of us. Willy Sebastián. Lola and Cando's oldest son, co-owner and general manager of the dealership. Not very tall, impeccably dressed in a way that suggested *his* wife didn't have to push him into wearing a tie, and quite possibly my . . . great-uncle? Second cousin, something removed? This is where I always got screwed up. Not that it mattered. What mattered was he was

Nana's nephew. And he was staring at me just as hard as I was staring at him.

"Excuse me, Dr. Machado." Willy's voice was smooth, with that trace accent I was now superfamiliar with. "And excuse me for staring, señorita. You just bear a remarkable resemblance to someone I know."

I'll *bet*. But it gave me the courage to find my voice because really—if he was seeing it . . . it wasn't just a figment of my imagination. "It's okay."

"Now, what is this research project of yours and what does it have to do with me?"

"Actually, is there somewhere more private we could talk?" Wow. Where had that voice come from? Sounded like me pulling a character voice—Calm, Self-Assured Woman on a Mission, but I wasn't acting. I'd noticed our cheery saleslady and the impossibly gorgeous receptionist and a few others scattered around the showroom avidly watching like we were the latest episode of *The Surreal Life*. Never mind that that's exactly how it felt like to me—it was still none of their damn business.

"Ah, *sí*," Willy glanced around, and all of a sudden, everyone got *real* busy with . . . stuff. "*Perdóname*. Let's go back to my office."

Once there, instead of sitting with the distance of some big desk between us, he gestured to a table with several chairs. It wasn't until we sat down that I realized Peter's hand had never left my back.

"I'd offer you something to drink, but something tells me that you'd like to just get on with it." His eyes were a sharp gray-green, kind of startling really, and obviously didn't miss much of anything.

I got on with it. And by the end of it, when he was holding the birth announcements and the printouts of the newspaper articles, he looked like he'd been hit by a truck. Yeah, welcome to *my* world for the past year, buddy, I felt like saying. But I managed to keep quiet, just letting him sit and process, staring from that *Herald* article with the picture of Lourdes to me, shuffling through the birth announcements, and finally winding up studying the picture of Nana that had been the first thing I handed him. My absolute favorite picture of her—in the peasant blouse and skirt, looking over her bare shoulder with her dark hair long and streaming down her back.

"I have to say, Caroline . . . this is an amazing story." Slowly shaking his head, he shuffled through everything once again. "And yes, my mother had a sister—but only one. And she was a nun."

"*No.*"

Sharp and tinged with panic, my voice cut through the room. No, no . . . there's no way I'd come this far . . . "No." Taking a deep breath, I tried to force a calm tone back into my voice . . . to keep it from shaking like a leaf. "Señor Sebastián, I know how bizarre it all sounds and that I'm asking you to accept a lot at face value—" Oh hell. Calm was dissolving and shaking like a leaf was winning.

"Caro, *calmate.*" Dr. Machado leaned forward. "Señor, is your mother still—"

Willy's face relaxed into a smile. "Is she still alive? Oh yes. Very." Accompanied with a roll of the eyes that had all of us relaxing and laughing. Or at least breathing again. His gaze met mine for a long minute before dropping to the picture from the *Herald* again.

"I was only seven, but man, I remember that day. They were so proud." Looking back up at me again, his eyes narrowed. "*Coño*, it really is amazing." Another few seconds' worth of silence, then he asked, "You really want me to ask, don't you?"

Biting my lip, all I could do was nod and watch as he left the room, still holding the pictures. The minute the door clicked shut behind him I was out of my chair and prowling around the perimeter of the room, looking at all the photographs lining the walls, a lot of them with Lola, of course, and in each and every one of those pictures, I could see myself. Or maybe it was just wishful thinking. While I did my caged-tiger thing, Peter and Dr. Machado were smart enough to not say anything reassuring or soothing or the least bit likely to make me snap into a thousand small pieces.

When the door opened behind me, I spun around from studying yet another picture of Lola and felt like I was about to snap into a thousand small pieces anyway.

"No."

"I'm sorry, *m'ija*." He honestly looked it, too. "She said to tell you she was very sorry, *pero, no*—she only had one sister."

And she was lying. I knew it deep down in my gut, my bones, like nothing else.

I thought I'd been prepared to hear anything. But I never could have anticipated this.

29

Very carefully, I slid the leather binder into my backpack, followed by my laptop in its padded sleeve, and zipped the backpack closed.

"Caro, come on."

"Come on, what? What else is there to say?" I set the green canvas bag on the floor next to my open suitcase. Pat me on the back for not just flinging it against the wall. Knee-jerk reactions wouldn't do shit right now—besides, I still needed all my carefully assembled data.

"That's just it. You're not saying anything."

"Okay." I straightened and faced Peter. "I can do this. I can continue putting the pieces together. It's just going to take longer. It's a setback, that's all."

"Caroline." His voice was soft, but harsh for all that. "You're just spouting what Dr. Machado was saying to you in the car—reciting it by rote. How are you really feeling?"

"Not just rote—it's true." I put the floaty blue sundress on a hanger and hooked it over the edge of the closet door. Wonder if I could not-so-accidentally leave it behind? Buried way in the back of Tasha's closet? Wasn't sure I ever wanted to see it again. "Academic investigation isn't about the quick answer. It can take years of resear—"

"Yeah, yeah, I *get* it," he broke in. "And in this case, it's total crap and you know it. This isn't just some academic assignment to be all objective about, Caro. This is your family—and you came so close. It's okay to be upset—"

"No. It's not." My fingers twisted in the thin leather straps of the sandals I'd worn before dropping them to the floor, but my voice, by some miracle, stayed steady and every bit as soft as his.

"It's not, Peter. I mean—am I disappointed? Hell yes. This is the closest I've been to Nana Ellie since she died. This is her *sister* who would've known her and I want nothing more than to talk to her. Forget want—I *need* to talk to her. To know what Nana was like when she was young. Did she always want to travel? Did she learn to cook as a little girl? When she married her husband, did she think she loved him and how does anyone know if it's a forever sort of love when they're seventeen anyway? How did she know when she was eighteen and ran off with Papa Joseph?

"I've got a thousand questions that I might never again have the chance to get the answers to, but I've still got to hold it together and stay calm and just think about my next approach." If I didn't, shattering into a thousand small pieces was a distinct possibility.

I said it all in that same soft voice, which, for some reason, seemed to make Peter more agitated. With every word, his pacing got more juiced, the tension practically vibrating off him and bouncing off the walls. It was tough to ignore—all that barely repressed emotion—but I tried, going back to folding clothes and neatly arranging things that were already neat because I needed to be doing something.

"Does it have to be *right* this second, Caroline? You can't let yourself have just one day, five minutes even, to let loose? Be pissed off about this?"

Dammit, why wasn't he letting this go? For the first time

234   caridad ferrer

since we'd met, he wasn't getting it—wasn't getting me. Calm gave way to jerky gave way to just giving up, flinging the T-shirt I'd been trying to fold for the last five minutes to the bed.

"Why is this bothering *you* so much, Peter? What do you have invested in it? Is it because for once you can't be the big hero? Can't be the mature adult and talk me through it because there's just not a damn thing you can say to make it all better?" My voice kept rising with each verbal jab, seeing in the way his fists clenched and his skin flushed a dark red that I was hitting close to home. "Can't come riding to poor, pathetic Caro's rescue?"

"Yes!" His open palm slamming on the dresser sounded like a shot. My eyes widened, no doubt a mirror of his as we faced off. "*No.*"

His hand slid from the dresser to hang by his side as he looked down, shaking his head. "Jesus Christ, Caro, it's not about *saving* you." His fists opened and closed, opened and closed against the sides of his thighs. Like me, he'd changed into shorts and a T-shirt after the aborted family meeting and the tips of his fingers kept snagging in the flaps of the cargo pockets, the faint rip of the Velcro somehow louder than even his hand hitting the dresser had been.

"I just want to help. I—" He gave his head another hard shake, like he was trying to clear it. "You looked like the bottom had just fallen out of your world, Caro, and I wanted to do something—anything. You know, after we got back here, I almost went back to the dealership—to try to convince Willy to talk to his mother again?"

More of the faint *schik-schik* of the Velcro, of my breathing falling into sync with the sound, watching his chest rise and fall in the same rhythm.

"You can't always fix it, Peter."

As he lifted his head, I could see his eyes were as dark as I'd ever seen them. "I know."

He looked so miserable, I almost couldn't say it—but I had to.

"And I don't *want* you to always fix it."

"I know that, too." God, I felt like I'd just kicked a puppy, the way his head dropped again and he rubbed the back of his neck.

"Some things . . ." My voice was soft. "Some things, I just have to do by myself. My way."

Amazingly, he smiled at that—rolled his eyes. "You know, you'd think if *anyone* should get that—"

A soft knock cut him off, followed by, *"¿Se puede?"*

"Yes, of course." The door opened and Jorge poked his head through, his gaze sliding from me to Peter. His glance at me was concerned, but at Peter—not exactly.

Oh man. The lingering scratchiness in my throat was a reminder that I'd pretty much just been this side of banshee.

"I am so sorry, Jorge," I started at the same time that Peter said, "Sorry, Papi, we—*I*—got a little carried away."

"We heard." Jorge's voice was fairly mild, but the look he was shooting in Peter's direction was just this side of frosted. "And we figured that since your . . . *discussion* was so loud, you probably didn't hear the front door."

I wanted nothing more than to have the floor open up right under me—maybe suck me into some alternate reality where I hadn't just been yelling like a cranky toddler at the top of my lungs. At my best friend. In his parents' house.

Peter, at least, was able to recover enough to ask, "Who's here? One of the girls?"

Jorge shook his head and looked at me. "No, it's for Caro."

"Me?" I exchanged glances with Peter as we went to follow

his father. But just before we left the bedroom, Peter caught my arm and held me back.

"Just so you know, I have never *once* thought you were pathetic," he whispered fiercely before releasing me. Putting his hand to my back, he walked beside me into the living room where we found Dr. Machado standing there, accepting a beer from Jorge. Out of the corner of my eye, I saw Ileana handing a *tacito* of Cuban coffee to an older man who was sitting on the sofa, the ivory of his short-sleeved guayabera, the traditional Cuban dress shirt, almost as stark against his dusky skin as the startling gray-green eyes that focused on me. And turning more fully, I saw next to him, accepting her own small cup of the fragrant coffee, but watching me with soft blue eyes, a white-haired woman.

"Holy . . ." Peter breathed out beside me. "It's her."

"You left these behind, *m'ija.*"

Still dazed, I reached for the sheets—the photocopies of the articles and birth announcements—that Willy handed me. I was still staring at Lola, because, you know, face-to-face, who else was it going to be? Face-to-face, I could see that our eyes weren't just the exact same muted shade of blue, but had the same odd flecks of gold in them that no one else in my family had. Face-to-face, I could see I wasn't only going to be decent looking in my thirties, but I was going to hold up pretty well into my eighties, too. A bizarrely reassuring thought in the middle of a *whole* heap of bizarre.

"And you left this, too."

Oh *God*, Nana's picture. I'd left Nana's *picture*? Guess Peter had been right about the bottom dropping out of my world, because I can't imagine any other scenario where I would have left this behind.

"Thank you," I said to Willy, holding it close against my chest, hoping he understood how much more was in those two words.

His eyes crinkled up at the corners and his eyebrows lifted. "Actually, I should thank you."

Me? "Why?"

"If you hadn't left these, I might not have gotten a hair up my ass to go prod my *mamá*."

"Willy!"

Just like that, a soft burst of laughter cleared the air. Some things were pretty universal, I guess.

"She talks a good game on the phone, but that face—it can't lie—and I wanted to show her the picture of your *abuelita*—see her reaction."

As he spoke, he glanced over at his mother who was shaking her head but smiling at the same time. See? Knew those eyes didn't miss a thing.

"It's been a very long time," she said in a faintly accented voice, addressing the room at large, but looking at me. I think outside of that exasperated look at Willy, she'd barely taken her eyes off me. "I was so young when Titi left, but it's funny—how similar it seems our lives turned out."

"Titi?"

She smiled—a lifetime of memory in the curve of her mouth. "That was your *abuelita*'s nickname—from Teresa."

"Oh," I sighed. Another tidbit—something to fill in the spaces that took Elisa Maribel Teresa de la Natividad Sevilla y Tabares to Nana Ellie.

Dropping to the floor on the opposite side of the coffee table from her, I asked, "What made you change your mind?"

Another smile, but this time at the quiet man sitting beside her. "Much as Willy would like to believe it was all his doing—" She arched an eyebrow at her oldest son and doggone it, was I seriously the only person on the planet who couldn't do that? "It was Cando who convinced me I was being a stubborn old lady and if not now, then when? So, after I told Willy that yes, once upon a time, I had *two* sisters, I had him call your professor." She nodded at Dr. Machado. "Who said he would meet us here and, well—here we are."

She held her hand out, palm up. I held the picture of Nana Ellie out to her, the two of us each grasping an edge and studying it.

"Joseph—your great-grandfather—took this picture, did you know that?"

I nodded. If he wasn't in the pictures, he had most likely taken them. Especially if they were of Nana.

"Did you know this was the picture he was painting her portrait from?"

My throat suddenly tight, all I could do was shake my head.

"It's no wonder he fell in love with her," she said softly, gently tugging the picture from my hand and showing it to Cando. "Wasn't she beautiful?"

"Runs in the family," he replied in Spanish, making her duck her head and glance away, looking just like she must have when *they* met. Catching my eye, she must've seen all the questions that were running through my mind.

"My parents disowned me," she said, setting the picture back down on the coffee table and settling back against the sofa cushions. "Marrying Cando was out of the question. And to this day, I'm still not sure if it was more because he was *mulato* or because he was poor." She sighed. "They were so stubborn and proud. You'd think that after Titi ran off, they might have learned to be a bit more flexible, *pero no.*"

"What happened?"

"With Titi?"

I nodded, vaguely aware that Peter was settling in on the floor beside me, that everyone else had taken various chairs and we were all leaning forward—the mother of all story times.

"Her marriage had been an arranged one although they'd been childhood friends and liked each other well enough. However, once she met Joseph, that was it. She wanted to ask her husband for an annulment on the grounds that she hadn't been mature enough at the time of her vows. Our parents said she would do no such thing, and if they found out she had, they'd have Joseph arrested. That night, she was gone. We never knew what happened to her— Armando, her husband, he tried, I think, but at the same time . . . he was very proud, too. I don't think he wanted to force her to be with him if it was someone else she wanted. My parents were furious and refused to look for her at all, saying she was dead to the family. They never again mentioned her and I wasn't allowed to talk about her. And we never heard from her—or rather, I never did. If my parents heard anything, I was never told. Which is why I never said anything—except to Cando."

She leaned forward just far enough to touch the picture again. *"¿Qué le pasó?"*

So I took over, filling her in on everything I'd learned, telling them snippets of the different stories—all the adventures— Nana used to entertain me with as a little girl when she was teaching me how to cook.

"Y déjeme decirte, esta niña sabe cocinar cubano como si ella naciera allí," Ileana interjected at that point, making me smile at the various enthusiastic male noises of approval over my Cuban cooking skills.

God—some things were just *totally* universal.

Then it was Lola's turn—more of her side of the story. Dr. Machado's hunch had been right on—Cando had been a ward of the *Casa de Beneficencia* and wanted to ditch the Valdes part of his name and history as he established himself as a ballplayer. And because of the disowning, Lola sure wasn't about to keep hers, so they compromised, and damn if Dr. Machado didn't sit there and look all smug when I glanced back over my shoulder to where he was sitting, listening.

"What happened to everyone else?"

"Well, I know Willy told you about María Carmen—or rather, Sister Charlotte Jeanne. I actually never really knew her since she joined a cloistered order in Switzerland when I was three. She lived there until she passed away about ten years ago. My parents—" Lola smiled, but it was sad and tinged with an old pain. "Being in this country, we could see the writing on the wall, *tú sabes*? And just before Castro took over, we tried to get them to come while they could, while they still had their money and the freedom to travel, but they told us we were overreacting and they didn't need our help or advice. So proud. *Y cómo los costó.*"

I watched as her hand blindly reached out and found Cando's. "The government came and took the houses, the tobacco fields, all the bank accounts. They made my father—*my* father, who had worn custom-made, three-piece suits every day of the week—go to work in one of his own factories sweeping the floors, because while he was a tremendous businessman, he didn't even know how to roll a cigar. Made my *mami* clean bathrooms."

I was almost afraid to ask—but in a way, I had to know.

"What about—" The words got jammed in my throat, making me force the last two out. "Nana's husband?"

"Armando was really a very nice man, Caro. Maybe not the right man for Titi, but a good man, with principles. Initially, he was one of those who believed that Castro couldn't possibly last—that he would fail. And in trying to wait the bastard out, of course, had everything taken away from him. That's when he began working to collect evidence and send it back to this country, to help *el exilio* plan to take the country back. And my father, finally believing what we'd tried to tell him, also helped."

Lola's hand clutched Cando's tighter. "And then they took them all away. Armando, my father, my mother, because they assumed she had to know everything they did."

"Then what?" The words trickled out of me, thin and weak. I knew, but I didn't know . . . didn't want to know . . . *had* to know . . .

It was Cando who finally answered, his voice raspy and soft. "Prison, *m'ijita* . . . and then . . ."

As his words died away, I closed my eyes, trying to clear my mind of the images that were suddenly scrolling through, like a nightmarish slide show. Of people who looked like Lola or Nana or Papa Joseph or Cando, held in some disgusting jail cell while soldiers taunted and abused them.

"What if she hadn't left . . ." I whispered.

Or what if Nana had been able to get an annulment? Would she and Papa Joseph have eventually left anyway? Or would they have stayed? My God . . . our family—

I opened my eyes, my gaze searching out and finding Ileana's. "What if she hadn't left?" I repeated, feeling kind of light-headed.

As I felt Peter's arm go around my shoulders, Ileana answered simply, "She did, Caro."

30

"*O*ye, dormilona—get your lazy ass up out of bed."

"Wha—?" Hands latched onto my wrist pulling me upright, while I blinked and spit hair out of my face, trying to get the bleary images to stop moving. At least long enough for me to focus.

"Sara . . . let the girl wake up, would you? I can't believe how you just barged on in here."

The bleary images solidified into one image of Sara leaning down and grinning—way too cheerfully—making me jerk back. "No way, we gotta get going if we want to get down there before things get crazy."

"Go where? What's crazy?" Aside from Sara. Just behind her, I could see Tasha, leaning in the doorway.

"Calle Ocho," she said. "*Carnaval.* And it's going to be crazy, no matter when we get down there, Sarita."

"So?" Sara kept pulling, forcing me from the bed. "The sooner we get down there, the more craziness we can enjoy."

"I suggest you just give up, girl. She's not gonna leave you alone anytime soon."

"Uh-huh." Waking up quickly was not one of my better skills. Had no freakin' idea what they were talking about, but I got that I wasn't going to be allowed to go back to sleep. I stumbled toward the bathroom and the shower, coming out ten minutes later wondering if I'd just experienced a really trippy, vivid dream, but no—Sara, at least, was still there, setting something on the bed.

"There. I already put your clothes out so you don't have to waste time trying to figure it out."

Combing my wet hair back, I looked at the jeans that did great things to my ass and red cotton sleeveless blouse. "What is this thing we're going to? And remember, Peter and I leave this afternoon."

"Yeah, but not until late." She waved it off, all no big deal about it. "We have plenty of time. We'll just put your luggage in one of the cars and go right to the airport from there. And where we're going is only one of the most massive parties ever. We'll save the beach for next time, but no way are you leaving without some kind of total Miami experience and it doesn't get a whole lot more Miami, *m'ija*, than Calle Ocho."

"If you say so."

"I do." She nodded firmly and crossed her arms, a physical exclamation point. "Now get dressed. Mami's got *café con leche* and *croquetas* ready, but don't eat too much."

"Why?"

"You'll see," drifted back as she left the room.

"Okay," I said to the closed door. After the last couple of days, I was too wiped to argue or even offer much of an opinion. I'd spent all day yesterday with Lola and Cando, looking through photo albums, listening to Lola tell me as much as she could remember about Nana as a little girl, telling me about her own life, both in Cuba and in this country. Mind-blowing stuff, a lot of it. Like how people realized Cando was biracial, but as long as he was a ballplayer, he was just "Cuban," and it was exotic and cool. The minute he became a regular citizen though, different story.

I recorded all of it and then was up for hours, transcribing until my fingers just wouldn't move on the keyboard anymore. Then passing out until Sara came in declaring I had to have the Miami experience to end all Miami experiences.

If Miami experiences were all about swimming in the sea of humanity, that is. All I could see were bodies upon bodies upon even more bodies as the shuttle we were riding on approached. Easiest way to get down there, I'd been informed. Park in a lot, use the public transport, go mingle among the masses and have a wild time.

All of us—Jorge and Ileana, Damario, Tasha, and Sara, me and Peter—spent hours just wandering up and down the main drag of Little Havana, which had been turned into a gigantic street festival. And what was truly cool was that it wasn't simply Cuban. I sampled foods from what seemed like every Caribbean nation, browsed through art and crafts from all sorts of cultures, heard Spanish spoken with a dozen different accents swirling around me. At one booth selling jewelry, I stopped and bought a silver car charm, a tiny palm tree, and a third, in the shape of a baseball to add to my bracelet.

"What do you think?" I asked, holding them up for Peter to see.

He nodded and smiled. "Those work."

Hordes of people around us were dancing, eating, yelling—it reminded me so much of the Fourth of July in Hampshire, just with empanadas instead of hot dogs and salsa instead of Sousa. Which led to my wondering—what kind of stories might live back at home? I mean, Nana Ellie couldn't have been the only one, right? That maybe, just maybe . . . Hampshire wasn't so boring.

Gave me a lot to think about on the flight late that afternoon—on the drive back to Middlebury, to Peter's apartment where I'd left my car over the break.

"You coming in or do you need to get right back to the dorm?"

I was glad he asked. Although I might've just gone on in anyhow.

"I'll come in for a while." I grabbed his backpack while he got his suitcase and we went in. First thing he did, after kicking off his shoes, was go to the thermostat and crank it up.

"Not one word," he warned. "I'm only putting it up to seventy."

I dropped my shoes next to his and flopped on the sofa. "Wasn't gonna say jack, dude. It's cold out there."

"Feels good, though." He dropped onto the sofa beside me, stretching his legs out and propping them on the coffee table. "Different kind of 'at home' from Miami, but it's good."

"Yeah." I watched as he leaned forward and grabbed the remote.

"TV or music?"

"Music, if that's okay."

"I asked, didn't I?" He rose and rummaged through his backpack; a few seconds later, Howie Day's "Collide" started drifting from the speakers. "Hope this is okay—after today, I'm too wiped for anything more raucous."

"It's good. I like Howie."

"Sara got bored with him. She's on a Matisyahu kick."

"Hasidic reggae?"

"She played me some. It's not bad." He shrugged and headed into the kitchen, calling over his shoulder, "You want anything to drink?"

"No, I'm good, thanks." Although I was dry-mouthed as all hell.

He sank back onto the sofa with, surprisingly, a bottle of Tazo in his hand. "I blame you for this," he said, following my stare.

"There could be worse things."

"I suppose." He took a long drink, then held out the bottle. "You sure you don't want some? I don't know how you're not dying after all the walking we did outside today and how dry that plane was."

"Okay." I took the bottle, took a sip, just enough to wet the Sahara insides of my mouth, but instead of handing it back to him, set it on the table. "Peter—"

He tossed his sweatshirt that he'd just pulled off onto a chair and turned back to me. "Yeah?"

I leaned forward and touched my mouth to his—that's all. Just let my mouth rest against his while my hands rose to his face. "Can I stay with you tonight? Please?"

31

Oh God. He wasn't saying anything—wasn't doing anything other than just sitting there, his mouth barely open against mine, his breath, these slow, shallow gusts that I breathed in, swallowed, as my hands slid back to his hair and hung on.

"Please tell me I haven't just totally screwed up our friendship." It had been an impulse, kissing him, asking to spend the night. Maybe the stupidest one I'd ever had and, God knows, I'd had some stupid impulses in the past, but then again— No way, Caro. No lying allowed here. This was one of those things I'd been thinking about the entire trip home. Had probably been thinking about for a lot longer than that, in all honesty. I swallowed again, harder to do against the huge lump that had just moved into my throat.

He *still* didn't say anything. But he moved, tilting his head, one hand rising to my face, the other to the middle of my back, pulling me closer, his mouth opening wider, his tongue coming out to just barely tease mine, to trace my lips before his teeth dragged lightly against the lower one.

Oh . . . oh *wow*. Easily one of the best first kisses—*ever*.

Until he stopped. Why'd he stop?

"Caro." His breathing wasn't so steady anymore. Good. I'd hate to be the only one afflicted by ragged, desperate breathing. "If you stay, I want it to be because you want *me*—not anything else."

"I understand."

"Do you? Really?"

I did. Like I said, I knew him. "You're worried that after all the emotion—how you've been here for me the whole way, that I'm acting on some misguided sense of gratitude. Or worse, still—that I want to be with you because I think you're safe, or something."

Yep. The wide-eyed stare let me know I'd hit the nail on the head. And that's when I did what was possibly one of the hardest things I've ever done. I pulled away—put some distance between us as I said, "Peter, the last thing you are is safe. I'm scared out of my head, but I want to be with you—whenever it's right for us. If that's not tonight, it's okay."

Oh man, not really, no, because I wanted him so bad, my body felt like it was wound tight and about to snap. But get this—I was finally, really getting what patience was about. Turns out timing's not only everything—it's also a bitch. But I wasn't about to screw this up.

As I grabbed my keys from the coffee table and stood, his hand slid from my shoulder and down my arm to my wrist, where it stopped. Looking down, I watched his long fingers close around my wrist, holding me still. Without a single blessed word, he stood, took my keys, set them back on the coffee table and, putting his hand to my back, guided me up the stairs.

Once up in his loft bedroom he turned to me, gave me another one of those mind-bending kisses before pulling back, saying, "Give me a second." While he disappeared into the bathroom, I stripped off the sweatshirt I'd thrown on over my sleeveless blouse on the plane, playing with the buttons on the shirt, wondering. . . . But before I could decide whether I should just get on with it or wait for him, he was back, snapping on the bedside lamp and dropping a small box of Trojans on the night table.

This was when I blushed. Of all times, can you imagine? I mean, not like there was any reason to be coy here—we both knew what we were going to do. I'd initiated it, for God's sake, yet I was embarrassed by his being with it enough to think ahead? Thing was, though, he was blushing just as hard as I was, but his voice was steady.

"I don't want you to think . . . I mean, I always keep at least a few around. Ever since—"

Again, I got it—felt that odd, easy communication that came so naturally with him. So my voice was steady, too. "It's okay, Peter. Just so that you know, too—" I licked my lips and took a deep breath. "I'm on the Pill."

Had gone on it right after I got back my collection of negative pregnancy test results. Swear to God, I don't know what had scared me more: the possibility of an STD or that I might be pregnant.

"Guess we're covered, then."

"Guess so."

He held out his hand and I closed the space between us, putting my hand in his, letting him pull me close. From that point on, everything went like it was set on slow motion—slow enough that I knew I'd be able to remember every tiny detail. Like how he curved his hand around the back of my neck while he kissed the front. Or the way his breathing got faster when my teeth teased his ear, tugging gently at the small silver hoop.

At one point, he just stopped, his hands tangled in my hair, holding me still as that intense amber gaze of his studied my face.

"God, you're so pretty." His hands left my hair, trailing down my neck to my shoulders.

I glanced away, suddenly shy. "Yeah?"

"Yeah." As he unbuttoned my shirt and pushed it off my

shoulders, he sucked in a sharp breath that made me look back up into his face.

"What?"

His hands were stroking my arms as he looked at me, his gaze moving over my body before meeting mine again. "I know I'm gonna sound like a total dog, but just this once, I've got to say it."

"What?"

"Just . . . *wow*."

I blinked at him. "Wow?"

He nodded with a sort of sheepish grin as I started laughing and just couldn't stop, finally managing to choke out, "Oh Peter, I'm sorry." Poor guy was paying me a compliment and here I was laughing, but there was just something about how he said it . . . I just *couldn't* stop laughing and from the way he was shaking as he hugged me tight, I could tell he was laughing, too.

"Hey, it's okay—it's allowed to be fun, Caro."

I pulled back slightly, wiping at my eyes. "Yeah, I *know*, but fun as in funny, ha-ha?" I mean, I thought one of those cardinal rules was no laughing at guys, that their egos couldn't handle it. Honestly, I didn't have enough practical experience to know one way or another, but I trusted him.

"Sure, why not?" He guided me down to the bed and stretched out beside me, propping his head on one hand. "Is there a law somewhere that says laughing isn't allowed?" he asked while his free hand stroked my stomach, making me squirm and giggle as he tickled my ribs.

"I guess not," I managed around another giggle that faded away as he stopped tickling, his hand warm and comfortable on my hip.

"I just want to make you feel good."

I dragged my nails along his stomach, grinning as he yelped and squirmed. "Me, too."

We lay there, laughing and talking and kissing, getting more relaxed and comfortable with each other until the second he shifted over completely on top of me.

"Oh God." I froze, my fingers digging into his arms. "*No—*"

He immediately eased us both to our sides, whispering, "I'm sorry, Caro, I'm sorry . . . it's okay . . . if anything freaks you out, it's okay, we can stop, all right?"

"What just happened?" My head was buried in the hollow of his shoulder as I tried to catch my breath. Tried to suck in enough air to slow down my heart rate that had shot up past aroused and straight into terror, making me break out into a cold sweat.

His voice was soft, soothing. "It's okay . . . no one's going to hurt you, Caro. I'm not going to hurt you. I'll never hurt you."

"I know that, I know." I rubbed my face against his chest, inhaling the warm, comforting scents of Armani and soap. "I just got—I don't know . . . it's like I couldn't breathe."

For a split second, with Peter's weight heavy on me, pressing me back into the mattress, my mind had flashed onto an image of Nichols, his body pinning mine, holding me down as his knee forced my thighs apart, brutal and painful. An ugly image that disappeared the second Peter rolled us back to our sides.

"It's okay," he repeated. "It'll pass . . . I hope. We just need to go slow."

"How can you be so sure?"

"I, um . . . did some reading." He was running the fingers of one hand through my hair, the other low on my back, rubbing in small circles, holding me close, but not tight. "I've wanted to be with you for a long time, Caroline. And I wanted to be ready.

Wanted to know what to do if you got scared. So we'll do whatever it takes to make it all right for you, okay?"

Reaching back, I grabbed his hands because that way he had of stroking my hair—not to mention every other part of me—scrambled my brain cells and I had a hard time thinking straight.

"You read about . . . rape victims?"

He nodded, the soft waves of his hair brushing against my cheek in a caress that scrambled my brain cells every bit as much as his hands had. No gushy declarations, no tears or drama. Just releasing his hands and sliding my arms around him and holding him close.

With everything he did, Peter made me feel . . . special.

We were lying curved together, my back against his front, his hand idly stroking my arm. "I love you." Putting his hand over mine, he curled our fingers together to make a loose fist. "I'm not saying it to put any pressure on you or anything. It's just—I don't ever want to be anything less than completely honest with you and *mmph*—"

Kissing was just such an effective means of shutting someone up. Enjoyable, too, as I rolled all the way over and plastered myself against him, laughing softly between kisses. I rubbed my palms against his cheeks—yeah, I definitely liked the feel of the scruff as much as the appearance. "I love you, too, you know." I rolled back over and curved myself against him again. "I like this completely honest approach."

"Me, too."

You'd think I'd have been exhausted, with the day—week?—year?—I'd had, but my brain was going a thousand miles an hour. Going over every detail of the last week—especially the details of the last hour or so and grinning like a fool into the dark. "Peter, I'm thinking of going home next weekend."

His voice was sleepy. " 'Kay."

"Would you like to go with me?"

His arm tightened around my waist. "Yes."

No hemming and fidgeting around for an answer—just a simple, easy response that had me turning my head far enough to drop a kiss on his shoulder. You know, whenever I would come across the phrase "warm glow" in some of the sappier of Amy's books, I'd blow it off as nothing more than flowery, romance novel language. But judging by what was going on in my midsection and spreading outward, I had to admit, it was a pretty apt descriptor for that kind of overwhelming emotion.

"I'm going to tell them about Lola."

"That's good."

"And that I'd like to invite them to come visit Hampshire."

"From everything you've told me about your parents, they'll probably be cool with that." A beat of silence, then he said, "Hey, Caro?"

"Yeah?" I said through a yawn. All right then. Looked like it was finally all catching up to me.

His sigh was warm against my ear, making me shiver. "Never mind."

"No, what is it?"

"Well, it's just—" His hand moved from my stomach to my thigh, stroking. "I figured since you're still awake and well, now I'm still awake, but never mind, I know you're tired."

"Not that tired."

32

"**M**r. Gordon's diazepam."

I took the bottle of pills and looked for the label. "Old guy finally cracked, huh?" Poor man had always seemed so twitchy and uncomfortable teaching high school biology. He really was better suited for life in a lab with microbes—they were quiet and probably wouldn't string up the dissection frogs like holiday lights.

"Caroline—"

"Dad, it's cool. You know it goes no further than me. Was just making an observation."

"Peter's nice." He raised his eyebrows as he measured more pills into a bottle. "Just making an observation."

Subtle . . . *not*. But that was all right—there was only so much mileage you could get out of poor Mr. Gordon and his new best friend, Valium. "It's an accurate one. He *is* nice."

Sliding from my stool, I went to pour a fresh cup of coffee since the initial early morning caffeine jolt was starting to wear off.

It was just the two of us in the back of the pharmacy this morning. Mom was up front with Peter, showing off things like the vintage pop drink signs and our century-old brass cash register that still worked and that, even though it was worth a fortune, no one would ever think of stealing, mostly because it weighed more than those huge stone horses outside P. F.

Chang's. So cool, that sense of pride Mom had over the pharmacy, even though she came by it through marriage. Made me hope that James would someday be able to find someone just as cool.

Since Dad had a strict "no beverage" rule at the drug counter, I settled into Mom's desk chair with my mug, watching Dad fill and label one last bottle. Putting his fists in his back, he stretched and came over to grab his own cup of coffee.

"Are we going to have one of those father/daughter talks?"

"About Peter?"

Taking a sip of coffee, I nodded.

"Much as it's sometimes hard for me to admit, Caro, you're an adult. And so is he. While every dad instinct I possess is screaming that I should say all this stuff about how it's too soon for you to get into anything serious after—" His voice cracked slightly, then he cleared his throat and added, "At least with him I know you're safe. He's a good man."

Yeah, he knew. He and Mom both. Back when I'd told them about Erik and Nichols and the rape, I'd also told them about Peter. I thought Dad was going to hug Peter when I introduced them yesterday. Following Dad's glance through the doorway, I smiled at the goony expression on Peter's face as his fingertips traced all the elaborate scrollwork on the cash register. I'd lay money he'd be back later with his digital camera, taking pictures to work into new projects.

At Dad's soft laugh, I turned back to see him shaking his head as he studied me. "I could also argue you're way too young to be getting into anything this serious, period, but I'd be a hell of a hypocrite if I did." He dropped into the chair alongside Mom's desk. "Considering I made up my mind when I was seventeen that I was going to marry your mom—someday."

One night, Amy and I had caught an old, old, *old* show called

The Many Loves of Dobie Gillis on TV Land—I didn't remember much about it other than some character with the unfortunate handle of Maynard G. Krebs kept repeating "married?" in this alarmed, high-pitched voice. That was kind of how I felt right now, but I settled for a reasonably calm, "*So* not anywhere near that, Dad. Don't sweat it."

"Who's sweating? Just so long as you don't do anything that makes me a young grandfather."

Augh. I dropped my head onto the messy surface of Mom's desk, praying a stray paperclip didn't stab me through the forehead. Or maybe that it did. He had to. Just *had* to, didn't he? What was *with* the man and this obsession with birth control? At the way he was laughing, I slowly lifted my head. And glared. He was messing with my head and succeeding.

"That's so unbelievably mean, Dad." Which segued into my begging, "Please don't say anything like that in front of Peter— not everyone has your bent sense of what's amusing." That only made him laugh harder.

"Nice to know I can still jerk your chain at least a little, Caro. I get my joys where I can."

"You seriously need to get out more."

"Your mother says the same thing, but I think it's just her way of saying she wants me to take her on that Caribbean cruise I've been promising her for years."

He held the coffee pot over my mug, motioning toward it, and after I shook my head no, refilled his own cup and settled back in his chair with a sigh. A few seconds later, Mom appeared in the doorway, asking, "Did you two caffeine hounds leave us anything beyond the dregs?"

Behind Mom, Peter smiled, quiet and private, a smile meant just for me, although I could tell by Dad's expression he'd caught it. He looked more than a little freaked, too, but I knew he'd deal—had as much as said that he trusted me. Hoisting myself to the one semiclear surface on the desk, I nodded Peter to the chair, while Mom dragged my abandoned stool over beside Dad's chair.

"So, we miss anything interesting?" Mom asked as she held out her mug for Dad to fill. More rhetorical, I figured, because really—not much interesting back here other than learning poor Mr. Gordon had finally cracked.

"Not much, just a little father/daughter conversation," I answered.

Mom laid a stare on Dad. "Jimmy, you didn't—"

"Mom, he didn't. It's cool." Didn't need Dad slipping and maybe saying something dorky about becoming a grandfather in front of Peter.

"I do have something I wanted to talk to you guys about, though." I let my gaze rest on Dad. "In a way, mostly you, Dad, because it involves you more directly."

Since he knew it wasn't about marriage or babies, thank *God*, he looked more curious than worried. "What is it?"

"I've—uh, been working on a research project at school."

"Oh?" Dad leaned forward, an avid expression on his face. Always nice to verify where I got the scholarly geek bent from.

I felt a pressure on my knee, warm through my jeans. Peter winked and nodded toward his leg, which he bounced a couple of times. Yeesh—hadn't even realized I was doing it. "Look, I could give you this involved, full-of-background lead-up or I can just tell you what I found."

"Either way, baby, you're not making much sense right now."

"I know, Mom." Just having Peter's hand on my knee wasn't enough. I put my hand over his, holding on tight. "Okay, *Reader's Digest* version is, I've been researching Nana Ellie's family. When I went to Miami last week, it wasn't just for spring break—it was because I was hoping to get some more information to help me find them and well, turns out, I did." I was trying to stay calm and mature and focused, but some "bouncing up and down like a little kid" enthusiasm crept into my voice as I re-iterated, "I found them."

"Them? Them who?"

Dad now looked totally confused. Couldn't blame him. Good thing I'd been getting a lot of practice lately in hitting people with a boatload of potentially life-changing information—I had a decent idea where to start.

"I found Nana's younger sister. Lourdes—or Lola. That's what everyone calls her."

A quiet "Oh," from Dad, while Mom shoved her glasses farther up her nose and leaned forward.

"Everyone?" she asked.

"Well, she has a husband, Cando, who was a major league baseball player, Dad, isn't that cool?"

"Uh-huh."

Okay, he'd think that was cool later, when it, like, penetrated. "And they own a car dealership in Miami and have three kids—Willy, Arturo, and Joanna—and *they're* all married and have kids and Willy runs the dealership and—"

"Caro, slow down."

"But—" I stared at Peter, who was looking like he was trying to hold back a smile.

Standing, he leaned in against me, his voice quiet. "Give them a chance. You've been working on this for six months, they've barely had six seconds."

Following his gaze, I realized he was right. Even in *Reader's Digest* mode, I'd been slamming them with information overload. Silently, I watched as Dad pulled his wallet from his pocket; opening it up, he flipped past the pictures of Mom and James and me, the studio portrait of Grandma and Grandpa that had been taken not long before the bad flu epidemic a few years back that took Grandpa and the broken heart that had Grandma following just a few months after, to finally, a picture of Nana and Papa Joseph standing with him at his college graduation.

"Her younger sister?"

"Yeah." Man, wait until he saw Lola's picture. Good thing I'd exhibited some restraint and left all that stuff back at the house.

Mom reached across to the printer and, grabbing a sheet of paper and a marker, wrote, "Be back at eleven, sorry for the inconvenience" in big block letters. Through the open doorway, I could see her taping it to the front of the pharmacy counter.

"I have a feeling this is going to take a little longer than the forty-five minutes we have before opening. The rest of the staff can man the front of the store. Let's go home and get the whole story."

"Okay." I slid from the desk. "And after we're done with the story, I want to talk about my birthday."

Mom glanced over her shoulder as she grabbed Dad's hand and pulled him upright. "Why?"

"Because, provided it's cool with both of you, what I want is going to require some planning."

"You have two voice mail messages."

"Let me guess . . . you're 'studying' again. Of course you are. Anyway, after you and Peter disengage your hips from each other, call me." Beep.

Bitch.

"Hey, baby, it's Mom. The hotel is set. Would you believe they called me back three times to verify I really wanted them to hold as many rooms as I said I did? Thought it was a practical joke. Good thing you were born a week early. I'd hate to be trying to

organize this around the Fourth of July insanity. Call me later. Tell Peter we said 'hi.' " Beep.

I flipped my cell phone closed and slid it into an open pocket of my backpack. "Well, Amy's still being insufferably smug— you'd think she'd give it a rest. My parents say 'hi' and between my family and yours, looks like we can rename the Hampshire Inn and Suites to *Casa de Sebastián y Agosto*. At least for the last week of June."

"Uh-huh."

Forget it. He was gone. I'd have to fill him in on the details later. I picked up my philosophy text and settled my head more comfortably in Peter's lap. We'd had lunch at the Organic Llama but rather than go back to my dorm or his apartment to keep studying for finals, we'd commandeered a bench on one of the grassy triangles bordering the union. The mid-May weather was just too sweet to not take advantage and while we still studied together all the time and could generally behave, this new intensity in our relationship still had a way of, well, overwhelming us on occasion.

Okay, *fine*. It had a way of making us jump each other like rabbits at a moment's notice. And we seriously needed to study for finals.

So, outdoors . . . public . . . definitely much safer. Or at least conducive to studying. Sort of.

"Peter."

"Hm?" His hand kept stroking the outside of my thigh. Jeez— maybe it was soothing for him, but for me . . .

"Peter."

He finally glanced away from his art history book. "What?"

"Are you genuinely that unconscious of what you're doing to me?"

A sidelong glance to where his hand was curved around my

thigh, bare in shorts and finally taking on a hue that wasn't fish-belly white. "Oh, you'd know if it was conscious."

"Oh, I would, would I?"

"Yeah, you would." His fingers started playing across my skin in this light teasing action that had me squirming and reaching beneath his T-shirt for his stomach, which was unbearably tick-lish, the two of us laughing and threatening each other with what we were going to do when we were by ourselves.

"Carolina? I mean—Caroline?"

Wow. Hadn't heard *that* in a while. Slowly, I sat up and turned on the bench. Erik stood a few feet away, a hanger with a black graduation gown in one hand, a clear plastic bag with a cap and cords in the other.

"It *is* you. I wasn't sure—the hair." The hand holding the bag rose partway to his head.

"Hi, Erik." I leaned down to pick up the textbooks that had fallen to the ground, my hand on Peter's leg for support—and as comfort. His body had gone all kinds of tense, but as I stroked my thumb along his thigh, just a small, subtle caress, I felt him relax, at least some.

Odd. After the gallery, it hadn't ever crossed my mind again how I might react if I ever ran into Erik. And now, wasn't really reacting much. He was just a guy I'd known once upon a time. Different lifetime.

"How are you doing?"

"Oh, well, you know—getting ready to walk the walk." He lifted the bag again, shrugged. "I'd bag it, but my parents are hot to celebrate the fruits of their finances, blah, blah, blah. You?"

"I'm really good." As I spoke, Peter put his arm around my shoulders and I hid a smile behind a light cough. How cute. He was being ever-so-slightly caveboy. Although he'd totally deny it if I called him on it.

"I see that." Erik's gaze flickered to where Peter's hand rested on my shoulder, stroking gently. "Peter, right?"

"Yeah."

Erik nodded, then turned back to me. "I looked for your name in some of the campus theater productions."

"I changed majors—not doing theater anymore." Art galleries *and* theater? Maybe Peter had been right about that growing-up hypothesis. "What about you? Still going to law school?"

"Yeah, Fordham. My fiancée—" The word rolled off his tongue in a way that suggested it still felt kind of foreign to him. "She was able to score a job in New York so it worked out pretty well."

"Congrats, Erik, really."

Well, what *else* was I going to say? "You sure you're ready to take that step, Mr. I Think It's Okay to Screw Around for the Health of My Relationships?" seemed kind of tacky under the circs. And for all I knew, he really *had* changed. In any case it didn't have a darn thing to do with me.

"Thanks." He ducked his head, shifted the bag and hanger again. "Well, I better motor." Our gazes met. "Take care, Caroline."

"You too, Erik." Strangely enough, I meant it. For the longest time, I'd felt this faint hurt if I happened to think of him. But couldn't remember the last time I had—thought of him *or* felt hurt.

Handing Peter his book, I stretched back out with my head in his lap, textbook propped on my stomach. He didn't open his, though—just sat there stroking my hair, his fingers occasionally brushing across my cheek.

"You know, I think he's always going to regret you."

Tilting my head back slightly, I saw that he was staring off in the direction Erik had gone. "What do you mean?"

"I don't know, exactly. Just this sense I get that he's always going to regret how he didn't do right by you. That he lost something special."

"It wouldn't have ever worked out, though, Peter." Talk about a sudden moment of clarity. I'd loved Erik, in a way. He was like those newer coasters at Cedar Point that you just couldn't wait to try—that were nothing more than a series of sharp turns and corkscrews and loops with no flat sections where you could catch your breath. They were dizzyingly wild and crazy and fast, but in the end, you maybe rode them once—just to say you had.

Peter was like a roller coaster, too, but he was like the ones that had the long, slow, gradual ascents with short bursts of furious speed and intense turns or breathtaking drops. The ride lasted much longer and because of the anticipation, the payoff was so much better.

Those were the ones you rode over and over again.

ACT III

33

I was in the kitchen, which was miraculously empty for the first time all day, checking on a batch of baked beans when he grabbed me by the hand and pulled me into the mud room.

"Peter—" Whatever I was about to say was cut off in the best possible way. I maybe should've never told him how effective I found kissing to be in shutting someone up.

Then again . . .

"It's your birthday and I've barely had a chance to talk to you, let alone give you your presents."

"Well, not such a surprise with what seems like five thousand relatives in the backyard, the front yard, the house—"

"And all your idea and you're loving it."

"I'm loving the sight of Dad and Granddad in guayaberas. Talk about something I never thought I'd see."

As they sat outside under the oak trees with Willy, Arturo, Cando, Jorge, and even Dr. Machado, the Cuban men teaching the gringos how to play dominoes and properly supervise the cooking of *puerco asado*. Heh. Roasting a whole pig in a pit in the backyard while salsa blared from one stereo and a baseball game from another. The neighbors would probably be having fits if we hadn't invited them all.

"And I repeat, you're loving it."

"Yeah." I hoisted myself up onto the washer, hooking my legs around Peter's waist and my arms around his neck. "But I have missed spending time with you—I'm sorry it's been so nuts."

"No, I'm sorry, I shouldn't bitch. This has all been so amazing." Sliding in closer, his hands crept beneath the hem of my tank top. "We'll be back at school soon enough—"

"Yo, where's Amy?"

My mouth a hair's breadth away from Peter's, I sighed. "Probably out back cleaning up in dominoes, James." She'd turned out to be the best player. Who knew? "Why?"

"Because she wanted a Cherry Vanilla Dr Pepper and we didn't have any more so I bought her some when I went to pick up more ice."

I gaped at my older brother. "Like, voluntarily? She didn't ask?"

"Yeah—so?" He shrugged and shifted the two huge bags of ice he held. Buried in one of them, I could just see a couple of bottles of Cherry Vanilla Dr Pepper, no doubt staying nice and frosty. "Resume tonsil swabbing. I gotta get the ice out there."

"You need help, James?" Peter asked.

I tightened my thighs around his waist. "No, he doesn't. Do you?"

He didn't because he was already gone and I was flabbergasted, heavy on the gasted. "I'm totally not believing what I just saw and heard. It's just a mirage brought on by the unusual heat wave we're experiencing as a result of global warming, right?"

"It's better to stay out of it, Caro. Their business."

"Stay out of what? I don't even know that there's anything to stay out of." But I was darn well gonna find out.

That one, infuriating, adorable eyebrow rose. "I've got presents for you."

I'd find out later. "You are *very* good at distracting me."

"Yeah?" His hands resumed stroking, my back this time, as he dropped small kisses along my neck, his hair teasing my shoulder and making me shiver.

"Oh yeah." I sighed. "But you said something about presents?"

"Must not be *that* good."

Yeah he was. So much so that sometimes? It was kind of scary and overwhelming and I'd have to crack a joke or something—like now—just to be able to catch my breath. I think he knew it, too, which is why he just smiled and dropped another kiss on my mouth—a sweet one—as he stroked my cheek.

He'd been prepared. Reaching down into a bag that was on the floor beside the washer, he pulled out a largish, flat package that he put in my lap.

"First gift."

"Ooh, I always like when it's first—means there's more," I joked as I tore away the dark blue foil gift wrap. And caught my breath in an entirely different way. "Oh my God, Peter. How on earth did you do this?"

"I asked Lola and your mom for the pictures, scanned them, and then played around until I got it the way I wanted." He tried to shrug it off, all casual and no big deal, guylike. Then his hand closed over mine around the edge of the framed print. "Do you like it, Caroline?"

"Oh . . . *Peter.*" His name eased out on a long, soft sigh. I simply didn't have the words to tell him how much what I was holding meant to me. What it contained—and the fact that he'd done this *for* me.

Pictures. Of Grandma—Nana's daughter, Dad's mother. Of Lola as a young woman and as she was now. Pictures of me as a little girl and one that was obviously a lot more recent, that I didn't even recognize. And of course, pictures of Nana—

my favorite, the one that Papa Joseph had taken, and of her as an older woman—the way I'd always known her.

And he'd taken those images and somehow managed to insert them within a lush, tropical garden landscape in a way that made them look as if they'd been right there when the photograph was taken. In the shade of a giant palm tree, he'd grouped the young-woman pictures of Nana and Lola and Grandma and me, seamlessly making it appear as if we were standing together, all laughing at something only we knew about. Farther off in the distance, he'd put the older-woman images of Nana, Lola, and Grandma as if they were looking back. And in one corner, a picture of Nana and me together that I remembered being taken one Easter, the two of us sitting on a sofa, but Peter had somehow manipulated it so that we appeared to be sitting on a garden bench, gazing at the four young women dominating the center of the shot. It was an amazing scene—skill and talent and love merging together to make magic.

"I took this picture." His fingers brushed over the shot of me I didn't recognize. "At Calle Ocho."

That's right—those were the jeans and red blouse Sara had insisted I wear, my hair loose down my back, head thrown back as I laughed at who knows what.

"Why haven't you ever shown me this picture before?"

"I kept meaning to, but then, I don't know—maybe you'll think it's stupid, but I sort of wanted to keep it for myself." He reached into his back pocket and pulled out his wallet, where he showed me a smaller version of the photograph tucked in opposite one of Ileana.

"I don't think it's stupid." Felt like my heart was about to expand past my chest, but I did *not* think it was stupid. "Thank you." Lame, but I just couldn't think of anything else to say. Luckily, he knew I meant a whole lot more—let me show him what it meant to me.

"I made copies of this." Lifting his head from mine, he tapped the montage. "For Lola and your dad." The familiar blush started rising from the collar of his T-shirt. "I think he liked it."

Oh please. I already knew Dad was liking Peter more and more with each time they met. At this rate, if anything bad ever happened between us, he was likely to keep Peter instead of me.

"And here's your other present." He lifted the framed print from my lap and dropped a small, wrapped box in its place.

Oh God, I'd almost forgotten that he'd said presents, plural. "Peter, after this . . . you really didn't need to get me anything else."

"Oh well, I'll take it back, then." He made like he was going to take it away, but he was out of his mind if he thought—

"Oh, no you don't." Smacking his wrist, I snatched the box up and started tearing the wrapping away while I ignored his laughing ass.

"God, you're easy."

"We'll see if you still say that when we get back to Middlebury."

Slipping the print back into the bag, he leaned back into me. "Oh baby, you know your threats make me hot," he teased.

Twisted boy. Chuckling, I lifted the lid on the box, along with a thin layer of cotton. "Um, Peter . . . what is it?" A delicate silver circle, small, about the size of his earring, but as far as I could tell, it wasn't an earring.

"It's a charm—for your bracelet." He lifted it from the box and now I could see the smaller link that was meant to attach to my bracelet. "I know it's simple and sort of abstract, but it's meant more to signify all you did this year than any one thing. Look out there, Caro." He pointed to the window behind me; turning, I could see what he meant. The Miami family mingling with the Ohio family, totally different yet with more of a common ground than anyone could've ever imagined.

I smiled as I watched Dad carry a couple of loaded plates of food over to where Lola was sitting with Cando and, after handing each of them a plate, take the seat next to Lola's. I don't think they'd stopped talking since Lola and Cando had landed at Hopkins.

"At the risk of sounding unforgivably corny, you brought it all full circle."

"Yeah, I did, didn't I?" I turned back to study the charm cupped in his palm.

"And at the risk of having you think I'm jumping the gun . . ." My gaze rose from the charm and found his. "I kind of see it as a promise, too."

Okay, now my heart wasn't going to just expand out of my chest, it was going to bust completely free and take my stomach and lungs right along with it.

"No pressure, Caro. Just me being completely honest again." The hand not holding the charm curved around the back of my neck, his fingers warm. "We both have a lot that we want to do and need to accomplish. Just . . . someday?"

While he was talking, I kept waiting . . . expecting scary and overwhelming to make an appearance, and there they were— but in a good way. Carefully placing my palm over his, I lifted our hands, the charm held between us. "Someday."

Seemed like people in my family had a tendency to make their minds up early about this sort of thing. Heck, at nineteen, you could argue I was actually behind the curve.

Peter released a long breath, his eyes clearing to the warm amber I loved. "I'll put it on your bracelet later." His voice was husky as he returned the small circle to its box and set it in the bag alongside my print.

"Caro, *mi vida* . . . time to come blow out the candles on your cake."

I stared at Ileana, who was standing in the doorway to the mud room. "Cake? I haven't even eaten so much as a *croqueta* yet."

"Whose fault is that? Hiding in here and doing the nasty," James cracked from behind Ileana. God, look at him, gnawing on what looked like an entire leg of pork, his face disgustingly shiny and happy. Amy could have him and good luck to her. I was going to take Peter's advice and stay *really* far out of it.

" 'Doing the *nasty*'? What are you, twelve?"

"*Oye,* get out of here with that thing, *m'ijo*. Leave your sister alone." Ileana turned and shooed my brother off, making him skitter backward with this fearful expression on his face that actually made him *look* twelve.

"Oh, definitely 'someday,' " I said to Peter. "If only to keep your mom around."

"Nice to know you have your priorities straight, Caro."

I stopped just short of the kitchen door. "What if I promise to show you my priorities later?"

His huge, gorgeous grin split his face. "Can't wait."

"Caro—*cake*!" Ileana and Mom. In unison. Unbelievable.

"You'd better get out there."

Holding hands, we made our way across the backyard to where Mom had set up what seemed like every table in Hampshire. On one of them sat a pair of huge cakes from DaVinci's—a dark chocolate fudge with orange buttercream filling and even darker chocolate ganache frosting, and next to it, a lighter cake—lemon with a simple vanilla buttercream for those who didn't want their blood-sugar levels zooming off into the stratosphere.

On the chocolate cake, a cursive *Happy Birthday Caro* was written in ivory frosting, while the lemon cake had a simple *Family* written across it. And gathered around the table and spilling all through the yard was my family. All of them—and all of them made up who I was. So what if they didn't know all of me? That was okay. So long as I did.

As Mom leaned over to light the candles on the chocolate cake, Dad took my chin in his hand and gazed down at me. "We're extremely proud of you, Caro. I hope you know that. And I think Nana would be incredibly proud of you, too."

He glanced over to where Lola was seated, in prime viewing position, with Cando beside her, holding her hand. "Maybe it's Lola you resemble, but from all she's told me, you're Nana, all over again. She never did what anyone expected, either."

Letting go of Peter's hand, I hugged Dad close, blinking back tears. Would've probably hung on to him longer, except an extremely loud, raucous, and tinged-with-a-slight-Spanish-accent rendition of "Happy Birthday to You" started echoing through the yard. Had me laughing so hard I could barely suck in enough air to blow out the candles.

Then, as I was pulling the candles out of the cake, I heard, "Well, it's a shame you can't stay for the Fourth of July celebration. Go all out 'round here and you just never know what's gonna happen. You know, one year, Caroline stripped down buck naked and marched around the Green to 'The Stars and Stripes Forever'?"

"Granddad!"

"What, Caro?" Granddad stood there in his new pale blue guayabera, blinking at me over a huge slab of lemon cake. "It's part of your past, honey. You should understand that, being the big family historian and all."

"Yeah, Granddad, but some stuff just isn't meant to be pre-served for posterity, you know?"

Or repeated in front of certain history professors with sadis-tic senses of humor. Dr. Machado was grinning at me in a way I just *knew* would come back to haunt me. Probably if I came down to UM for graduate work, which he'd been lobbying for all this week. Graduate work. I'd only just finished freshman year and the man was already planning my Ph.D. But it was exciting to think about.

"*Bueno*, you know, Peter once peed in the punch at a barbe-cue."

"Dad, I was *three*, for God's sake."

And that's when it occurred to me—standing there, with a glob of chocolate ganache melting on my tongue, and looking around. From my grandfather talking baseball with Dr. Machado and Cando, to Mom and Ileana and Grammy chatting as they cut cake and made absolutely sure no one was starving, to Dad and Lola, and even, God help me, to Amy, gazing up at James as he pushed her on the old tire swing—

"Hey, Peter?"

"Yeah?"

"I think an adventure came and snuck up on me."

His "You think?" lost of little of the dry, sarcastic impact, what with that streak of chocolate just below his lip.

Wiping it away with my thumb, I replied, "Yeah, I *think*." I lifted a shoulder. "So what if there weren't dashing Greek heirs or Russian dukes?"

His eyebrows drew together. "Hey, I'm glad there weren't any heirs or dukes to compete with."

I rubbed my thumb below his lip again—not because of chocolate, but just . . . because. "You so don't have to."

So no, no Greeks or Russians, but look—right in front of

me—a whole host of characters I could tell my kids stories about one day. Exciting events that had happened. Some that were sad or tragic.

There was love.

All the stuff good adventures were made of.

"I'm such a dolt." I sighed, wrapping my arms around Peter's waist and fitting my head against his shoulder "I didn't have a clue I was on an adventure—just lived the darn thing."

His arm rested across my shoulders, warm and secure. "I kind of think that's how it works, Caro."

"Yeah." I laughed quietly. "I get that now."

It just happened and played itself out, swirling around like river rapids and taking me along for the ride. And what do you want to make a bet Nana was probably somewhere having a piece of chocolate cake and laughing at me right now?

And as Peter leaned down and kissed me—a sweet, dark chocolate kiss—that's when something else occurred to me.

This adventure? With any luck, it was only the first of many.